Tell your stories—
Your legacy—

Tale Tellin'

Southern Style

Harriet Brill Outlaw

Harriet Brill Outlaw

Published by

www.IntellectPublishimg.com

ISBN: 978-1-961485-52-5

Cover design and artwork by Michael Ilacqua
www.cyber-theorist.com

V-9

www.TaleTellinBook.com

Dedication

I hope my fourteen grandchildren will tell stories to their children and grandchildren. Family gatherings should be a time of sharing memories of childhood and family traditions. I treasure the times we sit on my porch and just talk. And laugh.

Published in Memory of Kennard Balme

Kennard Balme deserves a permanent tribute to his memory. His legacy of preservation of local history, public service, and family dedication will live forever. This book is published in his memory because of his passion for writing and his gracious interest in the content of these tales. He and his wife, Penny, encouraged me to gather these tales and produce a volume of folk tales. Therefore, this tangible evidence of our respect, appreciation, and love of a great man is offered as testimony to his life.

Prologue

As I have grown older (and older) I have had time to stop and figure out what things give me joy. In my journals I have usually recorded events, but occasionally I found myself reflecting on joy, and I returned to that theme again and again. I had actually never given myself permission to do just that until recently: too busy doing those tasks that I thought others expected of me. As I started putting these stories on paper, I have found that this is fun and brings happiness. I am giving myself the freedom to do something I have considered trivial, so I justify the time spent on this as an attempt to preserve some of the past for future generations (so I don't feel guilty.)

Two of my favorite authors, Ferrol Sams and Frank McCourt, wrote incredible works late in life. My mother wrote her autobiography at age seventy-five after she became an invalid. I don't presume to even begin to be an author, but their work has shown me that it is not too late for me to attempt the task of recording stories I love.

I have always enjoyed stories. I enjoy talking with people about the days gone by. I have loved retelling those stories and eventually writing them down. Some of those which have been included in previous publications are gathered here in this volume. Some are ones I had just never gotten around to recording and have found joy in remembering them.

I started this entry as a "Word from the Author," then realized the entire book is actually from the author. I have put my joy on paper and perhaps someone else will glean a little joy from some of these stories, tales, and lore.

Table of Contents

Introduction

"Let me tell you a story"– what magical words. I've heard Wanda Johnson and Kathryn Tucker Windham use them in front of audiences eager to hear their stories. I remember my parents saying them on our front porch after supper or Sunday dinner. When those words are spoken, you quiet your thoughts and open your soul. When they are spoken from a storyteller sitting in a rocking chair, they are even more powerful. There is magic in the rocking back and forth, the creaks of the old wooden chair and the rockers crunching on the porch floor. The rhythm is the background music and somehow it always seems to match the heartbeat. It enhances the voice of the storyteller, rocking slowly as the story is beginning to take its hold on the listeners gathered around. Then, as the story spins, the rocking gets a little faster until somehow the chair just stops rocking on its own when the story reaches its high point. If you are lucky, when that story comes to an end the storyteller will start rocking once again and another story will fill the air. It does not matter one iota if it has been told before or is told a little differently each time.

There are all kinds of stories. Family stories are the glue that holds the past to the present. Notorious escapades of aunts, uncles, and grandparents seem far away until they come to life again in the story of your people. Our people – that is what storytelling is all about -our people, those on whose legacy we build each day. Those are the most important stories families can share.

"Fairy" stories are the canvas of the imagination. Princesses, goose girls, shepherds, talking animals – even trolls and wicked witches have worked their way into minds of people for as long as there have been people. Dragons, sea monsters, and creatures of the night are somehow tamed when they are in a story told on the porch; the storyteller wields the sword that destroys their evil deeds.

Then, there are those unexplainable mysteries inspiring tales of ghosts and spirits. Even if one is not sure there are ghosts, there is always fun in a good ghost story. Nearly everyone loves to hear a spooky tale now and then, but a real storyteller explains the story behind the mystery – or maybe not.

Folklore and legends are an essential part of American heritage. Who has not heard of Paul Bunyan or John Henry? What about south Alabama's very own Railroad Bill? Folk legends reflect our history through the characters that inspired them. Tall tales are closely related to legends. It is such fun to listen to a story that you believe almost until the very end, when you finally realize that those events are just too far-fetched to be true.

Storytelling is by no means a 'children only' event!! Adults are as intrigued as children by the spell woven when a story starts to unfold. National storytelling festivals jam-packed with listeners are witness to the popularity of the art. I am a storyteller, and I love the feeling in a room (or on a porch) when everyone becomes a part of the tale. I will never forget the day I was telling a story to a group of students, and the teacher began leaning further and further toward me until I was afraid he was going to topple over. That was one of the greatest compliments I have ever received.

I look forward to sharing some of my favorites in this book, but you should be told right up front that stories are much, much better when told aloud, or at second best, read aloud. A storyteller does not think about grammar or syntax in formal ways that authors do. In fact, the more the teller sounds like a character, the better the story is. The human voice and the speech patterns are the instruments that keep the story in tune. I apologize to my English teacher friends! In my old age I have embraced the skill of dangling participles and incomplete sentences when I try to write a story meant to be told orally! If this grates on your nerves, just try reading the story aloud with lots of pauses– that makes all the difference. In fact, try telling a story yourself, one you read or a memory you need to pass on. Just remember there is no right or wrong way to tell a story. It should take twists and turns created by the teller on an evening after supper, when the crickets are chirping, the tree frogs are singing, and the fireflies are blinking in time to the rocker. The rocking chair is much more comfortable when there is a child in your lap, and when that little head starts to droop against your shoulder, the evening is drawing to a close, making for wonderful dreams of things past and things to come. Sleep tight and don't let the bedbugs bite.

Tomorrow, I will tell you another story.

Tale Tellin'

Southern Style

CHAPTER 1 FAMILY STORIES

LET ME TELL YOU A STORY……

Anytime is a good time for telling stories of those memories that made life in the good old days. Time to tell stories to those who may never know what it is like to experience life without cell phones and computers. Time to sit on the porch and remember. That is how folklore is made. Come sit on the porch, chew a little sugar cane, and let me tell you about life in the good old days before electronics and air conditioning. When we told stories. Here are those family stories that made us a family.

MY HEART IS WHERE MY HOME IS

Speaking of porches, let me tell you about mine.

The author's front porch is a perfect place for telling stories and listening to the tales of the deep south

Home is where the heart is – I get it. But my heart is where my home is. I am one of those few lucky people in today's world who lives in a house that gives meaning to the term "a sense of place." Although this house is not the actual structure I grew up in, it is an exact replica, and somehow all those memories made in the old homeplace came to live here with us. The residue of powerful emotions from the old house dwells here and is felt in a real way. When people who remember the old house come to visit, they are soon recalling things that happened when they were there, blending the past with the present.

"We rolled a doll head down those stairs and scared poor Mike to death. I will never forget the look on his face. Maybe it seems mean now, but then it was hilarious."

"This is the spot where they laid out Papa's body. I can never come in this room without thinking of how that impacted me."

"We had such wonderful school-wide Easter egg hunts in this yard."

"We sat on this porch many a night and told stories."

Let me tell you a story about a house. Oscar and Harriet Brill each grew up in Bay Minette in the 1920s not knowing each other but had both later moved to Mobile for work. There they met, and were amazed at all they had in common, right down to the same birthday. Of course, they got married. What hard workers and determined people they were! They paid down on a little Mom and Pop grocery store in Toulminville and lived in the adjoining house, raising four children. Mother worked that little Hill Top Grocery day in and day out, and Daddy took over to close up the store after he got home from work.

Near the store, there was a house in which my Daddy had lived as a child for a while. Every time they walked past that house, Daddy would say, "Someday I am going to live there again." Sure enough, he did. They saved every penny they could and purchased the house when it came up for auction during the Depression. Life there was typical for a poor family in the 1930s. Walls were papered in newspapers, fireplaces were used for heat, and the ground could be seen through the cracks in the floor. There always seemed to be room for any kinfolk needing a place to live for a while, so the house was dubbed the "Big House." It is a good thing that house seemed to expand as needed, because five more children were added to the family within the next couple of decades.

The author's birthplace on Pleasant Avenue in Mobile was built circa 1835.

Year in and year out, life in the Big House was filled with work, laughter, grandchildren, celebrations, and even death. It stood against the storms and fought for life, winning that battle until the 1970s, when my widowed mother had to move, leaving a part of her spirit right there in that house. The house fell into disrepair, a grand old lady in her declining years, graceful, but broken and hurting. Death for the house was a blessing. After it was demolished the house lived only in our hearts and memories until my husband and I decided to build a replica of the Big House so my Mother could return "home" before she passed. Ground was broken to re-create that homeplace. Mother died before we could move into the new old house, but she saw it and gave it her blessing. On the last day she visited the house under construction, a baby hawk flew in. It would not leave even though the house was not closed in. On the day my mother died, six weeks later, my brother opened the back door and the hawk flew past him into the sky. That hawk showed us that my Mother's spirit would always be in this house.

The Benu is the Egyptian symbol of resurrection. The painting by Donnie Barret graces the floor of the entry hall of Benulee, the resurrection house of the author's original home.

This house, which we call Benulee, a name taken from the Egyptian symbol of resurrection, is home to yet another generation. And another. And another. Here new emotions are joining those already in residence. Through family ups and downs, the house represents the constancy of love shared here. My mind knows a house is not needed to hold on to your precious memories, but every day my heart counts it a joy that we can have a tangible reminder of those things most valuable.

My mother used to say that perhaps some houses have souls. If that is true, this one certainly does. Sometimes I think Heaven can't be much better than life right here in this house. But then, again, if Heaven is paradise and all will be perfect, the mansion prepared for me there will be just like this one – with a rocking chair on the front porch.

The author's home is an exact replica of the old house that once stood in Toulminville.

MISS ABBIE

I always told my children and grandchildren that there is no ghost in our home, but it is time for me to break the silence and come clean. Let me tell you about Miss Abbie who is here just as surely as we are.

We live in a reproduction home, an exact replica of the home in which I was born and reared in Mobile, Alabama. The house has a spirit of its own and is also home to an apparition who keeps me company with the past.

The original house was built in 1835 as a simple dogtrot style country home on the banks of Three Mile Creek, just north of downtown Mobile. Soon the dogtrot was enclosed, and a second story added to house the large family who lived there. The house had two main rooms on each side of the central passageway, and large front and rear porches. It originally faced the creek, but in the 1920s, the Fowler family remodeled it to face Pleasant Avenue. They added stucco to the front porch as well as the inside walls. Then the Depression hit; the Fowlers had to sell the house.

Oscar and Harriet Brill pose with their first four children in front of the Hill Top Grocery Store on Costarides Street in Mobile.

n my parents, Oscar and Harriet Brill, entered the picture. Actually, nily had lived in the house as a child, and he had always dreamed live in that wonderful house. He and my mother had married in e soon running a little Mom and Pop store, the Hill Top, on eet in Toulminville, a short distance from the "Big House." They a house connected to the Hill Top Grocery and raising four children House came up for purchase. Their hard work at the store, my dad's at Mobile Paint Company and a cottage industry repairing d enabled them to save a little money. For a family during the e purchase of a house was daunting, but they stepped out on faith. eral nest egg, they bid for the house and purchased it, loaded their ed into the house, which immediately became a real home in every ord.

they moved in, there were few other homes in the neighborhood, d War II workers were looking for homes, and small rental places around. Bragg Hill Apartments were built to the west of the house, of Stanton Road and Pleasant Avenue in 1947. They were built near the estate of the Bragg Mitchell Mansion, which still stands across the creek on Springhill Avenue.

There was another antebellum house east of our Big House, just across the sunken roadbed of the ancient Rondo Road (formerly Center Street), which originally crossed Three Mile Creek. That home was a real southern mansion built by a highly respected Mobile family in the early 1800s. It was one of those magnificent structures that had porches upstairs and downstairs, a cellar and several outbuildings. My mother became very good friends with the last one of the family to live in the house, Miss Abbie. They often visited over cups of tea in her parlor. Abbie was indeed a genteel and fine southern lady who spent her life teaching piano lessons, caring for the family home, and carrying on a legacy of southern manners.

Miss Abbie loved her home just as my mother loved ours. They were bonded by the love each had for their homes, not merely dwellings of sticks and bricks, but treasure boxes holding the memories of days past and the promise of days to come, the tangible cornerstone of everything else in life. These sister houses were two of the few houses that can claim ownership of a soul; for souls they did indeed possess.

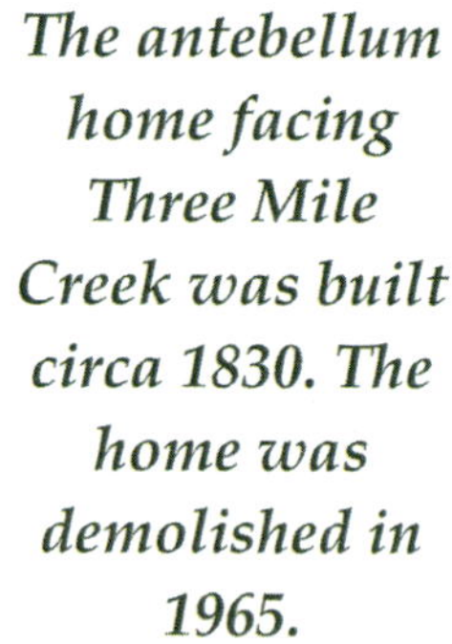

The antebellum home facing Three Mile Creek was built circa 1830. The home was demolished in 1965.

As the ladies shared many a story throughout the years, they often told of the presence of mysterious sightings and sounds. Miss Abbie told my mother the story of her ancestor, the Mistress of the House in the 1860s. When the Confederate forces were constructing earthwork mounds and batteries along the banks of Three Mile Creek, they were thwarted in cutting down a hundred-year-old live oak tree as the lady stood in front of the tree. The tree stood there until the hurricane of 1916 split it down the center and it thundered to the ground. The corpse of that grand tree lay there as a tribute to the beauty of nature.

Along the banks of Three Mile Creek on Rondo Road, an oak tree was split in the Hurricane of 1916.

During the Depression, people were allowed to come and cut branches to use for firewood. In the 1950s, a lovely home was built behind the tree – the architecture was designed to enhance the view of the tree. Many people told of seeing the lady in white standing in front of the tree. There were many neighborhood stories of soldiers on horses riding in the waters of the creek and sometimes people claimed to see a Confederate soldier in the yard of the antebellum home.

My mother had mysterious stories to share about our home as well. The Fowler family had told her that they had found a pair of Alabaster vases and a large brass key in the attic. They put them on the mantle in the parlor, but when they returned home one day after church, the vases were shattered on the floor and the key was missing. I grew up hearing these stories and honoring the heritage of the two houses.

The mantle in the original living room of the author's home was made of masonry and held a collection of salt and pepper shakers when the author was a child. But once it was where the mysterious alabaster vases found in the attic were placed – they were shattered!

Of noted interest were the painted window shades that hung in the parlor of Miss Abbie's house. The canvas shades had been painted in the 1830s and were protected for more than one hundred years by the outside shutters that Miss Abbie kept closed year-round. Miss Abbie was homebound in her later years and moved to a nursing home soon after I was born in 1947. She died two years later. After Miss Abbie's death, my mother purchased seven of those shades and put them in our home where they stayed until my mother sold our home in 1970. They hang yet today in the reproduction house we built so that the shades once again have a home. In fact, this house is actually here so that Miss Abbie and my mother could once again have a home as well.

My Own Apparitions

The final owner of Miss Abbie's home determined that the home had served its purpose and scheduled demolition of the house in 1965. Our family mourned the demise of the house but tried to accept the adage that houses are really built for people, not people for houses. Or is that really true when a house has a soul?

We watched the process of the house coming down and saved some of the wooden pegs that held the foot-wide joists in place for more than 150 years. I distinctly remember the last part of the house to remain in place was the center wall, which supported the massive indoor staircase in the center of the house. As I stood at the eastward-facing window in our living room looking across the ancient roadbed, I saw the wall come down. I screamed for my mother. The wall had clearly fallen on someone who was standing next to it and looking directly into my eyes. I can remember those sad eyes. My mother and I hurried to the site and told the foreman that I had seen the wall fall on someone. As you expect, there was no one there.

I was a freshman commuting to the University of South Alabama in the fall of that year. I returned home one evening about 10:00 o'clock and turned in the dirt lane. I noticed a figure in the front yard. It was clearly a lady who was dressed in black, with a white dust cap on her head. She was bent almost double and was leaning on a wooden walking stick I could see clearly. I turned the car to shine the lights on her and I could see her even more distinctly. The closer I drove toward her, the more transparent she became and by the time I was within 15 feet, she had completely disappeared. I was not afraid, but instinctively knew that this was Miss Abbie, homeless. I spoke to her inviting her to come into our home that evening. I woke my parents up to relay the experience, but they were not alarmed either. In fact, they seemed relieved to know that Miss Abbie had come to live with us. I asked my mother why she thought I was the one able to see the apparition, and she told me that Miss Abbie had loved me so very much and must have known that I would take care of her as long as I lived. A most interesting fact is that I had no memory of seeing Miss Abbie, and no one had ever told me that Miss Abbie was bent double with a spine disorder in her last years – that is why she was homebound and walked with a cane.

That Christmas, as a gift to my parents, I had taken a photo of our house and had an artist sketch the house in pencil. Of course, the artist, Rob Bearden, had no knowledge of Miss Abbie and yet she is clearly visible in the upstairs window of my bedroom in the sketch.

A pencil sketch of the old house was done by Rob Bearden, who had no knowledge of Miss Abbie. She showed up in the shadows of the upstairs left bedroom window.

My mother sold the house, and when it was demolished in 1978, we did not know ahead of time, and were unable to secure any original architecturals, but we were able to retrieve Miss Abbie – but not until 1993! My husband and I decided to build a replica of my homeplace and chose a lovely pecan orchard in Fairhope just like the pecan orchard of the original house. As we reproduced the Big House, we knew that this house would be as special as the original. The measurements are all the same; the windows, doors, creaks and cracks have all taken on the spirit of the old place. This structure has a soul because of the memories it keeps alive, but it gets better. After we had moved into our new home, I took a little visit to the old homeplace. You know what happened, don't you? I invited Miss Abbie to come home with me and live in our new home. I know that she did. I feel her especially in the corner of our parlor, the replica of the one which once had the clearest view of her homeplace. However, after we first moved in, that corner was a headache. The rain that leaked in could not be stopped. The drapes on that window were often askew, and the painted window shade was at different heights at different times. One day while I was studying photos of the original house, I realized that corner window had always been the location of a window shade with a castle painted on it.

The window shades were painted circa 1838 and graced the windows of Miss Abbie's house until her death in 1949. One of the originals hangs in the author's dining room.

That particular window shade had been given to another grandchild by my mother, so it was not among those which hung in our new home. I knew then what was distressing Miss Abbie. I went to the corner with the photo and explained to her that it was loved and well-preserved, but not in this house. I told he I was having a copy painted for her. From that moment on, the rain did not leak in, the curtains and shade stayed in place and I felt a great sense of peace there. She is here with me at my writing desk with her precious window shades hanging once again. I love hearing her walking cane thumping on the hard pine floors, and sometimes I see her shadow sitting in the parlor with a cup of tea. I sit and remember with her.

Note: The original castle window shade has now returned home thanks to Michael Brill. Miss Abbie is content.

Today a copy of the castle shade hangs in Miss Abbie's corner of the author's home.

DADDY'S MAGIC: A Father's Love

A father's love can do magical things. Let me tell you about mine.

Daddy was ready to enlist in WWII. He went to the recruiting office and completed the paperwork. Mother was willing to take on all of the responsibilities of raising their four children and running the store. When Daddy got to the desk, the sergeant shook his head. "I'm sorry, Mr. Brill, but you are needed too much on the home-front for us to send you to active military duty." Daddy was plant manager for Mobile Paint Company in downtown Mobile, which was rapidly becoming a major shipbuilding center. He was told that his knowledge of paint manufacturing was critical to the production of warships. So, he stayed in the port city, working every day to produce as much paint as possible for the government. The plant was under tight security and no one knew what was really taking place inside that large building.

Mobile Paint Company was on the riverfront for years. It later moved to Theodore where it is still a thriving business.

By the time I was born the war was over, but Daddy continued to work at the plant, while Mother ran the Hill Top Grocery and maintained the home. I looked forward every afternoon to hearing the sound of that old pickup truck and Daddy walking up the back steps. I waited at the back door for him, for I knew that he would pick me up, put my bare feet in his sweater pockets and take me out to pet the horses. After supper of beans and biscuits, we often sat on the porch rockers and talked.

It was just about time for me to start first grade. I was excited, but dreaded leaving home, mainly because I would have to leave my little stuffed red rooster at home when I went to school. You see, somehow, I had become overly attached to the rooster, to the point of obsession. I had it with me every minute day and night. One Friday night as I sat on Daddy's lap on the porch, I started crying and told him my fears of being without that little red rooster at school. He just held me tighter and told me he knew a secret that would fix everything.

Oscar Brill started work at Mobile Paint Company as a teenager and was there until he died at age 58. He was plant manager for most of his career.

The next day, he loaded me into the old Ford pickup and took me to the paint plant. As we walked through that immense factory filled with smells that I loved, he told me he was going to show me something very, very secret. He unlocked a large door and as we went inside, I saw one of the large mixing vats in the center of the room. He picked me up so I could see over the rim and he turned on the switch to start the large paddles stirring the paint. "This is what I did during the war. This vat holds the last batch of a rare, rare paint that our country used for our most secret weapons. This paint is invisible, and anything painted with it becomes invisible as well. It was used on only a few of the most important ships manufactured."

As I peered into the vat, I could see the paddles turning and I could see all the way to the bottom of the vat since the paint was invisible. Daddy put me down; he dipped a large ladle into the vat and poured some of the liquid into a Mason jar. He put the lid on and handed it to me. "I am going to give you a little of this secret paint and you can paint only one thing with it. Choose carefully what you paint, for you may never see it again." He gave me a special paint brush, and said the paint must be used at night, and the next morning the painted object would be invisible.

Oh, I was so excited. This was the answer to my little red rooster dilemma. I could paint it, and I could sneak it to school without anyone knowing it was there! I coated it with the wonderful paint from the Mason jar using the special brush, and, sure enough, my rooster was invisible when I woke up the next morning. I took it down to breakfast and no one but I could see it. When school started, the rooster went with me, sat on my desk, and the teacher did not say a word about it. That rooster reminded me that I was never really alone no matter where I might go. I don't remember when the rooster stopped going with me everywhere I went, but I knew I could always find it if I needed it.

My Daddy died when I was only 19 years old, but the treasures he gave live forever with me. Most of those treasures are invisible except to me, but one is tangible proof of a father's love and understanding of his child's greatest fears. When I was going through a trunk of his things, I found the little red rooster wrapped in newspaper. This is what love looks like: a little red rooster.

MYSTERY HOUSE

I am looking for an old house, a house my father lived in when he was very young. Can you help me locate it? Or is it a mystery house that never really existed?

My mother and I sometimes took drives to see places and people that were part of our history. We often went to Bay Minette to visit her parents' graves and then south of town to Pine Grove to visit Ethel Overstreet Jones, aa childhood friend of my mother's. After one visit in about 1967, she directed me somewhere to show me a house where my father had lived as a child for a short while about 1915. I took the snapshot shown here, but now I just cannot find that house!! I have driven miles in the area, and asked countless people including utility workers and mail carriers, but no luck so far. Now I am wondering if perhaps this house is simply a part of folklore and never really existed at all.

The house in the photograph was taken by the author in 1967 or so. It seems to have vanished.

There is a special reason I want to find that house. My father told me a story about the years he lived there, and I want to see if maybe what he told me is true. I never could really tell when my dad was "pulling my leg." This just sounded too real to be a leg-puller.

During the last months of the War Between the States, Blakeley and Spanish Fort were still holding their own in defense of the Port of Mobile. The Union forces had already taken Fort Morgan and were advancing northward to the forts along the waterfront. There was also a contingency of Union soldiers coming from Pensacola as well, and their advance was from the northeast of Blakeley – right through what is now the Pine Grove area.

The house where my father lived had been standing during the war and the lady who lived there had a small child, born while her husband was serving in the Confederate Army. He had never seen his own baby. Local people were frightened by the stories they heard of Yankee invaders and when the lady heard of the impending invasion, she took the only action she could think of in order to protect her child. She hid.

Now in many old houses, the crawl space between the first and second stories is about two feet high. The beams that were used to construct some old homes were about twelve-inch squared timbers, so when the crossbeams were put in, quite a roomy space was created, large enough for a person to crawl through. Just like the house I grew up in, there was a trapdoor cut into the floor of the upstairs of this old house so that the crawl space could be accessed. The woman held her baby and climbed into the space, pulled the door shut, and waited. She fed her baby and cooed him to sleep.

The story is a little fuzzy here. No one knows exactly what happened, but the woman and her child never came out of the hiding place. When the father returned after the war, he found no one in his home and hoped his wife and child had fled to a relative's home for safety. That night, however, he heard a baby crying from above his downstairs bedroom. He ran upstairs but found nothing. After this reoccurred several nights, he decided he could no longer live there and prepared to take a few meager belongings and go in search of his family. Before he left, he remembered the trap door and thought he should be sure nothing of value was hidden in the crawlspace and, you know what he found. He was heartbroken to say the least. He had a Christian burial for his wife and child in the old Brady Cemetery, then he left never to be heard from again. BUT the baby has been heard from again and again and again. Daddy said every resident of the house has reported hearing a baby crying. If you are downstairs it seems to come from above, and if you are upstairs, the crying seems to come from downstairs. That is because it is in the crawl space.

My father said it is true and surely my dad would not pull my leg! Is this house real or simply a picture that appeared by itself in my album? I hope to find out for once and for all. If it is still standing, I hope the baby is finally at peace and cries no more. Please let me know if you recognize this house.

SCREAMS FROM THE WELL

Aunt Voncille took me to see the crumbling cabin where the old folks had homesteaded when they came to Baldwin County from Croatia. Let me tell you what she told me.

The old homeplace was falling in, trees growing through the cracks in the floor, the porch completely shadowed with honeysuckle vine. While prodding around the old place, the mournful whistle of the train on the nearby tracks cried out echoes of early immigrants who came by rail more than 100 years ago. Our people were among those who faced the trials of ocean crossing and Ellis Island. They then made a tiring train voyage to the wilderness of the land around Perdido, Alabama. Some of them, like the Malovich family, spoke only their native language at home throughout the twentieth century. Families from Czechoslovakia and Poland also immigrated to this area, weaving a fabric made of threads from the old country.

This simple wooden cabin was typical of the first homes built by early immigrants. This one is attributed to the Weekley family.

They farmed, worked in turpentine and lumber mills, and for the railroad. Voncille told of her Uncle LeeRoy Weekley, who was station master for the L&N for more than half a century. Perdido was quite the boom town with the train depot the center of life there until about 1950. There were boarding houses, a hotel, a beauty parlor, and barber shop, several stores, a pharmacy, and thriving doctor's office. Voncille remembered them well. Residents of Dyass, Halls Fork, Rabun, and Lottie all came to Perdido for basic needs and to visit.

As we walked around the old cabin, I stumbled as I stepped into a sunken place in the yard. "Oh, yes," Voncille said, "I should have told you to be careful. That is where the well was. Once a well has been dug there will always be a depression no matter how much dirt you use to fill it in. And believe you me, we sure tried to fill it in."

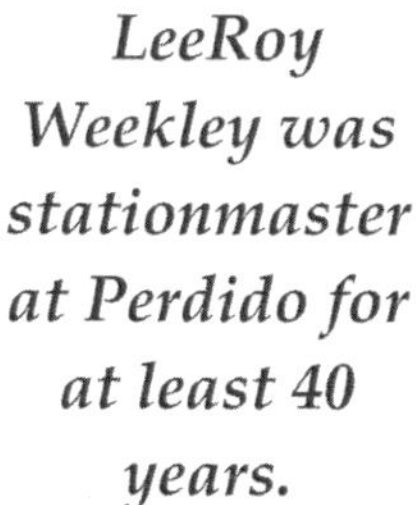

LeeRoy Weekley was stationmaster at Perdido for at least 40 years.

And she told me the story of the well:

"One day, a man with blond hair and blue eyes got off the train. He walked with a crutch made from a forked branch. You see, his left leg was useless; he dragged it with every labored step. This man did not speak any words to anyone. Everyone assumed that he was dumb, but he could sure talk with his own style of language.

"Well, this strange man went into the station master's office and made motions that he was seeking work, pantomiming shoveling and sawing. LeeRoy told him to go try a cabin across the tracks, and the stranger picked up his knapsack and dragged his bad leg right up the path to the Lonvic homestead.

"Guy Lonvic seemed to understand what the stranger wanted. He fed him a bowl of stew and then took him to the barn, brought him a black bear skin, and told him he could sleep on the hay in the corner of the mule stall. The stranger shook his hand vigorously. Many times, you do not need to speak to communicate. But there are other times that a lack of speech can be deadly.

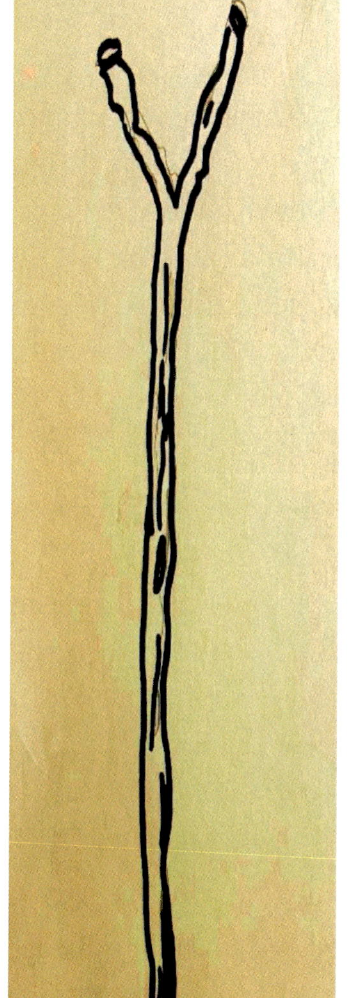

"The stranger caught on quickly to chores he was asked to do. He built a little fence around the cabin, milked the cow, gathered eggs, fed the livestock, and helped with the farming. Soon he was considered a part of the family. He was given a cot on the porch in the summertime. When the baby girl began to crawl about, he built a railing around the porch and he built a sturdy fence made of branches surrounding the well to protect children from falling in.

"For all the years he was here, no one can remember him ever making a vocal sound until his very death - when his screams echoed throughout the woods. In the middle of one of the darkest nights of the year, he was awakened by the scream of what we today call a panther. Anyone from around these parts knows that the real name of the wildcat is "Painter." You have probably never heard the screech of a painter, and if you have, you know it is the most heart-rending sound: like a woman screaming for her life. The stranger grabbed his crutch with one hand and the trusty old gun with the other and headed out into the deadly night to protect the people he loved.

"The family was awakened a little later by screams that seemed almost next to the house. In fact, the screams sounded like two painters in a fight. Guy pulled on his boots and grabbed an axe.

"The screams abruptly stopped. He waited awhile in the silence and figured the two cats had battled, and one way or the other, had departed. When he realized that the stranger was not on the porch, he lit his kerosene lantern and called for him. Now, yards in those days had no grass, just dirt that was swept clean using a broom made out of twigs. As he stepped onto the ground, he noticed some strange tracks. For a little distance, there were the common prints he was used to seeing - one footprint, one crutch print, and a trail of a dragging foot. But there were also prints of a painter. Then near the well, the ground was churned and trampled. The little brushy fence around the well was broken in one place and the dirt churned even more so at the edge of the well. There lay the old gun that was usually on the rack. And a tree limb crutch."

Voncille wiped her eyes with the corner of her apron. I am sure you have deducted what happened, just like Theola and Guy did. They could only think that a cat attacked the stranger, they struggled, and both fell to their deaths into the well, both screaming blood curdling screeches. They grieved for the stranger, and of course, they filled in the well, there being no way to retrieve his body from that abyss of death. They put a small wooden cross at the spot, which was once the well and was then a grave.

Soon after that, the family began hearing the same sounds that had awakened them during that fateful night. The first time they heard painters scream right at the well, Guy jumped up and ran to take revenge on the devil cat. You know what he found - never a thing. Sometimes people said they could hear the screams from deep in the well even in the daytime. They are the loudest when you stand on the spot where once there was a well that is now the unmarked grave of a faithful friend, willing to give his life protecting those who cared for him. To this day no one knows the origin of the stranger who found his way to the little cabin in Perdido, but all who hear the screams coming from deep in the earth know that his story will never be forgotten.

There are not many buildings left near the tracks in Perdido today. Somewhere under the overgrowth are the ruins of a simple cabin and a sunken spot where there was once a well and a wooden cross. Perhaps a local can remember just where it was, but I can't find it again. I miss Voncille and those who knew about the old days and where our people are buried -lying in long forgotten family burial plots. These are our people whose stories make us who we are today.

MILK BOTTLES

Sometimes memories make the best stories –even if the memories may not be exactly the way things happened. Let me tell you the story of the milk bottles as I remember it.

The Brill family ran the Hill Top Grocery store in Toulminville. They lived in the attached house until they bought the Big House on Pleasant Ave.

Dipping my little hands into the barrel of dried peas, I felt them flow through my fingers - great fun for a girl of four playing in her parents' store. At five o'clock Daddy came home from work and Mother went to the adjoining house to start supper. One evening, as Daddy began closing up the store, the screen door squeaked open and a strange woman entered on silent bare feet. She was quite thin, dressed in a most unusual fashion. Her colorful skirt was long and full, and she had a dirty quilt wrapped around her shoulders. Walking silently to the tall wooden counter she raised her hand, lifted a bony finger, and pointed to the milk bottles on the shelf behind Daddy. When he asked if she needed milk, she was silent, just kept pointing. Daddy handed her a bottle and she tucked it inside her quilt shawl. When Daddy told her the cost of the milk was a nickel, she looked down, turned, and left. During the Depression, Daddy often gave groceries to those in need, so he did not think this too unusual.

The next afternoon, the exact same thing happened. This time I paid closer attention to the stranger as she pointed to the milk, took it, and tucked it under the quilt. Daddy came from behind the counter and held the screen door open as she walked down the crooked wooden steps. We watched her continue down the dirt road and turn into a small lane where the Romas had camped until the week before. Back then we called them Gypsies. I loved to walk by the Gypsy camp, hear the music and smell the meals cooked over the open fires. I always wanted to see inside of one of the colorful caravans.

Dean Mosher, Fairhope artist and author, built this replica of a wagon used by Romas in caravans throughout the United States.

The third evening when the lady left with the milk, my father took my hand and we followed her. As she turned down the Gypsy camp lane, she walked to the edge of the clearing and disappeared into a mist. Daddy and I went home, fetched my brothers and mother, and a couple of shovels. I had no idea what he would do, but I soon saw with my very own little four-year-old eyes. Daddy and the boys began digging right where the lady had disappeared. My mother pulled me farther away when the shovels hit something hard. They saw there a crude coffin and creaked open the lid.

There lay the lifeless body of the woman who had come to get milk three days in a row. She was wrapped in the dirty quilt, and beside her there were three empty milk bottles. When my father reached to pick up the bottles, he noticed movement under the quilt. He pulled the quilt away and there was a beautiful little girl, alive and squirming there next to her mother. Daddy lifted the baby from the coffin and brought her over to Mother, "I guess this is a miracle." Mother wrapped the baby in her apron and hurried home to bathe and feed the precious child who had been kept alive by the milk.

I don't remember my parents ever talking about the night that my baby sister came. They named her Beverly and we loved each other more every year. When she was old enough to play in the store in the afternoons, she often looked toward the screen door that opened and closed on its own. We saw her smile at someone she was seeing there in the Hill Top Grocery Store. One day she asked about the beautiful lady who comes in the store late afternoons just as Daddy is closing up. Daddy told her that she must be an angel who comes to see the beautiful little girl playing in the dried peas.

Beverly and I are close to this very day, and I beg you not to tell her about the night we found her in the Gypsy grave, for she still doesn't know.

SYRUP MAKIN' AND THEM PIGS

Last week, we were taking a fall afternoon drive on the back roads of Baldwin County, soaking in the beauty of cotton and soybean fields, and an occasional stand of sugar cane. Then we came across something we had never seen before: a pig crossing sign. That reminded me that memories of pigs and syrup-making can get all mixed in together.

A rarely seen road sign was spotted in Spanish Fort near a dead-end street.

Fall is the time of year when the first frosty morning says, "Time to make syrup." I mean real cane syrup – not sorghum or molasses, but the kind made from good old southern sugar cane and is pronounced SURP, not SEER-UP! Time to make it is when the cane is perfect, after a good rain to make it juicy and before that first hard freeze.

I was lucky enough to be staying there on the farm one fall when the cane was stripped and cut, hauled in the old farm wagon, and piled next to the mill. Of course, we had already made a couple of visits to the cane patch to cut a few stalks to chew. Chewing that stringy pulp until there was no sugar left was the sweetest experience a child could know back then.

Uncle Sonny spent hours checking the mill and readying the cooking shed. When the big day finally came everyone was up early. By daybreak Uncle Sonny and Aunt Lucille had already milked the cows and neighbors had come from miles around to help out so they could claim a can of that delectable treat at the end of the day. That was a good thing, because syrup-making calls for many cooks in the "kitchen." I can see that mule walking around and around powering the grinding mill and remember feeding the stalks of cane into the jaws that squeezed that incredible nectar from the stalks. Most everyone took a swig from the jelly glass passed around to garner approval on that year's cane juice. The wooden kegs of juice were emptied into the kettle, a 10-foot-long rectangular cast iron tray placed over the brick firebox. The bubbling juice flowed down the tray through a maze of channels, constantly stirred with wooden paddles to keep it from scorching. As it started to boil harder, a foam began to form on the top and the work became even more intense. The foam was skimmed off with an old pot with holes punched in the bottom and put in a bucket to be fed to the hogs.

Syrup-making is an art almost lost. After the cane is cut, it is squeezed, and the juice cooked to just the right consistency.

The greatest skill of all was knowing when to "pull" the syrup. There was no thermometer telling the perfect time to drain the liquid. A few degrees can make a huge difference in whether the syrup will crystalize or not. The first pull was put in a mason jar and held up to the light. A beautiful amber color let the light shine through and made Uncle Sonny smile. The plug was pulled, and the first batch of syrup flowed into a five-gallon bucket, then poured into shiny silver cans and sealed. The workers all got a taste on top of the cathead biscuits Aunt Lucille brought hot from the kitchen. This went on for hours and hours, until almost dark.

When the final pull was made, a sense of well-being settled over the group. This time the jelly glass passed around to the adults held a clear liquid poured from a crockery jug Uncle Sonny kept in the washhouse.

Uncle Sonny and family feed the sugar cane stalks into the mill.

But the fondest memory happened a little later. Every farm had pigs back then. The skimmings of the syrup-making helped fatten those pigs and old folks said it made the bacon even tastier. As the buckets of foam were filled, it was my job to take them to the sty and pour them into the trough. However, somehow one of those buckets got moved over to the side of the nearby shed and we all forgot about it. Anyone knows cane skimmings are easy to ferment, like any extra sweet juice. A couple of days later while cleaning up the mill we saw the bucket, which by that time smelled like a brewery. I lugged it to the pig trough and watched those swine swill it right up.

After a while, we heard a most unusual sound coming from the pig sty. There we saw the biggest boar with his head stuck through the fence, howling in a way I have never heard a hog bellow. It was almost musical in nature. We walked a little closer and noticed one sow stumbling through the muck. Every time she stood up, she staggered and fell right back into the mud. Another pig was lying on his back with his feet straight up in the air. "Well, I'll be," said Uncle Sonny, "I do believe them pigs is drunk." You' ain't seen nothin' 'til you see a sty full of drunk pigs.

The reader may be wondering whether this story falls into the category of folklore. Yes, my friends, this is how folklore is born. By the time this story is told to the next generation those pigs will be singing "Sweet Adeline" and playing a hand of poker – and those hams will inebriate everyone who tastes them! In fact, when you tell it, I am sure you can add a little to it. I have some cut cane on my porch right now. Come on by and 'set a spell.' We'll chew some and tell stories.

OVERRRUN BY YANKEES

Yep, I hear the phrase "we been overrun by Yankees" all the time. In fact, my Dad said it back in the 1940's even after he married a northern girl.

I can write this because I am half Yankee, but I don't usually tell people that. My mother came south from Ohio during the great immigration movement in the early twentieth century. After she married my dad, who **was** a native Baldwin Countian, she always said, "I am Yankee by birth, but Southern by choice." She did indeed become a true southern lady in most ways. However, a few Yankee traditions crept in – like a love of rutabagas and turnip roots and sayings like "I stove my toe," meaning "stubbed."

Leafy and Henry Coon took their two daughters and headed south to the promised land.

From 1900 to 1930 thousands came and thousands stayed. Most of those who came from the Midwest came as groups. Nearly all of those from the Midwest were first generation immigrants from Europe who had entered the US through Ellis Island. In their communities up north, some found the cold unbearable and the soil not suitable for the crops they knew how to raise, so they bought a ticket south and loaded their meager possessions in boxcars on the L&N line.

Of course, they tended to settle near where people were of similar heritage. These pockets of communities shared common ethnicity and culture. Because of Baldwin County's size and poor road systems, most were actually quite isolated. They held on to their native heritage and others began to identify towns according to their common culture, such as German in Elberta. Baldwin County had about 20 distinct cultural groups for at least 100 years.

"The South Land" is Calling You!

Why Stay in the Frozen North?

Come to Sunny Alabama—live among the orange blossoms and let "the mocking birds sing you to sleep every night." All year 'round climate, where you can enjoy out-door life each month of the year.

A Semi-Tropical climate where truck farming, orange, and fruit culture are unsurpassed—the Robertsdale and Silverhill Districts.

Golden opportunity awaits the industrious man of moderate means, in this land of sunshine and flowers.

Write me personally, and tell me about what sized place you would like, and let me help you make a selection in a community among your own people, where schools, churches and social conditions will be the most satisfactory.

IMPROVED AND UNIMPROVED FARMS AND RAW LANDS.

WRITE TO-DAY---DO IT NOW!!

The sooner you come the better selection and deal you will be able to make.

ANTON F. WESLEY

ROBERTSDALE and SILVERHILL :-: :-: BALDWIN COUNTY, ALABAMA

Land developers advertised widely to attract newcomers to Baldwin County.

The Baldwin Times listed the following groups in the 1939 Anniversary Edition.

BALDWIN HOME TO MANY PEOPLES

Baldwin County has witnessed an influx of residents who hail from various backgrounds. The latest figures reflect the following estimated makeup:

Natives	26%
German	19%
Italian	17%
Czech/Moravian	11%
Scandinavian	9%
African Americans	9%
Greek	7%
French	3%
Polish	3%

The editor added one last group to the list:

Yankees	67%

I am not really sure that most of the early immigrants called themselves Yankees, but locals sure called them that because they actually moved here from above the Mason-Dixon line. My mother's parents came from Ohio to join a group of Amish friends they knew who had settled in Bay Minette. They stayed at the Hamilton Hotel, then a real estate agent took them out to the Phillipsville area where they bought a 20-acre farm.

My mother was called a Yankee at Pleasant View Elementary School and Baldwin County High School, but she actually was proud of her Ohio roots. So, I guess she was still Yankee 'til the day she died. At least I am half southern – the better half. Of course, the term Yankee is actually an endearment, since most of us here now have some Yankee 'blood.' Maybe the southern blood is redder, making us rednecks by birth.

"YANKEES WELCOME" sign once seen along Highway 59 heading to Gulf Shores.

Nowadays there is a different strain of Yankee blood around here. We love our Snowbirds and are happy when they decide to trade the cold winters and become a part of our bounty and beauty, but……we still call them Yankees. This Southern heritage has to rub off on them eventually – after all, "YA'LL" are Southern by Choice.

GIRL IN THE WINDOW

Leafy and William read the advertisement in the Chicago Tribune: "Bounteous Farmland in Alabama- Cheap." Let me tell you the story just as my Grandmother Leafy Coon wrote it more than 100 years ago.

"Your grandfather Bill and I packed up our little girls, your Aunt Margaret and your mother, Harriet. The southbound L&N train was hot, crowded with people seeking their futures in the Promised Land. Across the aisle sat a lovely girl with tears running down her cheeks, so I gave her a motherly shoulder to cry on. It was not long before she confided in me. Maureen was a loving daughter in her Amish family in Ohio, but when she realized she would bring shame on her family if she stayed, she took her cheese money and slipped away in the night. She, too, had heard of Baldwin County, and hoped to find work.

The depot at Bay Minette stood south of town.
It was the hub of activity most days.

The Hamilton Hotel was one of the hotels welcoming prospective home buyers. The Coon family stayed here until they found a house to rent in Phillipsville.

"When we arrived in Bay Minette, we all stayed overnight at the Hamilton Hotel. An agent showed our family some farmland on Phillipsville Road, and we decided to stay, but Maureen boarded the Homeseekers' Excursion on the spur line running south. At the second stop, she saw the grand Loxley Hotel and hoped to find work there. She was hired on the spot by the kindly owner; her Amish training served her well as she kept the hotel spotless and cooked delicious meals. She was given a room in the upper right corner of the railside inn.

Each stop along the rail spur running from Bay Minette to Foley had hotels. The Loxley Hotel was one of the finest.

"The hotel owner soon realized why Maureen had run away from home; she reassured her the new baby would be welcomed into their world. After the baby's birth, Mother and daughter lived there happily as long as that proprietor was alive. However, when she died the new owner was not pleased with a child living in the hotel. He made the little girl stay in her room all the time, with the understanding that if guests ever saw the child, Maureen and her daughter would have to leave. The little girl seemed happy in her room, busy with dolls and books, but she often looked out the window watching townspeople pass by and newcomers get off the train. When Maureen ran errands, she always looked up at the window, seeing her lovely daughter holding her doll. When I went to visit them I, too, saw the child at the window as I got off the train. She was always there. Maureen wrote me many letters – she was homesick but wanted her parents to hear from her never again.

The Eastlake style rocking chair was once in the old Loxley Hotel, where it was said to have rocked all by itself. It still does.

"When the great influenza epidemic hit the county, it was disastrous. The hotel shut down for a bit, but when the epidemic subsided, and it reopened, Maureen did not come downstairs. The proprietor went upstairs, heard her singing and the rocking chair creaking. After no one answered his knock, he opened the door. He saw the loving mother rocking her little girl. When she did not answer his questions, he approached them and realized there was not a breath of life in either one.

"After the burial, the hotel returned to business as usual – except for one little detail. Anytime a guest was assigned to the upper right bedroom the owner would be awakened during the night by the guest demanding to be moved. Many claimed they heard creaking and the saw the chair rocking. The owner put the chair in the attic, but still roomers heard eerie sounds. He finally closed off the room and never again rented it out.

"Later, when I went on the train to Foley, I looked at the old hotel and there in that window I saw a vision of a little girl holding her doll. The conductor told me that she appears many times as he passes through, so I told him the story, and he enthralled passengers for years with the legend behind the girl in the window."

A few people are able to see the image in the window even in more recet days. When the hotel was permanently closed and furniture auctioned, I bought this very rocking chair I am sitting in. I hope you will always take care of it in memory of Maureen and her beautiful little girl. And if you go to look at the spot where that lovely hotel once stood, wave to the little girl for me. She is still there waiting for her mother.

The Loxley Hotel in ruins was photographed by the author before the hotel was demolished. The little girl is clearly seen waiting at the upstairs right window.

A VISIT FROM THANKSGIVING PAST

Just as we are captivated each Christmas season by Dickens' Christmas Carol, Thanksgiving brings time for visits from the ghosts of Thanksgivings Past. This is the time for sharing those memories that make our heritage. The best stories are told by the old folks to the youngsters who have no idea what life was like in the "olden days" when their grandparents lived without a television – or even when their parents were young and had to walk all the way up to the television in order to change the channel.

Not too many people actually went over the river and through the woods to grandmother's house, but we could! We sang those words over and over in the old Willis Jeepster on our way to have Thanksgiving at Granny's. All my cousins came to the cabin where she and Grampa lived -- the place where Grampa was born, an unpainted house down a dirt country road. My family was usually the first to arrive and each time a different car pulled up, we all ran out to scream, grab a cousin's hands, and jump up and down in a circle. The women hugged and the men performed the age-old male ritual of back slapping and punching.

Families lucky enough to have an automobile were able to take trips to visit family for holidays. This Jeepster was a prized possession of the Brill family.

While the grown-ups caught up with each other, the children played those games we loved. There was a split rail fence around the house and the dirt yard inside the fence was swept clean, making the best playground in the world. We drew a hopscotch in the dirt and used broken pieces of colored glass for our markers. We played jump the river, where we took turns trying to make it over two sticks that were moved further and further apart after each round. Even with a running start, if your footprint was not clearly over the stick, you were out. At dusk, we began the scary game of hide-and-seek, and the only boundary was the woodline. The outbuildings, woodpiles, and farm machinery made great places to hide.

We dreaded to hear our mothers call us in for supper at dusk, but we were hungry, and it felt comforting to come inside the cozy old house. The cabin had a sink with a faucet in the kitchen, but the bathroom was still outside, down the path. Some of us washed up on the back porch using the cold, cold water from the pump. Those who were chicken washed up at the kitchen sink with some water Granny had heated on the stove. There were no full body baths while we were there for Thanksgiving. Granny and Grampa would use a large tin washtub brought in the kitchen when they felt they were in need of a real bath. Supper was hot biscuits and ham and we were allowed to eat all we could hold, sitting at the table since the adults had eaten before we came in. For most family meals, the children sat on the floor around some spread-out newspapers and the adults used the old farm table that had been scrubbed so many times, it felt as smooth as glass

The family stories about wagon train journeys all center around the chair used by ancestors in cross country journeys. (Photo courtesy of Harrison Inlow)

Granny and Grampa were proud of their newly installed electricity. We all begged Granny to turn off the light so we could talk and tell stories by only the light of the fireplace and a kerosene lantern. She reached up and pulled the chain hanging from the bare light bulb in the middle of the room. We sat on the wide planks of the floor, which did not meet perfectly so you could feel the draft coming in from under the house. Granny then told us all about how she had come on a covered wagon when she was about four years old. She showed us the very chair she sat in while on that wagon and let us take turns sitting on it.

In all the years past, the children had slept on quilts on the floor near the fireplace, but this year we slept in the loft because our parents brought electric blankets. The lightbulb hanging from the ceiling had electrical outlet connections where the cords of the blankets were connected. It is a wonder we did not all catch fire!

We awoke to the smells of turkey and sweet potatoes roasting in the wood burning stove. Pulling on jackets over our pajamas, we raced to the outhouse. The boys disappeared into the woods for a minute or two, but the girls crowded in the two-seater. We then gathered the eggs for Granny, which she fried up right away to go with the grits she had soaked overnight and started cooking at daybreak.

A Brill family Thanksgiving dinner was worth a photograph even in those early days of Kodak Brownie cameras. It was weeks before the film was developed, and results seen. Ah, the Good Ol'Days.

Thanksgiving Dinner was to be served at noon – country people eat on pretty regular schedules. The noon meal is Dinner, and the light evening meal is supper. The menfolk went deer hunting while we played outside and by noon were starving. The serving bowls and the turkey were placed on the table and we all held hands around it while Grampa returned thanks with a special emphasis on the "Thanks" this time. The adults fixed plates for the children who sat picnic style around the newspapers. The cornbread dressing and the marshmallows on top of the sweet potato delight were wonderful, but the best part of the meal was the laughter from the adult table.

The next day was the beginning of the Christmas season. Grampa hitched the mule to the wagon and took us into the woods to cut his Christmas tree which we helped decorate that afternoon. As we made popcorn garlands, we talked about Santa and what we would ask him to bring. We then pored over Granny's Sears catalogue, and we truly understood why it was called the *Wishbook!* Granny brought out the paper and pencils and we each wrote a letter to Santa before falling dead tired onto the pallets upstairs. Saturday morning was a frenzy of packing cars and saying goodbyes to those we loved so dearly and saw way too rarely. Our voices were a little subdued as we rode home, but the echoes of the week were still heard, "Hooray for the fun, Is the pudding done? Hooray for Thanksgiving Day."

Special thanks to Jeannette Ryan and Pam Gilpin for sharing their precious Thanksgiving memories with me. So many of them were so like those of my family, they needed to be put into words here, for memories may fade, but the written word lives on.

Photo by Penny Taylor

CHAPTER 2
PEOPLE FROM OUR PAST

Many times, real people of our history take on a larger than life persona.

Every story has the flavor added by time and teller.

PRINCE MADOC

Did He or Didn't He? Prince Madoc of Wales Discovers New World

As a little girl, I remember seeing the historic marker at Fort Morgan naming Prince Madoc as the first European to come to America. I have believed that "fact" ever since, even though scholars claim it is a myth. If so, it is a very believable myth.

For years, a marker stood at Fort Morgan recognizing the earliest discovery of America by a Welshman.

In my postcard collection I found a postcard of the historic marker that was placed at Fort Morgan in 1953 by the Daughters of the American Revolution. It reads:

In memory of Prince Madoc, a Welsh explorer who landed on the shores of Mobile Bay in 1170 and left behind with the Indians, the Welsh language.

Authority is- Encyclopedia Americana copyright 1918-Webster's Encyclopedia – Richard Hakluyt: 1552-1610, a Welsh Historian and Geographer- Ridpath's History of the World- ancient Roman coins found in Forts in Tenn. These forts resemble the forts of Wales of the 9th and 10th centuries and of the white Indians of the Tennessee and Missouri Rivers.

Legitimate historians are quick to point out that there is no proof of the visit of the Welshman long before Columbus landed on the shores of the New World, but traditional stories seem to persist. I guess people just love a good mystery. That is what folklore is all about.

Welsh legend carries the well-known tale of Madog (Madoc), one of the 13 children of OWain Gwyedd, king of Gwynedd in the 12th century. After the king's death in 1169, the crown was in dispute and at that time, Madoc left for an adventure on the high seas. He returned with exciting reports of the land which is now the Gulf Coast of Alabama where he had left a colony of 120. Persuading others to join him, his new party left from Lundy in 1171 on a return journey to the New World but were never heard from again.

Hatchett Chandler, long time manager of Fort Morgan, wrote that when England heard that Spain was taking credit for being the first to claim the New World after Columbus's journeys, they put forth their evidence of the earlier English claim. They made it known that the Welsh had long before established colonies on the continent. Poet Robert Southley, wrote an epic named "Madoc" in celebration of the prince's first voyage to America, wherein Madoc says he "stood triumphant on another world."

Madoc

Much later, discoveries in the New World added to the body of belief that the Welshmen had traveled north along the river systems. The remains of stone forts in North Alabama, Georgia, and Tennessee are said by some archaeologists to have been built well before the Columbus era and strongly resemble the forts built in England and Wales in the 9th and 10th centuries. Some compare them to Castle Dolwyddelan, the home of Prince Madoc. Hatchett Chandler printed a letter he found in the Newberry Library in Chicago -- an 1810 letter from Gov. John Sevier of Tennessee. Sevier wrote that he had interaction with

Cherokee Indians who said the forts had been built by white men who lived centuries earlier. He wrote that Chief Oconostota referred to the people his grandfather called Welsh and that there was in existence a book which reportedly was written with Welsh characters.

Historians agree that there was indeed a Prince Madoc and his castle ruins are still visible.

The most fascinating piece of the evidence believers put forth was gathered by artist George Catlin, a nineteenth century painter who spent eight years among the native American tribes, including the Mandans living along the Missouri River. They were known as white men with forts, living in towns laid out in squares and using Welsh style coracles instead of canoes for fishing. There were many elements of the Welsh language among their people and their hair and eye coloring were much more European than Indian. Gov. John Sevier reported the discovery of six skeletons wearing brass armor with the Welsh coat-of-arms engraved. Catlin's paintings reflect his observations among the Mandans.

Yes, I certainly understand that there is no concrete proof of Madoc's visit to Baldwin County, but then again, I have not seen any proof that he did not come. Such is the nature of legend and there are many proponents active in purporting the theory. It is sure fun to think about, anyway.

The marker was removed from its place at Fort Morgan at some point, either as a result of lack of historical evidence or of hurricane damage. It was returned to the Daughters of the American Revolution and stored at the Richards DAR House in Mobile. It was later moved to the Mobile Museum of History where it remains preserved. I mean, after all, if it was cast in bronze, it must be true.

OH, LEANDER

This story may not be found in history textbooks used in schools, but is one every child should hear, for not only is it entertaining, it could save a life.

The saga of Hernando DeSoto's exploration of the south is found in virtually every resource on early Alabama history. Children learn of his meeting with Chief Tuscaloosa, the Battle of Mauvilla, and his burial in the Mississippi River.

However, there is much more to the story – some details have come down through the ages without primary sources to back them up. Those stories can't be proven but they can't be disproven either. And they sure do make sense!

When DeSoto began his journey in Florida, he sent his ships back to Cuba with instructions to meet him later at the next big river to the west, which is the mouth of Mobile Bay. When the ships arrived at Gulf Shores, Hernando's beautiful wife Isabella was aboard. She is credited with planting the first fig trees and Nerium bushes in the New World. The Nerium shrubs were her favorite, and she walked by them every day calling for her husband using her pet name for him, Leander. As she cried, "Oh, Leander, come back to me," her tears watered the plants and their name Oleander came to be. Soldiers brought Isabella news of the Battle of Mauvilla and carried orders for the ships to meet DeSoto at the next large delta, the mouth of the Mississippi River. As Isabella sailed away from the Alabama shores, she could see the Oleander blooms and knew she was leaving behind hopes of seeing her husband alive again, and in her sorrow placed a deadly curse on the plants.

Oleander shrubs still thrive throughout the southern United States. They do well in sandy soil, bear long hot spells without water, and are tolerant of mild freezes. They can grow to almost 20 feet high and from April to November are filled with fragrant and pink, white, and red blooms. However, their beauty hides a dreadful secret. Oleanders are among the most poisonous plants in the world. Gardeners must be extra careful with the clipping of the bushes as their sweet odor is especially attractive to horses and other livestock. When I was a child, my father always warned me to never get near the smoke of burning oleander branches as it could cause blindness.

The shrub Oleander is a favorite planting in the deep south.
It, however, holds a deadly secret.

Many people have told me the story of the Girl Scout troop which was on a camping trip. The leader showed the girls how to cut branches of a nearby bush and shave the leaves away, making perfect skewers for roasting hot dogs over the campfire. The next morning, the entire group was found unconscious and most died. The Oleander sticks left around the campsite told the story.

I hope the reader will share the story of the Oleander bush with someone. You may save a life.

BOY WITH THE SNAKE TATTOOS

Walk among the cypress trees and wildlife on an island in Bottle Creek deep in the Mobile River Delta if you dare. Not only are there snakes, alligators, and other critters, there is the danger of unseen perils, for this is the location of the Curse of Mound Island.

It is hard these days being the mother of a teenage son. Things are sure not like the used to be. Or are they? More than 300 years ago in Montreal, Mother LeMoyne worried about little Bienville. She knew his adventuresome spirit would one day serve him well, but sometimes she wondered if she would live to see that day.

Bienville was only one of her fourteen children, but she knew he was special. Like his brothers, he followed in his father's footsteps and joined the French Army. By the time he was 18 he had been wounded fighting the British in Canada and was in France for recuperation.

The new I-10 tunnel under the Mobile River was adorned with sculpture designed by Julian Rayford. The symbolism reflects Bienville's fascination with the local native Americans.

King Louis XIV commissioned Bienville's older brother, D'Iberville, with the establishment of forts along the southern coast of North America to protect the land claimed by LaSalle. The expedition left Brest, France, in 1698 with four vessels and the teen-aged Bienville. By 1702 Fort Louis was founded in the Mobile Tensaw

Delta 27 miles north of present day Mobile, ideal for trade with the Indians, yet far from marauding pirates.

Immediately, D'Iberville sent his younger brother out to explore the delta and the Native Americans. Bienville was just the person for this. He was in his element, a natural linguist who absorbed every culture he encountered.

He had heard of a sacred site deep in the delta and talked his guide into taking him there. He paid him with a much-coveted fire stick, a blunderbuss. They canoed through a twisted maze of rivers in the delta. Approaching the island, what a spectacle he beheld. There through the fog of the cypress swamps rose an island majestically crowned by a mound more than 45 feet tall.

The island had been the center of the largest Mississippian chiefdom of the central Gulf Coast, composed of 18 mounds. The mounds had taken more than 100 years to build, using woven baskets filled with clay carried there by workers in canoes. The center had been occupied by about 2000 people of the Pensacola culture, related to the Indians of the Moundville complex further north.

By the time Bienville came, it was sparsely occupied, but still revered by cultures such as the Mobilian Native Americans. Bienville's guide was so fearful of the site that he turned his back as Bienville climbed the tallest mound and entered the crude temple standing there. On the altar were the stone (perhaps ceramic or clay) figures that held power over the people: a man, a woman, a child, bear, and owl. His next action seems out of character for the man who respected and interacted with the local Native Americans, but remember he was still very young. He took the figures and delivered them to his brother.

John Sledge, one of the most respected historical authors in our area, writes of the Mound Island theft in his recent book, ***Mobile River***. He quotes from D'Iberville's journals, "The Indians who see them here are amazed at our boldness and amazed that we do not die as a result. I am taking the images to France, although they are not particularly interesting."

D'Iberville died in 1706 in Havana. Coincidence? Or Curse?

Bienville grew more and more involved in the Native American culture. He had himself tattooed with snake designs from neck to foot. The skin was pricked with a bone needle and ash was rubbed into the wound to dye the image under the skin. In 1720, Bertet de la Clue wrote, "They have their skins covered with figures of snakes which they make with the point of a needle. Mr. de Bienville who is the general of the country has all of his body covered in this way and when he is obliged to march to war with them, he makes himself nude like them. They like him very much, but they also fear him."

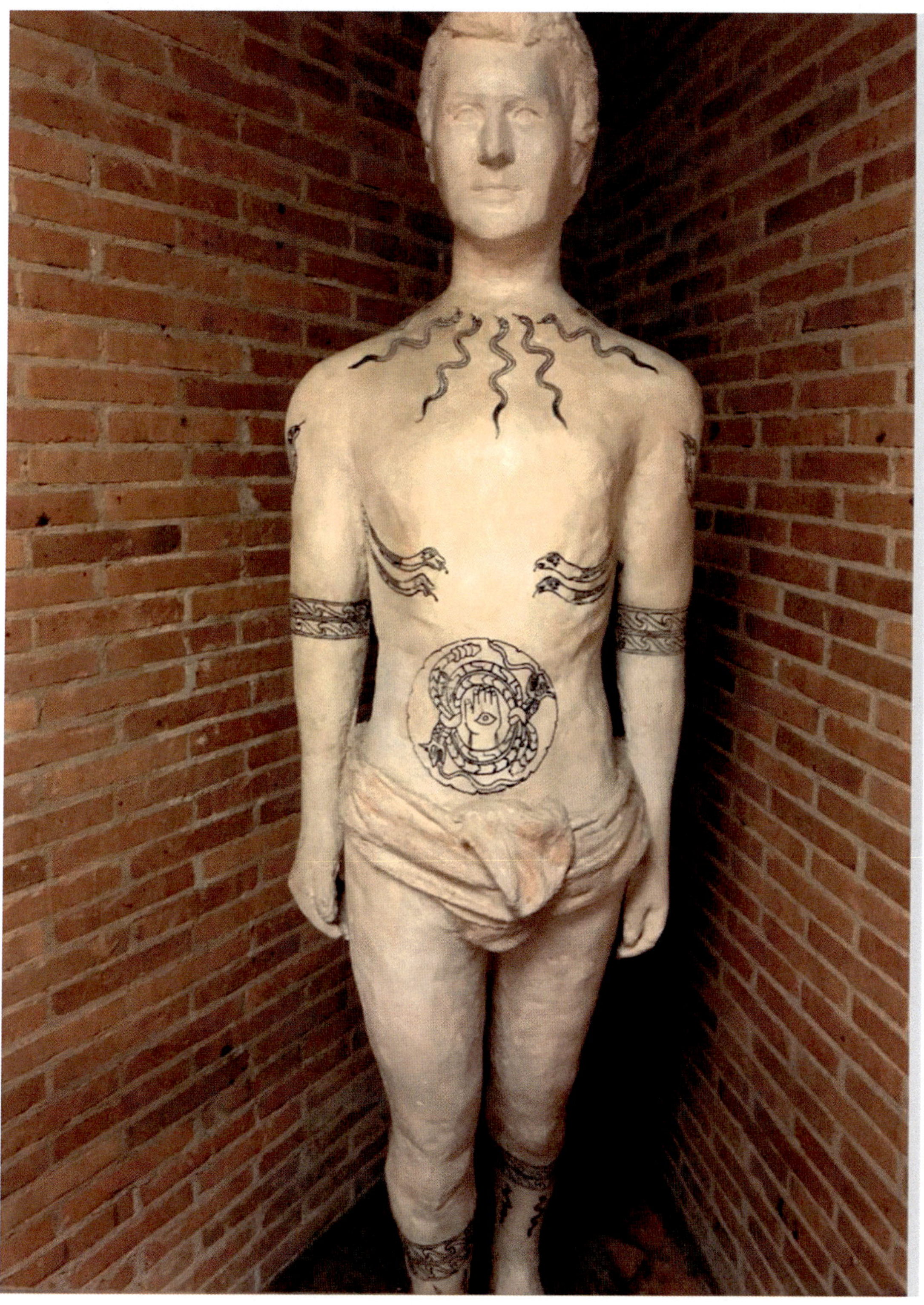

There is a statue on display at the Fort Conde museum based on research done by Jacob Laurence of the History of Mobile Museum. He said it is really conservative, that there were probably many, many more snake tattoos in intricate patterns. Another local folklorist and historian, Julian Rayford, spent countless hours studying Bienville. He designed the bronze figures on the Wallace Tunnel. One is a figure of the Indian holding the famous disc modeled after the one found in Moundville. Some say that 'Judy', as he was known, really meant this figure to be of Bienville in his Native garb. The other figure is of Bienville in traditional clothing.

Sean Herman is taking the reins left dangling with Julian Rayford's death. He and his wife Amanda are owners of Serpents of Bienville, a project to preserve the folk heritage of our area. Sean is also an amazing artist. His Bienville Disc design is his interpretation of Bienville's tattoos and artifacts discovered in our area. He performs his tattoo magic on many satisfied clients.

Bienville must have overcome the curse as he lived a long productive life, eventually being appointed governor in 1732. After more than four decades in the New World, he returned to France, and died in Paris at age 88. Could his tattoos have been his act of contrition? Perhaps the gods heard his pleas and removed the curse from him.

Where are the figures now? Are they bringing death and destruction? John Sledge still has hopes the religious figures will be found one day in the dusty storage room of some museum in France. Or could they be in Havana?

Historic Blakeley conducts tours of the Bottle Creek Mounds occasionally. The area is now a National Historic Site administered by the Alabama Historic Commission. Access to the island is strictly controlled. The curse is there anyway, so unless your body is covered with snake tattoos and you go there naked, you should beware. I think the next time I go I will take Sean along. Or maybe I will get my own tattoo first.

Tours to Mound Island and the Bottle Creek Mounds are conducted on a regular basis from Historic Blakeley State Park. It is quite strenuous, but well worth the effort for those hardy enough. It is well protected and not open to the general public without prior arrangements.

I often wondered what Bienville's mother said when they were reunited years later. It has to be something like, "I knew it. As soon as you leave home, you go and get a tattoo!" Just like mothers 300 years later.

Visit www.serpentsofbienville.com to find out more about Sean and Amanda Herman and their project. ***The Mobile River*** *by John S Sledge, 2015, is available at local bookstores.*

BATTLESHIP PETE

I well remember riding across the Highway 90 and 98 Causeway before the Interstate 10 Bay Way was built. I could see the huts out on the little patch of land my Daddy called Goat Island. Sometimes I was lucky enough to catch a glimpse of Battleship Pete, the man who called the island home. I felt important because my father had been to that island and knew the legendary character personally.

One Thursday night my Daddy told Mother that he would not be home the next night. He said he and a buddy were going to spend Friday night out at the "Camp" with Battleship Pete so they could get an early start fishing on Saturday. I could hardly wait to hear all about his adventure. I loved imagining what it must be like to live all alone on that island we could see from the Causeway every time we crossed Mobile Bay. We could see it best just as we crossed the narrow Admiral Semmes Bridge drawbridge, and I often envied the man that lived there.

As Daddy cleaned his catch at home that Saturday night, he told me they had slept in bunk beds in a cabin Battleship Pete had built for guests. There was a jukebox in the middle of that hut, run by a generator. They used jugs of fresh water they had brought with them and cooked their food in the cooking shed. Pete had a separate sleeping hut and there was an outhouse. (Daddy had to explain what an outhouse was…) "Yes," Daddy said, "There were goats all over the little island. Pete keeps them there to clear the underbrush that used to cover the island. He also has chickens and rabbits."

Legends may call Battleship Pete a hermit, but he was certainly not one! He had many friends and came to town at least once a week. Let me tell you his story. Peter Felix Bernard was born up north in 1869 and started working in the shipbuilding industry at age 16. He worked in several shipyards in Canada and the US as a boilermaker. In 1902 he helped build the *New Jersey*, one of the BB-16s, part of the Great White Fleet used in the North Atlantic when Teddy Roosevelt was determined to circumnavigate the earth as part of his Big Stick plan. That was about the time Peter's friends started calling him Battleship Pete.

Most of what is known about Battleship Pete is recorded in booklet by Merlin J. Miller.

He married a Canadian girl and they had a son. He left them in Washington to find work, but when he returned, he could not find them. Pete continued to bounce around, eventually settling in Mobile working at Mobile Shipyard and Shipbuilding Company and later at Todd Shipyards. He retired from shipbuilding when he turned 62 in 1931, but his life was hardly over!

He boarded in various places in the area of Mobile around St. Emanuel, Eslava, and South Royal Streets, and began keeping a boat at the foot of Eslava Street, according to Lawrence Stauter of the famous Stauter Boat family. He spent days in his old boat, mostly catching crabs which he sold to Southern Fish and Oyster Company. At age 76 he thought he would take a stab at running a restaurant, so he opened one at 220 South Royal Street. He closed it four years later in 1949. All this time he was active at the Union Hall of the CIO and had lots of friends.

I guess Pete lived the life of leisure as long as he could stand it, because just a few years later he opened an oyster bar at 270 South Royal street. A sign painted by Fasco Beverage Company hung over the door: **Pete's Place Cold Drinks**. During the years Pete ran the bar, *Shipbuilder* magazine ran a story about Pete. As fate would have it, a man who knew Pete's son showed Pete, Jr. the article. When Pete, Jr. came from Detroit to visit his father, the local newspaper ran a story about the reunion. Pete, Jr. had followed his father's footsteps in the industry, and he brought the old man news that he had a 25-year-old grandson living in Florida.

Their visit was short, but it did connect Pete with his relatives. His older sister living in California also visited Pete in Mobile when she was 87 in 1953. He learned that his son had died in 1958, and he began to spend more and more time on his boat and would often sleep over on the little patch of land about a mile from shore. So, at age 88 he decided to end his city life routine and move to the island.

The island was actually created during the Civil War as a defense battery protecting the city of Mobile. Battery McIntosh was built with pilings driven into the bay bottom and filled in with soil barged in from miles away. It rose 24 feet above the water, had a magazine, seven cannons, and the troops who manned them. The walkway built surrounding the battery was constantly walked by sentinels on guard duty. After the war, it was left to nature's will, and visited only by boaters, until Pete decided to make it his home.

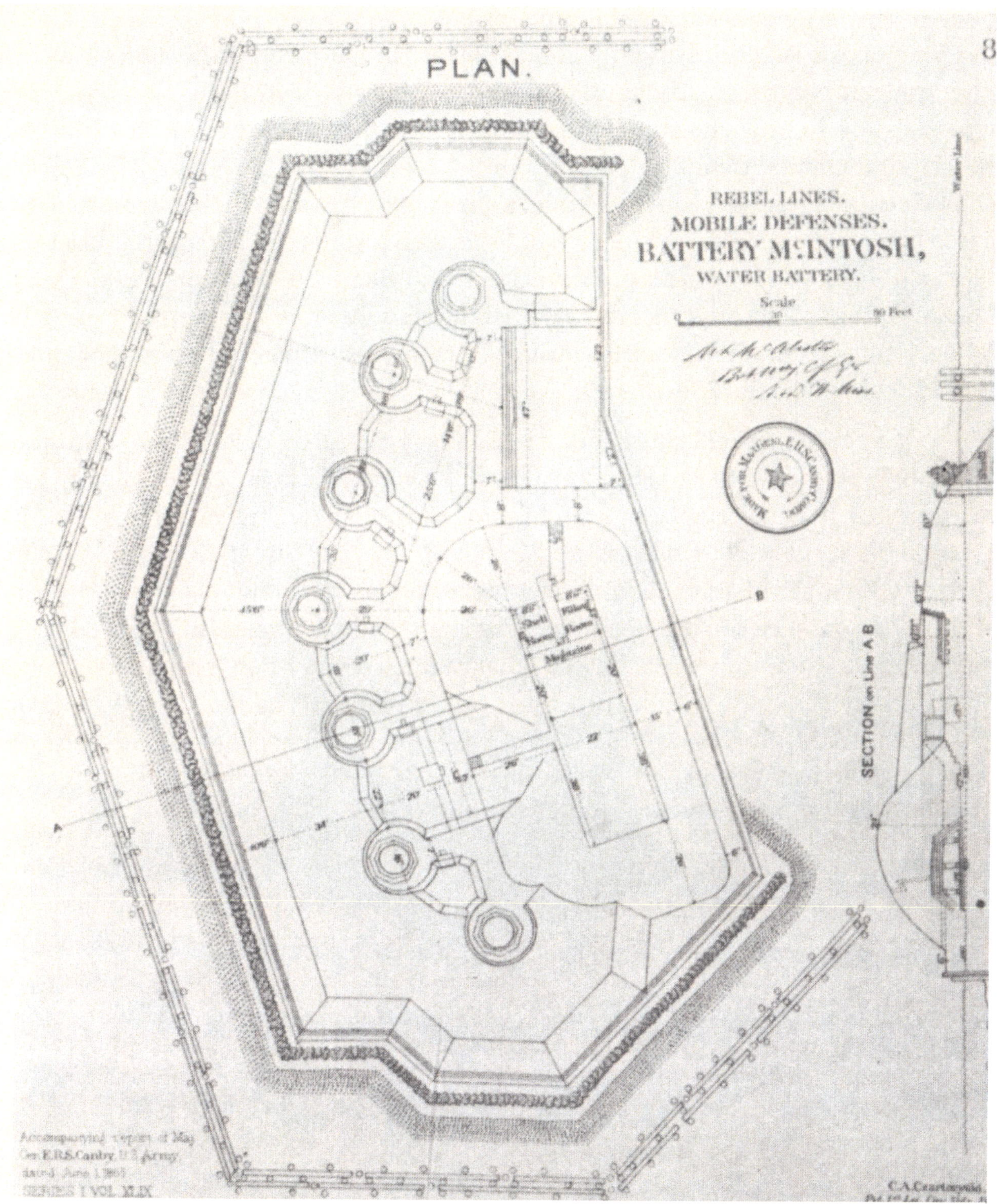

The island was man-made as a defense post for Mobile named Battery McIntosh.

Pete had already been keeping his boat at Autrey's on the Causeway and the owners Billy and Queenie Rice became his best friends. When Pete started staying full time on the island it was only about 12 feet high and had quite a nice stand of pine and gum cypress. It was covered with debris, which he used as building materials for a crude shack. His friends at Autrey's kept an eye out for him and collected his mail. Friends helped him build a bunkhouse, a cooking shed, and a chicken coop. He survived the terrible flood of 1959 by quickly throwing together a tree house where he stayed for two days, but he lost his chickens and rabbits. He replaced them with this next pension check and made the decision that added to his reputation. He brought goats to the island and Pete himself started calling his home Goat Island. He had a pier built on the Spanish River side of the island. It was 10 feet wide and 32 feet long.

More people can tell you about his death than about his life. He continued religiously attending Mass at St. Vincent's in his old neighborhood. He also bought his supplies in Mobile, usually tying his boat at the Eslava Street dock. On April 3, 1966, as the 96-year-old Pete was crossing St. Emmanuel Street, he stepped off the curb into the path of an oncoming taxi. He was taken to Mobile General Hospital and friends contacted Queenie, who came right away. He remained in a coma all day and was pronounced dead at 9:00 that night. To grant Pete's wish, his friends organized the longest funeral procession ever held in Mobile. Cars came from miles and miles to process to the Catholic Cemetery where he was laid to rest in Potter's Field section. He had left enough money for the funeral, but not enough for a headstone, so his grave is unmarked to this day.

Never has the quote "Gone, but not forgotten" been truer. Battleship Pete's story has been told and enhanced throughout the years. This larger than life character has become a folk legend. You may not able to find his grave, but you can possibly see Goat Island. The best view is from the deck of the USS Alabama or from a boat. It is about half the size it was when Pete lived there, and who knows how long it will be before it is completely gone.

Even though the name Battleship Pete matches the island location, he actually got the nickname from his years in the shipbuilding industry. However, the USS Alabama is a wonderful place to get an up-close view of the island – what is left of it

My goodness, how few years can pass before we have lost information about people who lived and walked among us. If not for the newspaper articles about Pete, we would have only the myths that sprang up around his life on Goat Island. In my mind, he had lived there for at least fifty years, but in reality, he spent only the last eight years of his life there. For example, even though I knew Pete lived on Goat Island before the USS Alabama was brought home to berth at Battleship Park, I connected the two and assumed his name came from the fact that he lived right next to the grand old Number 60. So now we all know the rest of the story, and I hope you talk about it every time you see Goat Island.

TEACHER'S LEGACY

Some of my fondest memories are of the days I dressed as a 1920s schoolmarm and was the teacher for student field trips to the Little Red Schoolhouse.

This is a story of a building that has a soul. Maybe the spirits of the teachers and students who taught and learned there were so powerful that the emotions still remain there. At least that is what I believe. This perfect little one room schoolhouse was built in the community of Bromley by the local residents who valued the education of their children above worldly goods. Mrs. Rebecca Tompkins had already been teaching children in her home when, in 1919, the men took it upon themselves to fulfill Mrs. Tompkins dream and build a real schoolhouse. Some of these men had recently returned from World War I and they were determined to make a difference for the future. They were granted some funds from the Julius Rosenwald fund which helped build hundreds of schools for African American children in the southern states. The school system provided some money as well and agreed to pay the teacher. The community raised funds, too, but more importantly they contributed their blood, sweat, and tears to build the wooden structure on Magnolia Church Road. The timber was cut from the Tompkins' land, and each nail was driven by a local citizen. By 1920 the building was almost complete and classes at the Bromley School commenced there in January of 1921.

The materials, desks, and books were scrounged from discards from other schools. Even though the books may have been second best, the teaching was first rate, and many children later graduated from Baldwin County Training School in Daphne. This was the only high school for Black children at that time. An unusual percentage of Training School students went on to earn college degrees and many of those former students became teachers and administrators in the Baldwin County Public Schools.

Water was pumped from a well, and the restrooms were at the end of the outhouse path. The school was heated by a coal burning furnace which stood in the corner of the room. Mr. George Tompkins converted his truck into a makeshift school bus to transport the children living further away. Other teachers assisted

Mrs. Rebecca through the years until Douglasville School was built in Bay Minette, and teachers and students were transferred there. Then the lonely little school stood all alone.

The Little Red Schoolhouse is open to the public at Baldwin County Bicentennial Park in Stockton. It is the only existing Rosenwald School in Baldwin County.

However, she was not forgotten. The community saw that she was preserved until she was moved to Whitehouse Fork school to be used as a kindergarten. Then when Delta school was competed in 1990, she was no longer needed, and was in danger of demolition. A group of citizens under the leadership of Mr. Sam Watson, grandson of the Tompkins, and Dr. Dolores Cooper formed a foundation to preserve the building and it was moved to the school system office complex on Hand Avenue in Bay Minette. There she was refitted with old desks, a slate board, a furnace, and a teacher's desk which had been saved by Mr. Leslie Smith and Mr. Wesley Grant. A rare recitation bench salvaged from the Lottie Langham School was given a place of honor at the front of the room. Additional restoration work was done in 2005 under the leadership of Dr. Faron Hollinger, and retired teachers conducted field trip experiences for students to learn about school in the 1920s. It was during these years of reenactments that I felt so close to the teachers and students who had been in that little school years before.

Volunteer schoolmarms give students a taste of a typical school day in a one room school in 1921.

Every day that I came into the little one room, I felt connected and honored to be a part of the continuation of learning experiences. As time passed, I began to notice unusual things upon my arrival. One morning, when I arrived, there were arithmetic problems written in perfect penmanship on the slate board. Assuming there had been others in the building, I cleaned the slate and went on with the day as planned. The following week when I opened the door, I noticed that the <u>*ABC*</u> blocks on the side table were arranged in order. They were in a perfect line of the alphabet. I thought that maybe children of a caretaker or other office worker had been playing there sometime during the week. Another time, the portrait of George Washington had been raised out of the reach of little hands, and the teacher's desk had been straightened and cleaned.

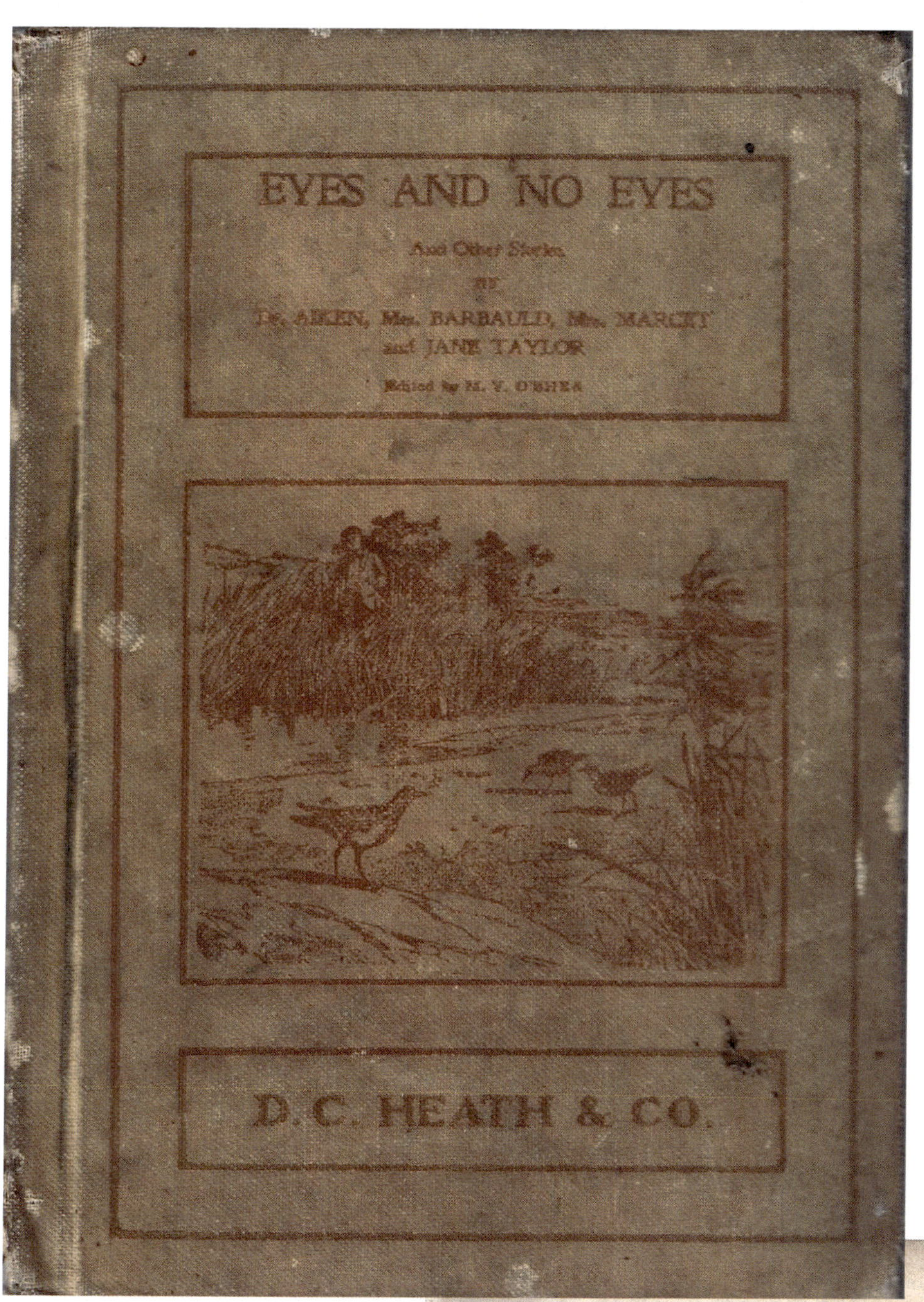

The book here was mysteriously found on the teacher's desk one morning. It was open to the inscription page showing it was used in the school while it was still in Bromley.

3rd Grade
435
#6
Bromley School Library
Seven day Book

began to look forward to the next visit to see what the unseen presence was saying to me. One day, I saw a book on the recitation bench. I knew the book must have been in the library cabinet at the rear of the schoolhouse the prior week. The book was opened to the cover sheet, and I read the inscription, ***"Bromley School #14/ Seven Day Book"*** – this book had actually been used by those teachers in Bromley, and no one had ever realized this book was one of the originals. I took the book with me to the Baldwin County School Archives for cataloguing and preservation of this relic. The very next week, the most amazing incident of all occurred, for there on the slate board was written, "Where is my b…" Needless to say, the book was returned to the Little Red Schoolhouse and left there for an unseen teacher to use as she teaches her many pupils who must come there for their lessons. The teachers who taught here left a legacy that will live forever.

GRAND PIANO MAN

Each summer my husband and I celebrate our wedding anniversary at the Grand Hotel, and for more than forty-five years we have danced to the magical music of Jack Normand, the Grand Piano Man.....

Old folks around here call it the Hotel, not the Grand Hotel Marriott Resort, Golf Club and Spa, its real name. It is simply the Hotel to those of us who remember when it was just about the only hotel around here. This rare treasure on Point Clear holds memories that reverberate down the halls, throughout the grounds and especially in the dining room. The sounds of the memories join the wonderful creaking of the wooden floors and remind guests of things that have happened here for more than a century. The stories of those memories can fill volumes, but there is one that is my very own story.

An old postcard shows the Grand Hotel in all its glory. Located on Point Clear, Alabama, she remains the queen of resort hotels.

When my husband and I were married, we spent our honeymoon at that most romantic of places, the Hotel. Dinner was magnificent, as usual, and the dance floor was crowded with guests dancing to the tunes of the resident musician, Mr. Jack Normand. He found out we had signed in the Honeymoon Guest Book and asked us our favorite song. Actually, we were at a loss to name a tune, so he chose *When a Man Loves a Woman*, the Percy Sledge hit. That was a mystical night, but it was not to be the last one. When we returned to the Hotel each year for our anniversary, Jack remembered us without fail and played our song. After he died in 1990, we mourned with the world and thought our anniversary dinner would not be the same, but we were wrong. Jack still remembered, and we still hear his magic music every year.

Just before World War II, a young Jack Normand was hired by Ed Roberts to mark the re-opening of the newly remodeled Grand Hotel. When Pearl Harbor

Jack Normand moved his family into a historic home located on the bluff overlooking Mobile Bay. The home remains in the family for the second generation. Pictured is his son, Robert who lives there with his wife, Denna.

was bombed, he joined the Army Air Force, playing in the Air Force Band. After the war, he returned to New Orleans until he was lured back to the Grand Hotel in 1951 for a six-week contract that turned into 40 continuous years. As years passed, he was joined by his children and the Jack Normand Trio became the Normand Family Band. Jack and his wife became icons in the community and reared their five children in a lovely old home overlooking Mobile Bay.

Everybody loved Jack. His charm was a part of the hospitality of the hotel. A master at the piano, and more so a master at the heart, was Jack. He had an uncanny knack for remembering which tunes were special to guests and when he noticed a returning couple, like us, come into the dining room, he often interrupted his set with the favorite song of that particular couple. No wonder he was loved!! The band sometimes played on Julep Point, a terrazzo tile open-air dance floor, where couples danced under the stars. Those stars over Mobile Bay inspired Jack to create a medley of *Stars Fell on Alabama* and *On Mobile Bay*, which was always the band's final tune of the evening. Even after the band packed away instruments and headed home, the strains of the tune seemed to be a part of the salty breezes that blew gently across the hotel grounds. Actually, those sounds have never disappeared. We know because we have heard them.

Jack Normand played nightly in the dining room of the Grand Hotel.

The first year after Jack's death, we walked the lovely grounds of the Hotel after our anniversary dinner. We walked past the dining room, which was dark, having already closed for the evening. My husband and I suddenly stopped in our tracks and looked at each other. We both heard the melody of a piano playing our song. So, of course, we danced right there on the lawn. Others have experienced the

Grand Piano Man's music as well. Often people comment on the taped music played outside the Hotel late at night. But, of course, the music is echoing from days long past.

After Hurricane Katrina, which claimed the grand piano that Jack loved, we feared the sounds had been washed away. When the hotel re-opened after repairs, our anniversary night was special, but not quite the same. Our late-night stroll past the dining room was sadly quiet this time. As we walked on to Julep Point, we were thinking of all that storm had taken, but were thankful it did not steal our memories. As we began to dance on the old floor in silence under the stars, the sounds of a grand piano grew more and more distinct. The melody was clearly that of *On Mobile Bay*. The last tune of the evening was borne on the salty bay breeze blowing gently across the grounds. If you listen, you can hear it. Dance to the sounds of the Grand Piano Man.

Guests dance to the music of the Jack Normand Band under the stars at romantic Julep Point, Grand Hotel.

HOSPITAL HAUNTS

We had heard that some guests experience "special effects" in the Holmes Medical Museum in Foley, so we joined a group touring the rooms preserved from the past, hoping to find out for ourselves.

When we entered the Holmes Medical Museum reception room we were greeted by a most energetic and knowledgeable docent named Bob, who relocated to the sunny south a couple of years ago. Although he was not around when Dr. Holmes ran the clinic here, he has become an expert on all things related to the legendary hospital.

The city of Foley offers the public a look into the first hospital in Baldwin County. It is located on Laurel Street in Foley.

"You are entering the museum through the former Cook's store that was here for the years the hospital was operating on the second floor. You will see some artifacts used in medical practices from the past, and as you go upstairs, you will enter the rooms of the hospital just as they were left 50 years ago." He handed us the self-guided tour cards and we headed to the stairs.

We joined a family from Massachusetts and clomped up the wooden steps that were installed recently to accommodate visitors to the museum. About halfway up, we began to feel that we were being transported back in time. Even the odor that began to waft over us was eerie. The new stairs now enter the hospital in what was originally the operating wing and adult ward rooms, just the place I had come to investigate.

The east wing of the hospital houses the doctors' offices, nurses' rooms, exam, and waiting rooms. The far room was the office of the first Dr. Holmes, Sibley. He practiced from this area directly above the drug store. He dreamed of having a hospital, but it did not materialize until his son, Buddy, made it happen, opening the overnight facility in 1936. Dr. Buddy's wife Philomene was as well-known as he was. She delivered many babies by herself and actually managed the hospital on her own while her husband served in World War II.

Patients needing major surgeries were sent to Mobile, but the Holmes performed minor and emergency procedures.

My father had often talked about a cousin who had been terribly wounded in a tractor accident more than 80 years ago. He was loaded into the farm pickup and taken to the newly opened hospital in Foley. My father ran inside to alert the nurse that they had an emergency case in the truck parked out front on Laurel Street. Dr. Holmes ran down the steep old stairs and quickly assessed the injuries. His wife Philomene rang the bell hanging at the door. Immediately four strong men emerged from the pool hall across the street. Dr. Holmes had the stretcher ready for them; they quickly loaded my cousin and carried him up the stairs, taking the right turn at the landing where the stairs split into two corridors. They took the one heading into the hospital rather than the left that led to the regular examination rooms

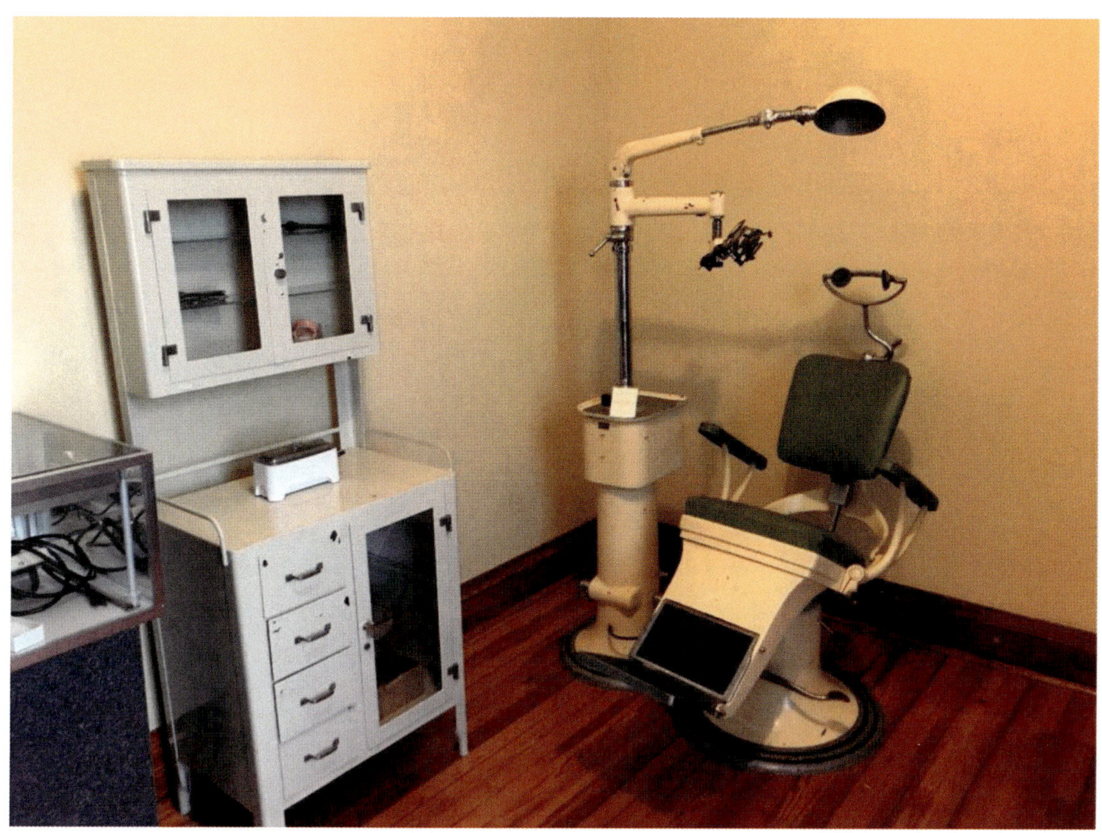

Patients were treated in the exam room. The original equipment used by Dr. and Mrs. Holmes remain in pristine condition just as they were left in 1958. Photo credit: Penny Taylor

Sadly, the injuries were mortal. A leg had to be amputated and the patient placed in the men's ward, where he received excellent care. But this was one of those times when the best care in the world could not save a life. He lingered for about two weeks in terrible pain. Gangrene had set in the wound and it was too late to save his life. My father often talked about visiting my cousin the hospital and referred to the smell of sickness that pervaded the room. A scent so powerful that the residue of it remains there today. That was my first sense of the past that met me as we toured the museum. My body sensed the smell of death as I entered the spotlessly maintained ward. No one else could feel it, but I knew that my cousin had endured terrible pain there.

We continued the tour through the halls and saw rooms displaying tools of the medical profession from more than a half century ago. It looked like the staff had just closed the doors and 'up and left.' In fact, that is just what happened. When Dr. Buddy C. Holmes had been successful in helping build the Foley Hospital in 1958, his practice moved to the new facility with modern equipment.

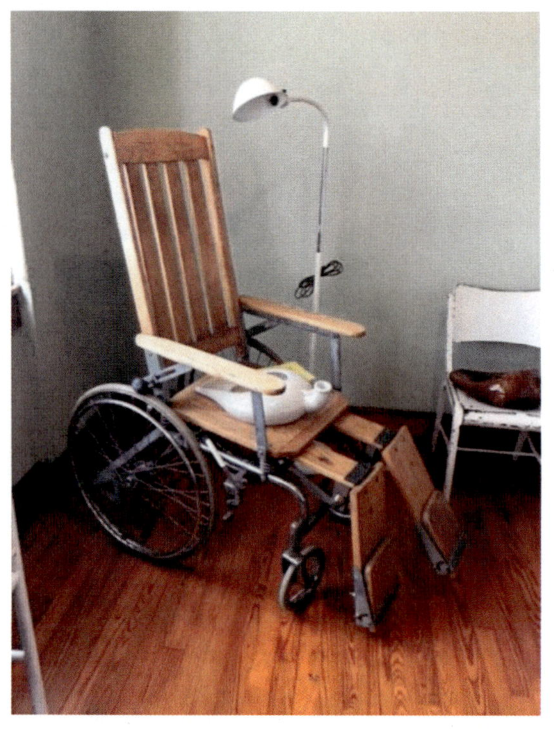

Wheelchair used to transport patients within the hospital. Photo credit: Penny Taylor

We saw the very wheelchair that transported patients. We saw the very beds and bedpans used to serve patients. We entered the nursery, which displayed procedures for "birthing babies." I guess the hospital is most famous for the number of babies born there. Those 'babies' still get together every once in a while and celebrate the heritage they share. Dr. Homes and his wife delivered more than 300 babies, who now dub themselves Holmes Babies. A scrapbook on display holds photos and birth certificates of most of them. We had fun seeing baby pictures of many of our friends, including Ken Underwood of Magnolia Springs.

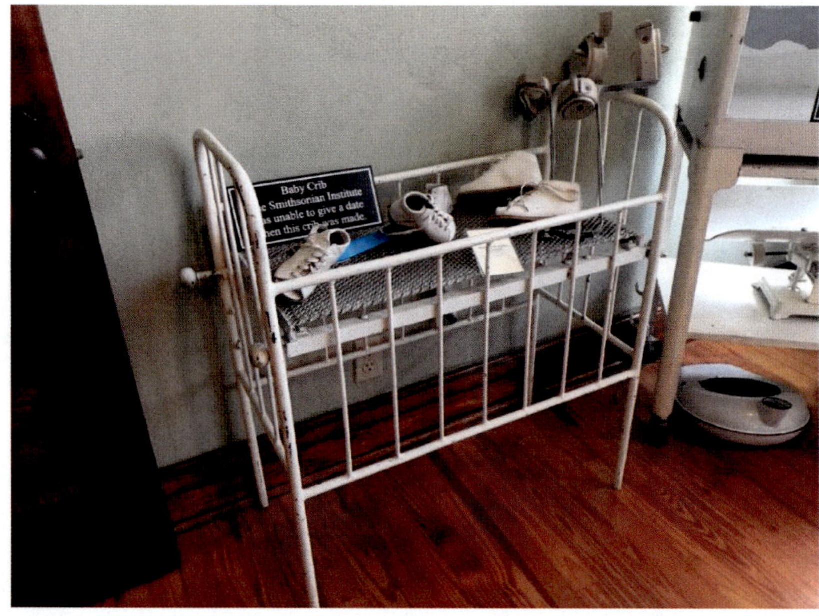

Many babies were born in the Holmes Hospital and are proud members of the Holmes Babies Club. Record of births are available in the museum. Photo courtesy of Penny Taylor.

We left that room and continued down the hall. The family that was with us suddenly realized their four-year-old was not with us and the mother returned to the nursery to fetch her daughter, who was happily dancing and laughing. Her mother asked what she was doing, and she said she was talking to the little boy in the iron crib and making him laugh.

I was then reminded that when the paranormal crew recently spent a night of investigation at the hospital, they discovered many orbs and electrical responses, but all of them appeared to be content and no negative readings were made. The little girl proved that to me.

We then heard heavy footsteps rapidly running up the original stairs that came into the upstairs hall. We turned to see who was allowed in that restricted area, but no one emerged from the stairwell. All of us in the group heard the same thing, and we only stared at each other in wonder. Then the sound of the stomping boots was heard retreating behind us, hurrying to the operating room. And there was that odor.

Emergency patients had to be carried up the narrow staircase on stretchers. When the staff rang the bell, volunteers came from the pool hall across the street to carry patients up the stairs. Photo courtesy of Penny Taylor

Many people say that Dr. Sibley's office is often cold, no matter what the thermometer says. We walked behind his desk, and, sure enough, the strangest cold penetrated through our bodies. The cold was chilling, and we felt the goosebumps run up our spines, making our hair stand on end.

Just outside his office is the room from which a woman is often seen in the window at night. Several folks swear that early in the mornings, when from their autos on the street, they see a lady looking out of this window toward the rising sun. I just know that her child is in the children's ward and she is waiting to hear from the doctor. Such intense fear can't be erased by time.

There are some people and places that remain vibrant and alive forever. The Holmes Hospital is one of those places. Ask any Holmes Baby, and then go feel it for yourself.

LADY ON THE STAIRS

Guests at the Swift-Coles Historic Home are often enthralled by the story of a lady who eerily appears in the old house.

As tour groups stand in the hallway of the Swift-Coles Historic Home, a light sometimes flickers at the top of the stairs. When that occurs, the docent tells the story of the lady in black who often floats down the stairs and around the house.

The Historic Swift-Coles Home is open to the public and serves as an event venue. The home was first built in the late nineteenth century on the banks of the Bon Secour River.

The front hall is actually the oldest part of the house, a dogtrot enclosed by Mr. Charles Swift when he bought the 1882 cabin. Mrs. Swift had the walls lined with bookcases and furnished with desks. The Swifts built a one room school for their eleven children and the children of the mill workers, but there were times that lessons were conducted here in the Library, as they called this hall. One teacher, a lovely lady from Mobile, boarded here with the Swift family. Her bedroom was one of the rooms connecting with this hall. She rode the riverboat home to Mobile some weekends, but soon wanted to stay here all the time because she began to feel she was a part of the family. Her name was Augusta.

Augusta always wore a long dress, even when it grew out of fashion. Her hair, prematurely white, was worn in a bun on top of her head. The dignified lady was a strict teacher, but the children knew she loved them as if they were her own.

The Swifts built a schoolhouse for the local children and paid the teachers. It was located near the site of the current Swift School in Bon Secour.

Augusta became an active member of St. Peter's Church and soon was teaching Sunday School, which was held in the nearby Swift family home. In the summers, she helped with Bible School classes also held in the house. She began to stay here more and more weekends and even during the summers.

Unfortunately, she became quite ill one winter with influenza. The Swifts insisted that she be nursed in an upstairs bedroom where it was warmer on those cold windy, winter nights. As her illness progressed, her family moved her to their home in Mobile, even though she begged to stay in Bon Secour. She died and was buried in Mobile, pleading to be returned to the home on the river until her dying breath.

Perhaps her dying wish was granted, as Augusta seems to have returned to the Swift home after her death. Her first appearances were shadowy visions of a lady in a long black dress.

The most convincing report of Augusta's presence came from workers who were refurbishing the center room after Nik Coles bought the house in 1976. He hired three local men to remove the bookcases and sandblast the paint off of the walls. The workmen told everyone their experience here in this room.

It was a hot summer afternoon when they were busily working, using power equipment and crowbars to rip bookcases from the wall. They each reported the same experience, so it must have really happened. The muggy day suddenly took a drastic turn. It became very dark outside and a cold, cold wind blew right through the doors at each end of this hallway. Suddenly, a dramatic bolt of lightning struck, the electricity died, and all their equipment was silenced.

They felt frozen as in the dead of the night – but a light appeared at the top of the stairs. Their eyes were drawn to the source of the light, which started moving down the stairs. They soon saw that the light was emanating from the white hair of a woman in a long black dress. Her hair was in a bun and glowed in an ethereal manner, a halo surrounding her head. They heard her dress rustle on each tread as she descended the stairs. She appeared distressed and stopped at the landing. She wrung her hands and then spoke to the men, "Pray tell, what are you doing to my library?"

Of course, the men could not move, but the apparition did. It seemed to glide past them and take a seat at Augusta's desk. When the workmen regained their composure, they immediately disappeared out the front door, never to return to work there again. No amount of coaxing from Nik Coles could persuade them to continue their work.

Later it was discovered that they were not the only ones to experience her spirit. When her desk was moved to another town by the family member who inherited it, there were reports that the apparition followed the desk, appearing in the guest room where the desk was installed.

However, she returns here as well. Lately, Mike, one of the docents, was working on his computer in this hall. He was suddenly aware there was a lady's long black skirt passing by going into the parlor. He followed it into the room and felt a cold chill over his entire body. When he went to report his sighting to the other docents, they were alarmed at his pallid color and shaking hands. They were all convinced that the spirit was there that day and appeared to one of her favorite docents.

Augusta is only one of those inhabitants of the historic home. Maybe you will be able to see her – or hear her - on your next visit there.

The narrow stairs in the front hall of the Swift-Coles Home are said to be the haunt of the lady who comes to check on her wards and her library. Photo courtesy of Penny Taylor

MEME'S RESTAURANT

There are a few people around who remember eating at the world-famous seafood restaurant named Meme's at the end of Highway 49 right on the Bon Secour River. It is now a part of the folklore of the Gulf Coast. If you are in the Bon Secour area, chances are you will smell a pot of gumbo simmering (not boiling) on a stove somewhere. But are those smells from the day and time from more than fifty years ago?

Amelia Swift was one of the 11 children raised in the historic Swift Coles Home in Bon Secour by Charles and Susan Swift who ran the Swift Lumber Company. Meme, as she was known, married Charles Wakeford and they built a reputation as the finest seafood cooks in the south. During World War II they lived in the original house and were said to have hosted many a seafood fest, a homefront contribution to the war effort on the home front, giving the boys a taste of southern hospitality. The kitchen in the Big House was always full of laughter and there was always something cooking on that old wood stove.

Meme and Charley Wakeford moved from the Big House to one of the fishing cabins on the river. Here they opened a store and Post Office.

After the war, they decided to move into one of the fishing cabins on the river and then they ran a post office from one room of their home. People often came in and asked where they could buy good oysters, so they opened a small oyster bar in 1953. Soon it grew into a full-service seafood restaurant and little did they dream the heritage they would build there. At first, the restaurant was in a cement block building and later a River Room was built over the water. Boaters could dock right at the front door, and it was advertised accessible by "good" roads. Dirt roads and potholes only added to the charm of the destination and many famous people made the trek to dine on the best gumbo ever made. It was at first made by a French Creole cook, but once when she was ill, Charley stepped in and used the recipe he had learned from Meme's mother who he called 'The Madam.' He used her spoon that was flat on the bottom due to years of stirring the rich gumbo, and the diners raved so much that recipe was used from that time on. Charley made it known that good gumbo must be cooked very, very slowly and stirred almost constantly.

Meme's Restaurant was operated by Amelia Swift and her husband Charley Wakeford. It was one of the most popular seafood restaurants in the area, often frequented by famous guests. The names are listed on the menu.

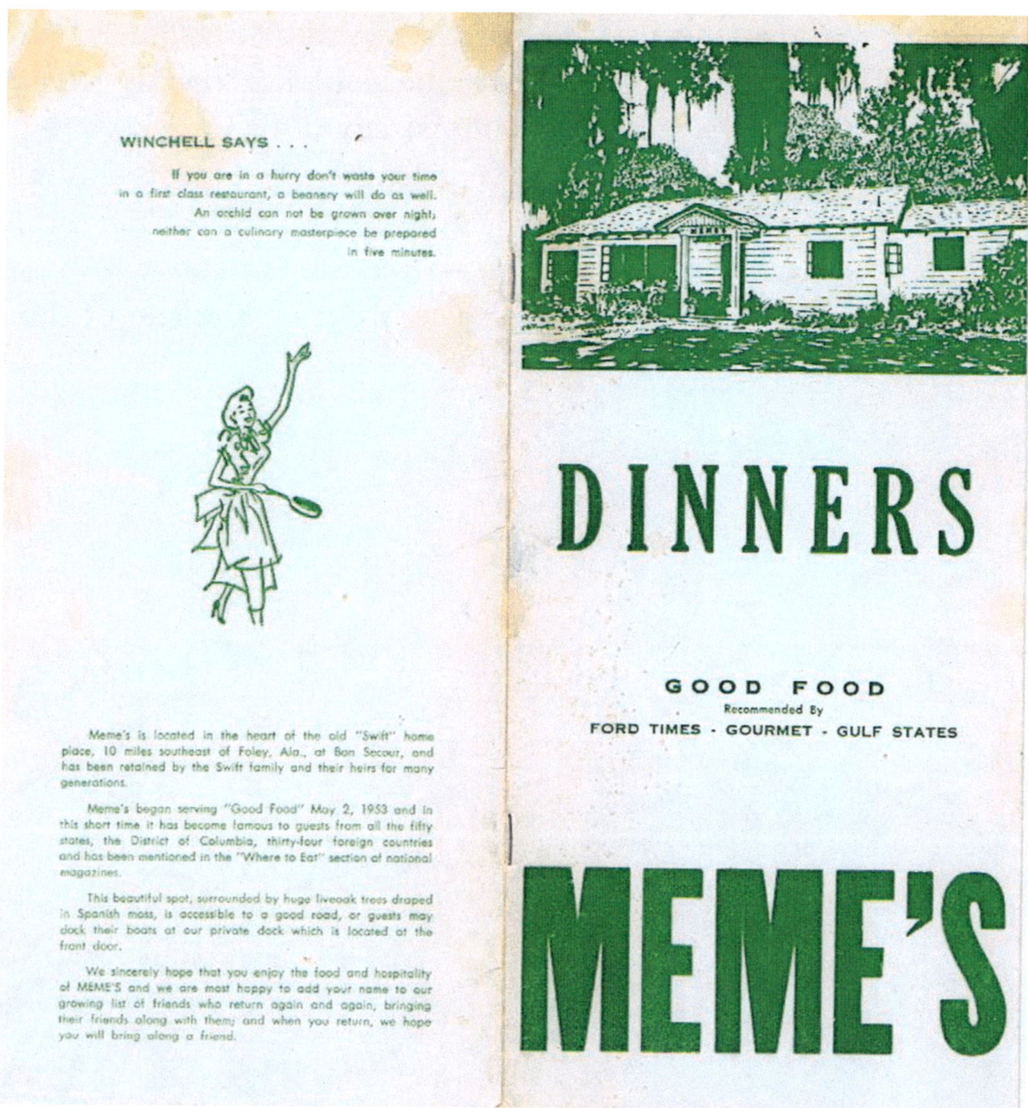

WINCHELL SAYS . . .

If you are in a hurry don't waste your time in a first class restaurant, a beanery will do as well. An orchid can not be grown over night; neither can a culinary masterpiece be prepared in five minutes.

Meme's is located in the heart of the old "Swift" home place, 10 miles southeast of Foley, Ala., at Bon Secour, and has been retained by the Swift family and their heirs for many generations.

Meme's began serving "Good Food" May 2, 1953 and in this short time it has become famous to guests from all the fifty states, the District of Columbia, thirty-four foreign countries and has been mentioned in the "Where to Eat" section of national magazines.

This beautiful spot, surrounded by huge liveoak trees draped in Spanish moss, is accessible to a good road, or guests may dock their boats at our private dock which is located at the front door.

We sincerely hope that you enjoy the food and hospitality of MEME'S and we are most happy to add your name to our growing list of friends who return again and again, bringing their friends along with them; and when you return, we hope you will bring along a friend.

DINNERS

GOOD FOOD

Recommended By

FORD TIMES · GOURMET · GULF STATES

MEME'S

The menu lists a deviled crab dinner for $3.50 and a seafood platter cost a whopping $4.00, with drinks and dessert included. One specialty was broiled oysters on toast, and another was "Fish Baked in a Paper Sack." The gumbo could be shipped frozen to almost anywhere.

Meme's became a hot spot for political gatherings and a few election campaigns were kicked off there. The menu had a list of famous people who had graced her doors, including most of the governors of Alabama during her years of operation. Listed are guests from all fifty states and more than 53 foreign countries, including His Royal Highness The Prince of Durrani, Hessan. After Charley died, Meme continued to run the restaurant with the assistance of Rose Weeks, who stayed on as Meme's caretaker after the restaurant closed.

It seems the restaurant never opened back up after the devastation of Hurricane Frederic in 1979. There are now no remains of the restaurant on the grounds except maybe the concrete slab. The ruins of the house stood for years as a reminder of the horrible storm that changed all who were here then. But that is another story… In the meantime, take a whiff of that delicious gumbo simmering on the wood stove somewhere along the river – maybe it is from the Tin Top, which is building a legacy of its own with a new establishment right on the site of the original Meme's.

LIBRARIAN OF BAY MINETTE

Bay Minette old timers often sit on their porches telling stories. On the porch of the historic home of Bert and Mary Blackmon, I learned about the resident spirit of the Bay Minette Library.

The ding announces the arrival of the elevator to the second floor of the Bay Minette Library. The door opens, but no one is there – nothing particularly unusual unless there is suddenly a distinct smell of roses in the upstairs hall - for then the very real spirit of the library is present. Bert Blackmon had witnessed the phenomenon and was more than willing to tell the rest of the story.

The Bay Minette Library was once housed in this building, which serves today as the voter registration office.

Nearly every library staff member and many patrons have some story to tell concerning the strange goings-on that happen frequently in that lovely old building that was once the Baptist Church. However, the unique happenings began before the library moved from its original location, the small colonial brick building that now serves as the Voter Registration office.

The things that happen are simply leftovers from the very first librarian in Bay Minette, Mrs. Ann Gilmer, who motivated the Women's Civic Improvement Association to create a library for the fast-growing county seat. Mrs. Gilmer became the first director and continued in that position for 25 years. She spent countless hours cataloguing cards, shelving books exactly in Dewey Decimal order, and lining them up in precise, uniform manner. Even when Pearlie Overstreet followed her as director in 1943, Mrs. Gilmer volunteered many hours to the library. After her death the library staff realized how much work Mrs. Gilmer had done and they tried to keep things as orderly as she had, but they must have not been meeting Mrs. Gilmer's expectations, and she just had to come help.

One morning when a librarian arrived at work, she was alarmed that one drawer of the card catalogue had been pulled out and was lying on the floor. All of the cards were still in the tray, except for one which was several feet away. The librarian put the card in its correct place and replaced the drawer in the cabinet. Two weeks later when the librarian arrived to open the building, she saw several books on the floor. Fearing a burglary, she called for the police. When the officer investigated, he could find nothing in disarray except the five books on the floor. Shrugging her shoulders, Pearlie placed the books on the shelves in the places they belonged, realizing that these books must have been formerly shelved incorrectly. From then on when there were mysterious happenings, she would thank Mrs. Gilmer for her help. Pearlie told her staff they had best do their jobs correctly because they were always being watched. The good-natured librarian never felt intimidated by the presence, but Bernice was not so sure about it. Often, as she was cleaning, a book would drop to the floor: one she had not yet dusted. Her eyes wide and wary, she would look all around and the lights would go off and back on. Bernice reported that one night she just said aloud, "You just leave me alone. I have work to do." That did the trick, and Bernice was never bothered again. All these happenings took place in the old building.

When the library moved into the historic First Baptist Church building, the presence of the librarian went along as well.

Charlotte Jones Cabiness Robertson was the director when the library was moved across the street to the former First Baptist Church. Many people thought that Mrs. Gilmer would remain in residence in the old building, but Charlotte invited her to come with her as she moved the portrait of Mrs. Gilmer to the new location. Charlotte says there is no doubt she came.

Charlotte says that the aroma of roses is a sign that Mrs. Gilmer is around. Many people ask about the roses, and some even complain that someone's perfume is giving them a headache. Evidently Mrs. Gilmer is enchanted with the elevator which would have saved her many a stairstep climb from the basement in the old library up to the main floor. She uses it often. Charlotte reports that the elevator still operates at times when a librarian is alone in the building. Every director to this day makes sure that Mrs. Gilmer feels welcome, and that she knows her library is loved.

The elevator still opens and closes at uncanny times - so if you take the elevator, be aware that you may not be alone. Especially if you can smell the roses.

RAILROAD BILL

Daddy was a little boy when his father took him to the Bay Minette depot to see the body of Railroad Bill. He told me about it while we were sitting on our front porch one evening. Even though there were a few mismatched, creaky rocking chairs, Daddy preferred to sit in a straight-backed kitchen chair, leaning back on rear legs that had been worn down. He propped one foot on the cement porch railing and said, "Let me tell you a story about Railroad Bill."

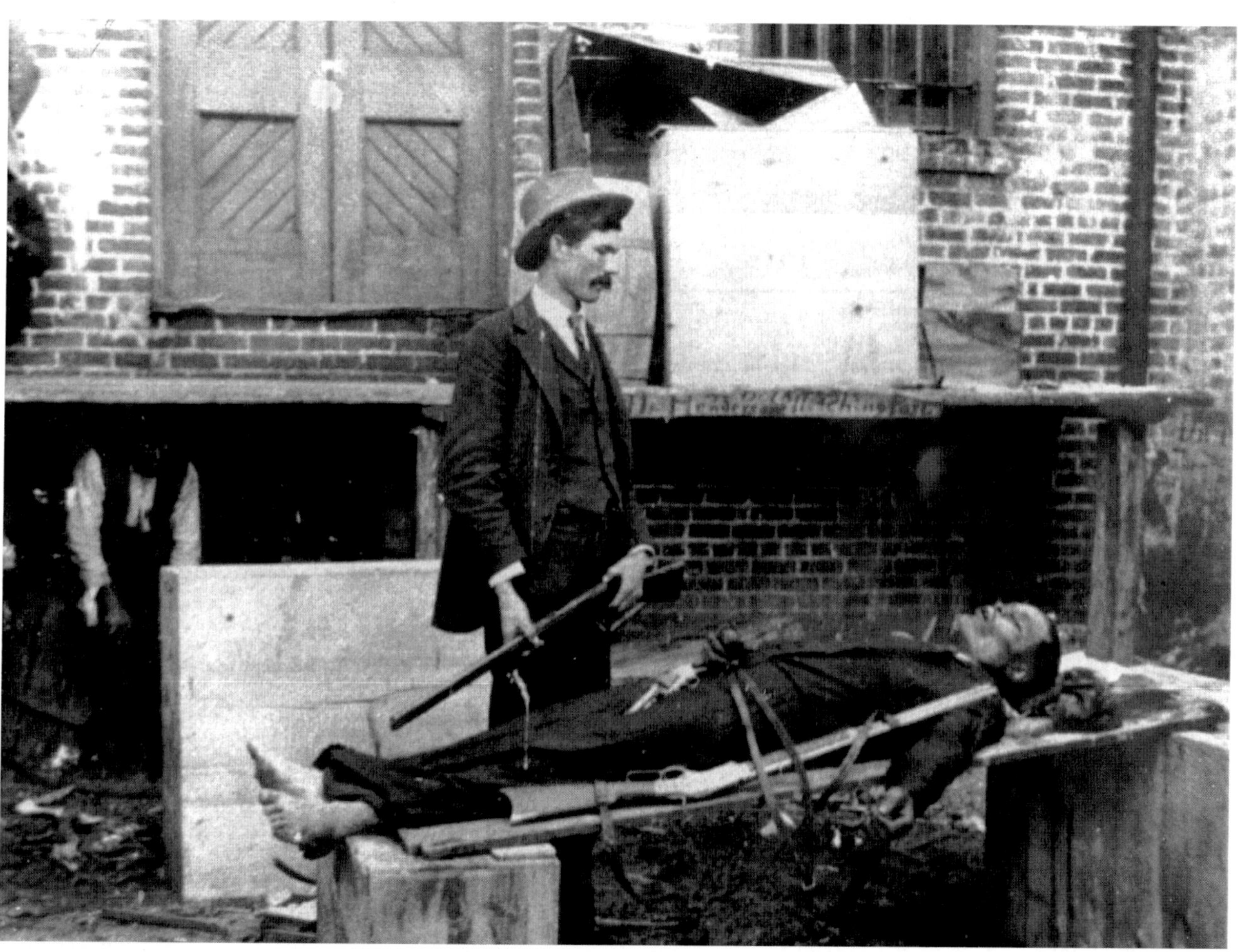

Railroad Bill was a subject of many stories in the deep south. He was actually known as a Robin Hood character for people living along the rail line. The rail company felt differently, however, and after he was killed, his body was displayed up and down the rail line between Bay Minette and Brewton.

Railroad Bill is Baldwin and Escambia Counties' claim to a reallio, trulio outlaw. This story has its roots in true historical facts. As legends do, when he became a folk hero the facts became blurred. His real name was Morris Slater, born to parents who were former slaves. He went to work early on to help put food on the table, but after his parents died, he left home and joined a carnival. There he learned conjuring and all sorts of magic tricks. When he came back to Baldwin County, he worked in little turpentine stills, and, as most backwoodsmen do, always carried his rifle. In fact, even while he was working, he carried the rifle stuck down his right pants leg. This made him walk with a straight-legged limp. One day he caught the attention of a deputy sheriff who was determined that Morris would either purchase the required permit or relinquish the gun.

The deputy came up to Morris and said, "Hand over that there rifle or else buy a permit." Morris just turned and limped away. That got the deputy's goat, and he was then even more determined. The next time he approached Morris, Morris once again just turned to walk away, and the deputy pulled his gun and fired in the air. Morris turned and fired, the buckshot shooting the deputy's ear right off his head. Knowing he would be arrested and found guilty, Morris jumped a slow freight train and rode into a new way of life.

He hid out with some of his friends, and took his old circus name, Bill McCoy. Hitching rides on freight trains between Bay Minette and Brewton, he stayed on the move to elude the law. One time when he jumped on an open boxcar he found it full of canned goods. Figuring he was already a fugitive anyway, he picked up a couple of crates and tossed them off. He then jumped the train, retrieved the booty, and took it to some locals in the nearby shantytown. Starving families were so thankful for the food that he continued this practice He even took to throwing goods off the train so people living along the tracks could come right along and pick them up. These people began to tell tales and sing songs about Railroad Bill, their very own Robin Hood. If Bill happened to be nearby and needed a place to hide out, he was welcomed in the homes of his people, who always had canned beans, thanks to Bill's escapades.

All of a sudden, the railroad had quite a different outlook. There were Pinkerton agents and lawmen after him all the time, and large rewards were offered. Men on the hunt told of the many times they almost had Bill, but something strange would happen. Remember, he learned conjuring when he was young, and he could often turn himself into an animal. Once when a posse was on his trail, the hunting dogs were joined by a stray dog and they lost all scents they were trailing. Another time, a grinning fox appeared in front the dogs, and everyone knows a dog is going to choose to hunt a fox anytime he can. The fox disappeared into a hollow log, and a skunk came out the other end of that log, putting an end to that hunting trip.

Lawmen pledged to take Bill, dead or alive. Sheriff McMillan was elected on that promise. He got a note one day from Bill: "I wish you hadn't made that statement, Mr. Ed, because I love you and don't want to kill you, so don't come after me."

But Bill did shoot Ed McMillan when he came after him. Efforts to rid the county of the outlaw were intensified. However, every time a lawman would get close to Bill, he would somehow slip away. One time, they saw a cat run out of the house where they thought Bill was hiding, and no sign of Bill was found inside the house. From that time on, Bill was associated with mysterious cats, which would appear and disappear at the strangest times.

The hunt for Railroad Bill ended when a man was shot in a general store in Atmore. Some say a posse happened on the store and was sure the man they saw sitting on a barrel eating cheese and crackers was Bill. Others say the lawmen had been tipped off and ambushed a man there. The man was shot dead. The L&N agent rushed there and took the body to the funeral home where it was embalmed. The Constable posed with the body strapped to a wooden plank and souvenir hunters paid 50 cents for a copy of that photograph.

They took the body from town to town to show people that Bill was dead. The last stop was Bay Minette. That is where Daddy saw that body and witnessed something he never forgot. As the coffin was being closed, a strange mist escaped and then the coffin was empty. There under the coffin bier was a grey cat with a curious grin on his face. That cat went right to the caboose and made himself at home. The coffin slammed shut. The railroad officials said they buried the body, but no one could every recall where. They said they didn't want the man to be idolized as a martyr, so the burial was shrouded in mystery.

People still talk about the last day that anyone saw Railroad Bill, at least in his human form before it changed into that gray cat. The Bay Minette depot was moved out to Highway 59, where there is always a gray cat strolling around just as cool as can be. He sleeps peacefully in that red caboose. The workers at the Chamber of Commerce there say the cat will not be caught, but they feed him, nonetheless. I guess they know about all those times Railroad Bill fed the people along the tracks and they think he deserves some payback.

The original depot and a caboose were moved to the main highway and serve as the Chamber of Commerce Office and Visitor's Center. The caboose is still a refuge for a strange cat that may actually be Railroad Bill.

Regardless of what is true, Bill is a legend who will live on in songs, such as the one sung by Janice Joplin, and sometimes people see a tall, lean man walking alongside the railroad tracks between Bay Minette and Brewton. He has a stiff legged limp.

CHAPTER 3
LEGENDS OF LORE

Some stories are obviously at least part fiction, but they sure are entertaining. Usually, the storyteller's demeanor lets the listener know the story is one that has most definitely been enhanced through the years. My husband says that when a legend is better than the truth, write the legend. Just don't call it a documentary. This is certainly not a documentary.

BLACK RIBBON

Throughout Baldwin County's history, many northerners have come to resorts for respite from the bitter cold winters or the heat of the cities in the summertime.

One of the most developed resort communities along the Gulf Coast was Portersville near Bayou la Batre in Mobile County. Further east, Magnolia Springs was especially popular among Chicagoans. Many resorts back then sprang up around places known for their healing waters, and the spring at the head of the Magnolia River was famous for its purity. A lovely little gazebo called the Wishing Well was built at the spring.

Along the pristine river were built hotels, a golf club, and many private homes. One of the most famous hotels was the Woodbound, which had three stories and a tall observation tower. Local rumors held that there were many visitors who were in some way tied to syndicated crime families in Chicago – strictly rumor, mind you. Without a doubt, there were many colorful guests at the hotel. Advertisements in mid-western papers touted amazing waters and delightful winter climates. The most memorable manager was Horace Dunbar; a happy bachelor living in his apartment in the hotel. Daily he walked to the Wishing Well, where people met to "take the waters" and visit.

Late one evening as he approached the spot, a lovely young woman was sitting there all alone. She was dressed in black, had a lace mantel over her head; a cameo brooch secured a wide black silk ribbon around her neck. As he approached, she lifted her fan to cover the lower portion of her face – oh, but her eyes -- her eyes were magnetic, and Horace fell under her spell. They made plans to meet at the well every evening, and a courtship ensued. After they were married, she moved into his apartment in the Woodbound. She was secretive about her past, but that did not hinder the love Horace felt for his wife.

The bride rarely talked to guests and when she did, she hid her face behind her fan until she got to know them. She eluded all questions about her family or her prior life. During the first years of her marriage she continued to wear black clothing, but as time passed, she began to dress in more colorful clothing and was even one of the first ladies to wear a bathing suit to take a dip in the river. However, she never removed the black silk ribbon fastened around her neck with a cameo brooch.

Once the most luxurious resort hotel on the southern coast, the Woodbound Hotel was located on the Magnolia River.

One afternoon when Horace went upstairs to their apartment, he was unable to rouse her from her nap. He summoned the resident physician, who made an immediate diagnosis: the lovely bride was suffering from an allergic reaction and her throat was swollen so that her breath was extremely labored. The doctor administered a medicine, and then told Horace the black silk ribbon would have to be removed so he could perform a tracheotomy and she could once again breathe. Horace unpinned the brooch and the ribbon fell away. The husband and doctor saw then what she had been hiding with the ribbon.

Magnolia Springs was named for the natural springs that feed the river. There was a gazebo structure built over the spring and was lovingly nicknamed "The Wishing Well."

Just at that moment, she gasped and took a deep breath. As regular breathing was restored, her lifeless body began to regain some color, but she was still unconscious. As she began to moan and stir a wee bit, Horace picked up the black ribbon, and looked at the doctor, who nodded to him. The loving husband replaced it around the ugly scar that was on his wife's neck. The scar was rough and red: the kind of scar that could only have been made by a noose of hemp rope used for hanging. Without a word, he and the doctor made a solemn vow of silence. Perhaps she would never know they discovered the reason she wore the wide black silk ribbon. When she awoke, she immediately lifted her hand to her throat and was reassured that the ribbon was in place, hiding her deep, dark secret.

We don't know if she ever told her beloved husband the story of her past that left the sign of an attempted execution on her perfect neck. They lived a lovely life in the Woodbound until it burned in 1911, then moved away and as far as anyone knows, never returned to Magnolia Springs. The doctor was diligent in his notes and he was the one who wrote this beautiful love story in his journal. Each person in our family who inherits this treasured journal reads the story and vows to keep it safe. Some stories are just too good to keep locked in a journal, so now you know about the Black Silk Ribbon.

BRIDE OF YANCEY BRANCH

Everyone who walks over the Yancey Branch Bridge hopes to catch a glimpse of the lady in white. Let me tell you the story of the Bride of the Branch.

Recently, a late afternoon jogger ran along the walking trail on Whispering Pines Road in Daphne. As she crossed the wooden bridge over Yancey Branch, she saw a lady dressed in a bridal gown in the boggy bottoms of the stream. As she slowed down, she heard a wailing cry. She stopped and stared as the vision dissolved into a mist. She was one of the lucky ones who saw the Bride of the Branch.

This story has been told for more than 150 years, because the traumatic event that left the ghost bride on the murky banks of the creek happened about 1850. I know this is true for I once heard it from an ancient man who was the child of former slave on a nearby plantation – the home of the Bride of the Branch.

Joline was the lovely daughter of the owner of a large plantation near Loxley. She often accompanied the man driving the wagons loaded with cotton and produce to Wharf Landing to sell to brokers. The road to Daphne crossed Yancey Branch by way of a wooden bridge on the Old Spanish Trail. Yancey Branch is still today a slow-moving stream until heavy rains bring rushing water, causing the banks of the creek to quickly become a boggy mire, which the locals call quicksand. On one of her trips to Daphne, Joline met and fell in love with a bayboat captain, Joshua. They were soon planning marriage, but a tragic turn of events led to heartbreak.

Joline's father was respected throughout the south, but few knew of his weakness for a game of cards. Unbeknownst to his family, he had already lost his plantation to a doctor in Mobile. The doctor, one of Joline's rejected suitors, offered the man a chance to win back his plantation in one more game, if Joline's hand was his stake. In a bayside tavern his weakness sealed the fate of his beautiful daughter. When Joline's father realized what he had done, he wept to his daughter of her impending marriage. She dutifully told her father she would honor the debt and prepared to leave.

Yancey Branch runs through neighborhoods and Village Point Park. It is visible from the walking bridge on Whispering Pines Road. Standing on the bridge, the wailing sounds of Joline and Joshua are often heard.

She boarded the doctor's buggy dressed in her white wedding gown. They left her home forever, Joline appearing calm for she knew that Joshua had devised a plan to rescue her. A terrible downpour began at dusk as they approached Yancey Branch. On the other side of the bridge, a masked highwayman met them and demanded they dismount. The doctor drew his gun and fired at the disguised Joshua. The frightened horse reared, throwing the doctor and Joline into the muddy roadway. The doctor was trampled to death, but Joline jumped up to go to her wounded lover. She ran toward Joshua calling his name but became disoriented in the blinding rain. She stepped into the boggy quicksand, and was pulled to her death, leaving behind only echoes of her voice calling to Joshua.

When Joshua regained consciousness, he heard his bride calling his name and began a frantic search for her. He walked for months along the banks of the branch. Sometimes he thought he saw her, but each time he approached her, she disappeared into a mist sinking into the quicksand. One day, his lantern was found near a muddy quagmire, and he was never seen again. However, Joline has been seen many times, always in her white wedding gown with her wet veil clinging to her face. Sometimes witnesses on the wooden bridge say that they hear a shivering wail, which may be the rustling of the sweetgum tree branches or the slushing of the stream, but most can distinctly hear her calling, "Joshshshsuaaa!"

CATMAN

When camping at Gulf State Park about 35 years ago, I was up in the night rocking a fussy baby by the campfire. There at the edge of the campsite I saw a strange man with long, long hair. He sat on his haunches and watched me. He cocked his head, intently listening to the lullaby I was singing, "Go to Sleepy Little Baby." Tears rolled down his face. Let me tell you the story of Catman.

Billy and Nancy Mae Morgan hated the snow in Pennville, Indiana. The newlyweds yearned to live near the ocean, so in 1910 they came as far south as they could -- all the way to the Gulf of Mexico. Here they built a little cabin on the shores of Lake Shelby and lived every day enjoying the sunshine and water. To welcome a little boy into their lives, Billy handcrafted a baby bed shaped just like a boat. The couple had not lived on the coastal waters long enough to know the signs of impending danger, so when the Hurricane of 1916 struck with fury, their cabin was swept away, and the couple was never seen again. However, stories of their little boy began to circulate among the natives and those same stories are told today around the campfires at Gulf State Park.

Legend has it that the Catman of Gulf Shores was swept away in a hurricane while in his boat-shaped cradle. It landed in the fork of a tree with the baby unharmed.

One of the first tales occurred after the Hurricane of 1926. Rescue crews saw a creature high in one of the few trees left standing after the destructive storm. Since all leaves and pine needles had been blown away, their view was unobstructed. Assuming he was stranded, the crew headed toward him only to see him scamper down the tree with amazing skill and disappear into the underbrush. They told others about him, comparing his physical abilities to those of a cat, so people began to reason that the son of Billy and Nancy Mae had been in the cradle boat when the storm hit, had been safely carried to a fork in a tree where it was lodged. A mother panther (locals call them "Painters") took him as her own and raised him in the scrubby, sandy forest growth. Thus, the name Catman stuck in Baldwin County folklore forever.

The legend was fed by numerous other sightings, most by respected members of the community who shared them as they gathered at churches and shrimp boil parties. The road connecting the communities of Gulf Shores and Orange Beach followed a Native American pathway, and this was where Catman made most of his appearances. Night travelers along Catman Road sometimes glimpsed the creature darting into the brush. He was described as having long, long hair, running on all four legs at times, but able to run upright as well, and able to climb trees with remarkable speed. During WWII, telephone operators were trained by Mr. John Snook, owner of Gulf Coast Telephone, to patrol the beaches for possible German invasion. One of those ladies clearly saw Catman at the edge of the forest. In the 1950s thrill-seeking teenagers often made a sport of daring late-night adventures along Catman Road, but most of those stories were exaggerated to impress others. There was never a verified tale about Catman in which he was aggressive or dangerous to any human.

The road closed to traffic in 1972 but was later converted to a biking and walking trail running from the campground at the Gulf State Park to Highway 161 in Orange Beach. The paved pathway closes at dark, probably due to the stories told about a strange creature often seen in the scrub woods along the trail.

Now, to my encounter with the mystical man. While up late one night rocking our baby son near the campfire, I saw an old man at the edge of the clearing, sitting on his haunches. Sensing he was of no danger to us, I continued singing to Baby Paul. Catman's long hair was now thin and gray; his skin wrinkled. My eyes locked with his and tears rolled down his ancient cheeks. He was under the spell of the tune I was singing, "Go to sleepy little baby, Go to sleepy little baby. When you wake, we'll patty patty cake and ride on the pretty little pony." With the first streaks of dawn he melted back into the underbrush.

I think the magic was in the lullaby. My mother sang that song to me, and in Pennville, Indiana, her mother had sung it to her and her sister, Nancy Mae. I am sure Nancy Mae sang it to her precious baby boy as she put him to sleep in his boat-shaped cradle near the sea. I am so glad he heard it once more and remembered his mother's love.

Is Catman still around? I sure hope so.

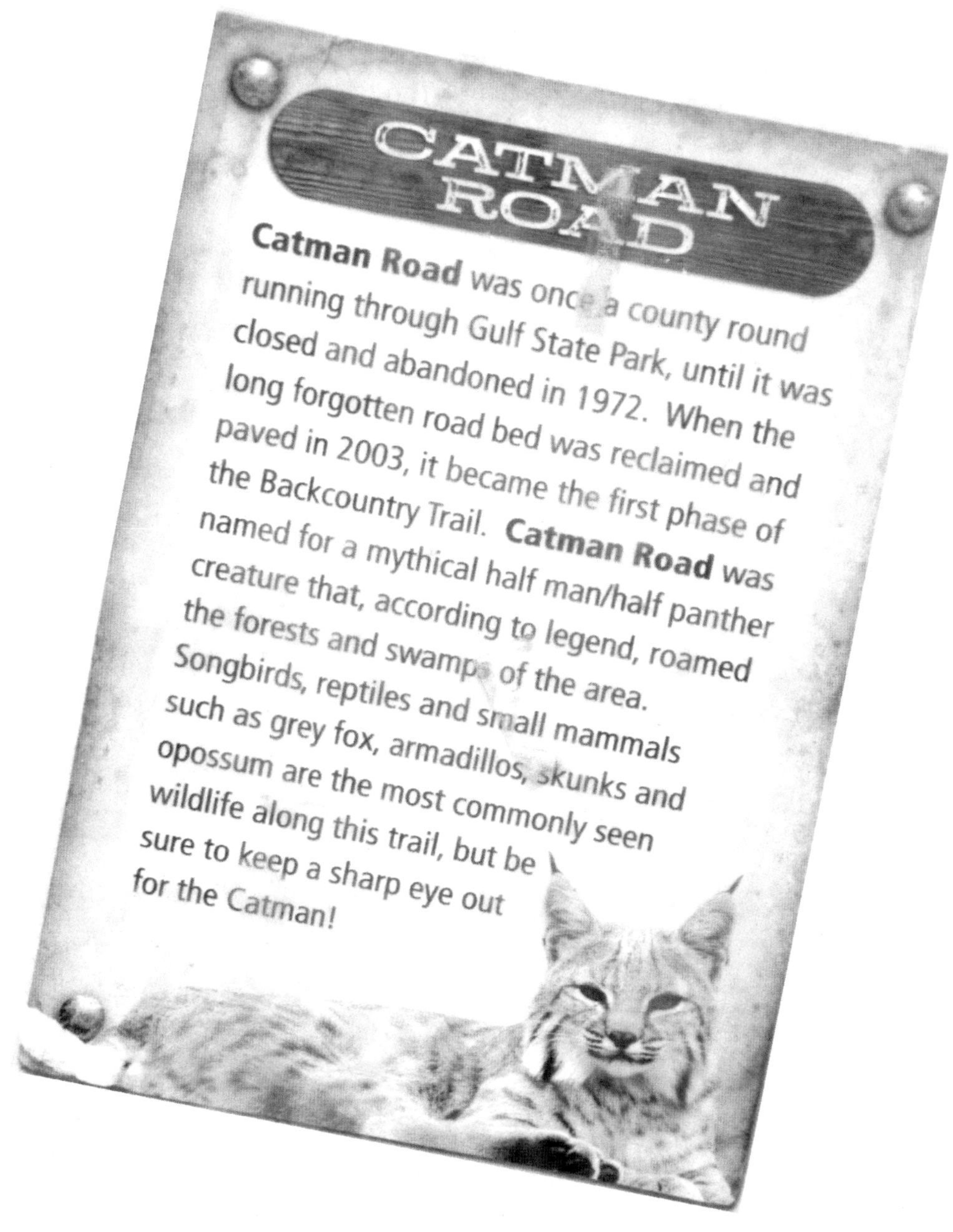

ROCKING CRADLE

I was fortunate enough to actually meet the woman. I was working at the ancient Creole cemetery cleaning and recording the graves. Many of the headstones were so deteriorated that I could not make out the names. I sensed a presence behind me, and there she was. She thanked me for caring for the gravesites of her family members and then the Woman of the Swamps told me her story.

Come, mon Cherie, sit here and let me tell you my story. I live deep in marshy bogs where alligators, they bring me to see their babies. I live in dark shadows of cypress limbs where water moccasins, they come, wrap around my ankles. Spanish Moss drape over us and hide our secrets. My name is Jeanneá, but River People call me Woman of the Swamps; these people who come for potions and charms and blessings. These people who are my people; who share my French forbearers.

Swamps in the south are home to many species, both animal and human.

Thomas and Marie come from the old country many, many years gone by, perhaps to escape the French Revolution but never say. They come to the banks of these rivers where they live on gifts of water and land. Thomas, he fish and trap and make a cabin of pine logs for his family. The family, it grow to three children. Marie and Thomas good parents; Marie she rock each child in the cradle in her bedroom. The children grow; learn to use the gifts of the swamps and Mama' Marie she teach them to read and write in English and in the French. Marie she keep the cradle in her bedroom hoping that once again a baby she can rock to sleep there.

When older, the two boys they go to school in Louisiana where cousins stay. The girl, Almeda, she learn things her mother Marie know. Marie she know about plants and their secrets. She teach Almeda of the plants to heal and also plants of death. Almeda often go with Mamá to help bring new babies into the world of the River People.

Now, Marie know she once again will have new baby to come. She think baby will come two months away, so she send Almeda to buy supplies. Thomas go on fish boat. After Thomas and Almeda gone, Marie she then know baby will come that day. She prepare for baby and baby come while Marie all alone. She hold the dark haired girl, swaddle her, put her in cradle. She sing a French lullaby as she rock Baby Girl to sleep. Marie, she then return to bed, never to wake here again for she pass over to wake on the other side.

When Almeda come home, she find Marie's life gone and new baby in the cradle. She cry, but know Marie want her to be strong and so the girl she become a woman that day. The priest, he send for Thomas and boys to come home for the burial. All is sad here in the cabin, but Almeda she do things Mamá taught her, and she care for baby and family. She work hard every day; sometime young Almeda, she sad and lonely. One night, when baby cry, Almeda sit up, and she see cradle rocking. She hear a French lullaby and baby girl go back to sleep. Almeda smile and know that Mamá here to help her. One day Almeda hang clothes on line and late feeding baby, so she rush into the bedroom and there she see Mamá bending over the cradle, singing to baby. Almeda feel love fill the room and she no alone now.

Almeda teach baby wonders of the swamps that Marie taught her. She good sister and mother to baby. Even when baby grow big, the cradle stay in the bedroom and rock all by itself when someone sad. When baby grow to woman and Thomas pass over, Almeda she marry Nicholas Frost and live in this cabin. Marie she came again to rock the new babies.

The cradle that seemingly rocks all by itself is really rocked by an invisible mother.

After Almeda marry and have more babies, Baby Girl, now woman, go to swamp where she live with alligators who bring her to see their babies. She live in dark shadows of cypress limbs where the water moccasins, they come and wrap around her ankles. The Spanish Moss drape over her and hide her secrets. She make potions to help River People who come to her in the boggy bayous.

Ah, mon Cherie, you know now that Almeda name the baby girl Jeanneá. Sometime Woman of the Swamps come here to visit the graves and to look in the window of the cabin to see if cradle still rocking. It always is.

SNAKE LORE

A reminder – these commentaries draw from the art of storytelling tradition. Local vernacular and rhythm are not the same written as they are orally. So, I hope that sometimes you will do like my good friends Susan and Jim Langley do – read them aloud. Stop and talk along the way and tell your own stories.

I am really afraid of snakes. Not a phobia, because that means unfounded fear – and mine is definitely founded. Actually, I inherited it from my mother. It is in my DNA.

It pains me something terrible to write this commentary, but I have to do so. If I don't, I will have nightmares about snakes. It seems like every day I hear some snake horror story. I have almost quit using social media sites because people are determined to post photos of snakes in the craziest place, like a child's tire swing or inside the power switch box. Once I see a photo, I just can't erase it from my mind, and it comes back to me at night, and I hate those snaky dreams.

Why do people feel they have to share those tales about snakes? What is it about them that makes them irresistible story material?? Whatever it is, it has been around since Adam and Eve.

Alabama's official storyteller, Kathryn Tucker Windham, tells about folk snakes in *Alabama One Big Front Porc*h, and my front porch is exactly where I first heard those tales. I heard all about Hoop Snakes. You know, they can grab the end of their tails in their mouths, form a hoop and go rolling faster than they can slither. That's pretty fast, and even faster if it's downhill. They will chase a victim, unwind, and leap at their throat. Not exactly leap, that is. They have a poisonous stinger in their tails, and they aim their tails at the prey. There was a little old stunted popcorn tree in our backyard. It was crooked and skinny. My Daddy told me that an ol' hoop snake was chasing him. When he saw it unwind, he jumped out of the way. So that hoopsnake stinger stuck right in that tree. It has never been right since.

A hoop snake can bite its own tail and roll faster than any human can run.

My brother told me about a farmer finding a snake in the henhouse. "That old chicken snake had come in the coop and swallowed what he thought was an egg. It was really a china doorknob. The farmer had put it there to keep the hens laying. Then that ole' snake slid right through the handle ring of a glass jug. Next, he reached far enough to swallow an egg whole, which they do, you know. Well, when that egg hit the glass ring, it was stuck, and so was that snake. Old snake couldn't go forward nor backards. He drug the ring, the doorknob, and the egg around that chicken coop until he died, I guess, or maybe that farmer or his wife took care of him. Oh, yes, the farmer took the dead snake with its internal and external attachments to the country store to show it off. That's what they did in those days."

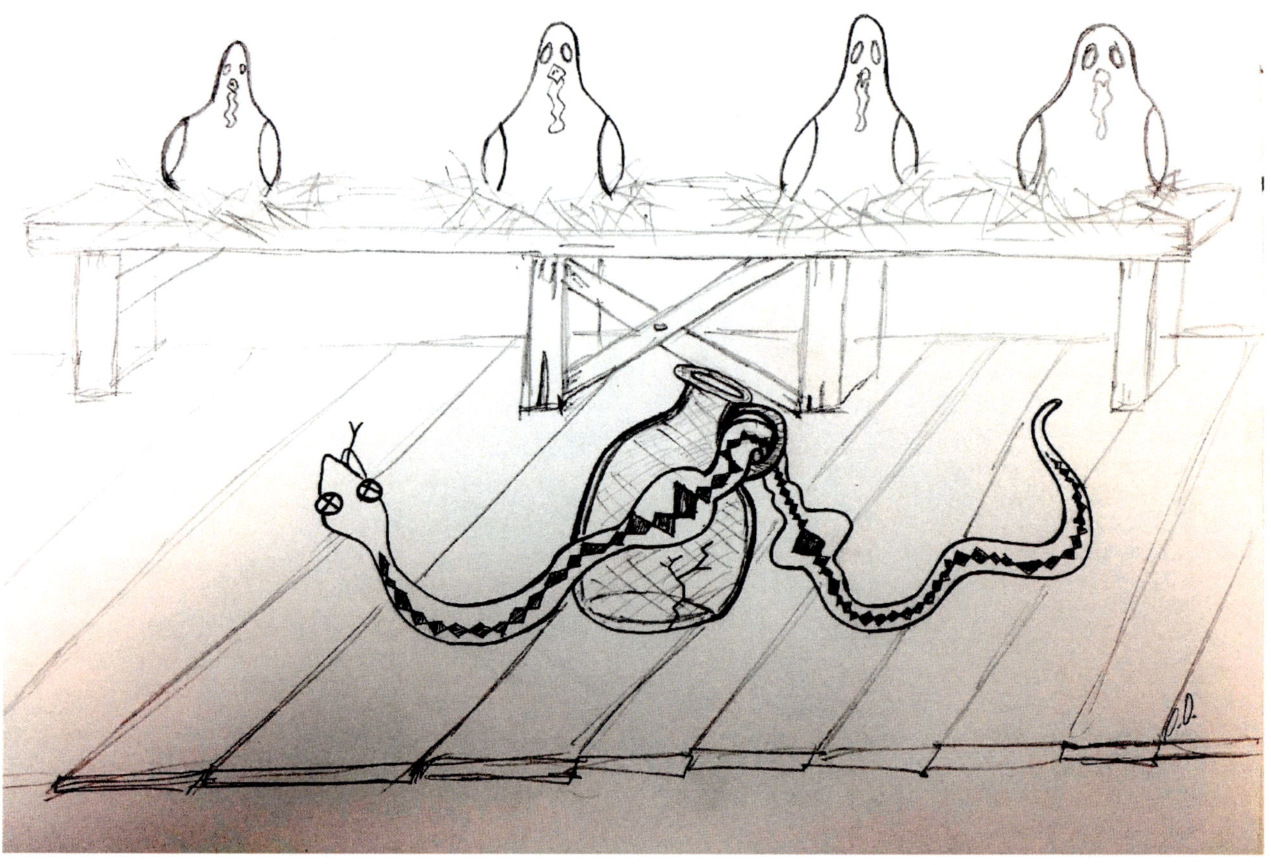

A snake caught between a jar neck and a china doorknob met its demise at the scene of the crime. Art by Paul Outlaw.

You probably know that snakes have curative powers, too. In fact, the term ***Snake Oil*** has its roots in the magic that comes from snakes. Huckster salesmen roamed the country peddling bottles of magical potions that would cure whatever ailed you. My Grandma bought a bottle and took a big swig every night after supper. It made her sleep awful good.

My son spent a year wrangling in New Mexico. He came back with a rattlesnake skin around his hat. He said he killed that snake with a stick, and of course I had a conniption fit. But, after that, he never had a headache. Probably not, because a snakeskin around your head will prevent migraines. If you put the rattles on the headband, you are sure to have good luck. They ward off evil.

Paul Outlaw, wrangler, killed a rattlesnake with a stick and used its skin for a hatband to help cure his chronic headaches.

Snakes can also be used to do the work of the devil. My friend said that her family always talked about Lula, who was picking cotton and came upon a coiled snake. She made the mistake of looking right into those evil eyes and was hypnotized. Her mother saw her spellbound, threw her picksack to the ground and snatched up her daughter. The girl was not bitten by the snake, but perhaps that would have been better. From that day on, she was just not right in the head. Many times, she went into a daze, staring into space. Sometimes while in the "spell" she talked to some unseen being. Don't ever let a snake's eyes capture you. Look away. In fact, run away.

There are lots of things I do to wrap a sense of safety around me. I will never bring in a potted plant that has been outside. Too many tales around about snake eggs hatching and taking over the household. Always carry a snake stick when you go walking in the woods. Once I tried spreading that snake repellent all around the house, but when I realized that snakes already inside that ring of powder would just stay there, I decided never to do that again. It really stinks, too.

They say that snakes come out a whole lot after it rains for a couple of weeks. They are seeking dry ground. But then, again, snakes come out when we have a dry spell. They are looking for water. I guess this means the snakes come out any time they want to.

So... those snakes are out there right now. Thank goodness for nature loving folks whose DNA is a little (well, a LOT) different from mine. Maybe Critter Gitters or Wildlife Solutions will come wrestle those critters out of my attic or underneath my house and take them somewhere else. Please just don't post those photos.

And as for you, readers, don't email me any pictures or tales of near misses about you and snakes. I don't want any nightmares tonight.

OL' TWO TOE

Living around swamps, deltas, creeks, and forests where alligators are abundant, there are bound to be quite a few alligator tales. I heard this one when I was a child.

Ol' Two Toe first made himself known in the swamps near the Bon Secour River. Here the Bertram brothers were trappers known for the fine pelts they took to Patterson's Store every winter. One day, as they checked their traps, they found a trap that had been sprung, and there in the trap were the two middle toes of an alligator that had pulled himself free by sacrificing those two toes. The brothers told everyone about those toes because they were enormous.

Alligator hunter displaying hides hung out to cure.

It was not long before others began noticing alligator slides bearing the prints of a huge alligator with his right rear foot missing the two middle toes. Fishermen said that sometimes they could see two red eyes that were further apart than any other 'gator's ever seen. Reports grew more and more alarming. One farmer heard his pigs hollering and when he went out to check, there was a 'gator with a pig in his huge jaws. The 'gator took off, disappearing into the dark. The farmer heard that pig squealing until he heard the splash into the murky waters. Another local man ran out to confront the alligator raiding his henhouse; that 'gator raised up on his hind legs and ran off just like a human. People began fearing that monster; missing children or livestock were credited to him. The hunt was on to rid the county of 'Ol Two Toe.

Those Weeks boys were the best alligator hunters in all of the south. They claimed they had killed the nuisance and brought in a gallon pickle jar filled with alcohol and the right rear foot of an alligator with the middle two toes missing. That jar stayed on display at Patterson's Store for a long time until one day it was broken by accident. Mr. Patterson picked up that alligator foot and saw that it had been stitched up with fishing line, discovering the hoax those boys had pulled. So, the hunt for 'Ol Two Toe resumed with a fury.

Patterson's Store in Bon Secour was the commissary story for Swift Lumber but also served local customers.

By this time, 'Ol Two Toe had taken off to the north. He was spotted all along the Eastern Shore of Mobile Bay and eventually on up into the Delta. Hunters and fishermen told of those huge eyes. Well, at least those who escaped death told about them. Nearly every time those eyes were spotted, disaster struck the fishing or hunting party. Witnesses reported their boat had been overturned by a monster. 'Ol Two Toe was still claiming his revenge for those lost toes. Some locals even claimed to be driving along a dirt road and suddenly outside the window they saw a 'gator running alongside the car – right up on his hind legs. A hunter reported that he found the remains of a large deer in an alligator nest on the banks of the Tensas. There were so many sightings of him that every swamp man knew 'Ol Two Toe was breeding, and each of his offspring had only two toes on his right rear foot.

Five Rivers Resource Center on Highway 90 in Spanish Fort houses a wildlife display for the delta area. Ol' Two Toe or one of his descendants is stuffed but may not be dead. Photo courtesy of Penny Taylor

Maybe all of this came to an end when alligator hunting was once again made legal. That first season, David Lenore and his buddies won the lottery to go on the hunt and killed an alligator that beat all records up to that point. That alligator was preserved and put on display at the Five Rivers Nature Center on the causeway. Right there he is today. You can go see for yourself. Be sure you notice his right rear foot, the one with only the two outside toes intact. Maybe it's 'Ol Two, or maybe one of his offspring. You can decide whether you think this menace is still out there. Regardless, smart fishermen still fear the night they see those two large red eyes in the swamp. If they know what is good for them, they head on in for the night before disaster strikes.

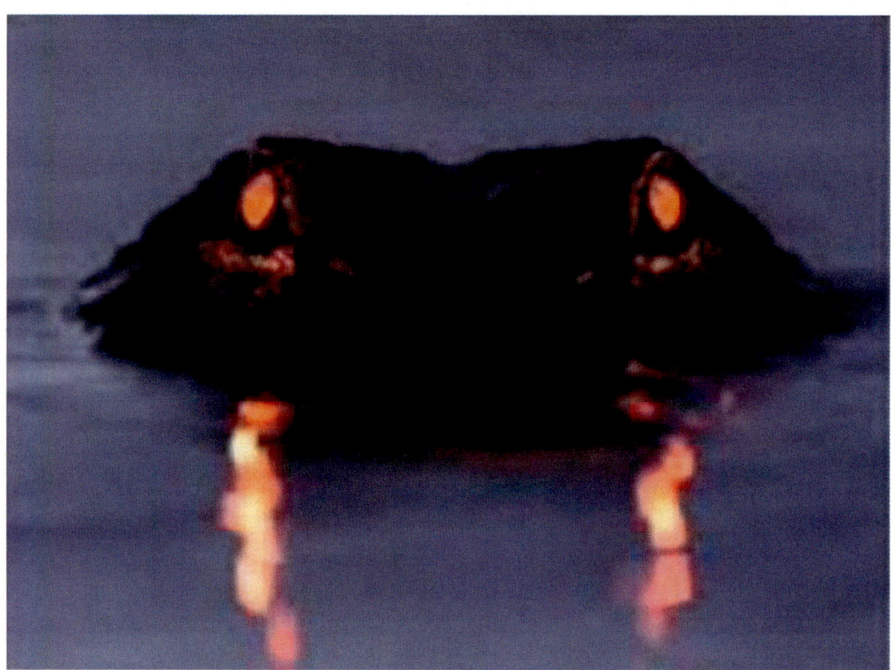

CHAPTER 4 WATER, WOODS, AND WEATHER LORE

Many people refer to the Gulf Coast as "Where the Land Meets the Sea." The abundant forests and plentiful waters are a vital part of Southern culture. It is only fitting that stories of the connection with nature are told again and again.

GRAND OLD LADY OAKS

I just planted three Southern Live oak trees. I know I will not be around to see them mature in 75 years or so, but when you plant an oak, you are planting for the next generation, continuing our southern heritage and respect for the Grand Lady Oaks.

BLAKELEY

Of all the many varieties of oak trees, the Southern Live Oak, is the most iconic throughout the coastal southeast. Its branches bending low toward the ground before rising upward are the perfect places for sitting with a good book on a summer afternoon. And, yes, the Spanish Moss is hanging from its branches.

Southern Live Oaks grow in salty soil and in the shade, so they are found only along the southeastern coastline of the United States. Their crown can spread up to 80 feet and they reach 5 or 6 feet in diameter. They can live to be over a thousand years old – mainly because the root system is so widespread that they rarely are uprooted by storms. They only shed their leaves just as the new ones grow in the spring, so they are green year-round. Southern oak wood is extremely durable, and, in fact, was used to build "Old Ironsides."

The most famous Southern Oak trees in our area hold some of the best stories, and tales are told under those shady branches. Almost every courthouse square in the south has several oak trees and old men gather there to talk about the weather and tell stories. My favorite is about my notorious Uncle Buddy – so many "greats" back that my grandmother could not even keep it straight. I've never told my children because my grandmother said that refined people do not talk about their infamous kinfolk. Mmmm, I think it would be a shame if this story was not passed along, the story about the condemned criminal.

My grandmother was part Choctaw Indian and her grandmother had told her this story. In those days, trials were not conducted in the same way they are today. They were swift and the sentences were carried out immediately. Uncle Buddy was one of those mixed breed Indians who had sided with the Americans during the Indian Wars, actually fighting against the great Creek Indian Leader Red Eagle. After the war he was granted some land in the new county named Baldwin, where he built a log cabin and cleared land for his crops. When American settlers began flooding here for a new life, one of them settled on land that Uncle Buddy was sure was his. He warned the settlers to leave; they did not, so he shot and killed the man.

The town of Blakely was once the county seat. Judge Harry Toulmin held court at the tree before the courthouse was built.

He was arrested and brought to trial in the county seat of Blakeley before the courthouse was built. He stood trial before Judge George Toulmin who was sitting in the fork of a large southern oak tree. The jury sat on a limb on the opposite side of the tree. Buddy was pronounced "Guilty" and sentenced to hang the next day. He was strung up a short distance away at the Hanging Tree in Blakeley. His wife took his body home and buried it on the homeplace, but her cabin had been taken over by homesteaders, so she moved back to north Mobile County where some of her relatives lived. The Mowa Tribe today grew from these peoples.

The Jury Tree was damaged by 1979 Hurricane Frederik but stood until 1992. I remember going to the memorial service held for that tree! The hanging tree is still there in Blakeley. When I see it, I know I am connecting with the past. That is what oak trees do: they connect us with the past.

The Hanging Tree is well-marked in the old town of Blakeley, now a historic state park. It stands in front of the courthouse site.

Imagine a tree still alive that was there when my Uncle Buddy was hung. If you go to see the Hanging Tree, be sure to walk a little further down the path to see the Hiding Tree, where a Rebel soldier took shelter after the Union overran the breastworks at the Battle of Blakeley.

MONTROSE

Everyone loves to drive down a road where the oak trees form a canopy, and some of the finest are along the shady roads in Montrose. The Montrose Garden Club has adopted the mission of maintaining the avenues of oaks planted by Captain Frank Stone about 1938 soon after the highway was paved. They even published a tribute to Southern Oaks in their book, *Live Oaks and Gentle Folks.* The club has also published *In Full Bloom* and *Montrose,* using the profits for Heritage Oak preservation. They also help to maintain the Historic Montrose Post Office, which is set amidst those oak trees on Adams Street. Recently, they had Scenic 98 designated as a Blue Ribbon Memorial Parkway, installing historic markers at each end of the trail to honor all who have died in service.

Once mail delivered to Steadman's Landing was brought to the miniscule Post Office in Montrose. It is preserved today as a historic site.

DAPHNE

The Jackson Oak in Jubilee Point Park Preserve in Daphne has seen its share of history, too. These are the branches that do indeed talk. They witnessed events that we can only read about and imagine. This oak saw the earliest French colonists settle the place they named Belle Rose. Later, its branches shaded soldiers who stood listening to Andrew Jackson as they prepared to fight the British in New Orleans.

The historic marker says that Jackson stood on a branch of that tree to address his men, "Probably the only occasion in Jackson's long career that he was on a low limb."

Protecting trees is now a common civic goal, but in the early 1900s, trees were seldom considered during development projects, and the voices of women were not considered important. When 1926 state highway improvements on Highway 98 in Daphne threatened a tree that was the center of town gatherings, Elodia Hall Van Iderstine gathered her fellow members of the Daphne Study Club. They armed themselves with pitchforks, hoes, and scythes and stood in front of that tree. The machine operator was forced off his bulldozer to try to negotiate with the angry ladies. Sadly, the state prevailed, and the tree was removed, but those ladies gave birth to a movement.

Kudos to those who are expending extra effort and expense to preserve our heritage oaks. An example is the new extension of Bishop Road in Fairhope which circles an amazing tree. As drivers slow down to make the curve, I hope they take time to appreciate this miracle of nature.

FISH RIVER

If you've been around here for twenty-five years or more, you certainly remember the hubbub around the ancient tree near Fish River on Highway 98. It became known as Inspiration Oak, but now visitors to the county park can see only the seven-foot-wide stump of the tree that brought tree lovers from all over the world. It was thought to be 500 years old at the time of the great tree dispute starting about 1990.

Visitors can now only see the stump remaining of the Inspiration Oak whose demise captured attention all over the world.

The oak's 27-foot circumference was girded by a chain saw, reportedly at the request of the owner of the property as a result of a land dispute. Locals were enraged and a major effort was led by Stan Foote of Fairhope to save the tree. Funds were raised and the property was purchased by the county. A team of experts made massive efforts to save the tree by enclosing the damaged trunk in a greenhouse and grafting the gashes. Worldwide news coverage brought people from Australia, Europe, and Asia to witness the effort. A guest book was kept at the site, souvenirs were sold in a gift shop, and the *Save the Tree* campaign continued to receive donations.

Extensive effort to save the girded tree were made possible by donations. Arborists were involved in the methods used to try to preserve the life of the tree. A tent lovingly named ICU covered the surgery effort to regain flow to the branches.

After three years of intensive care, the tree was finally pronounced dead and the greenhouse surrounding it was dismantled. The six-foot fence enclosing the park was locked in 2000 to protect curiosity seekers from the danger of falling dead limbs. In 2003 the tree was finally cut down, and "cookies" of the trunk were sold at $20 each to schools and museums for use as timelines. More than $3,080 was raised – that's a whole bunch of cookies. The analysis of tree rings showed the tree was actually about 90 years old. However, in most old folks' stories it will remain the tree that was alive when DeSoto came to the New World. Plans for the 2.8- acre Inspiration Oak Park have been bantered about, but right now the seven-foot stump sits lonely at the center of the fenced area.

I hope you will take a drive through an oak lined street, or better yet, take off your shoes and walk down the dirt lane at Blakeley.

Daphne
Ala

SPANISH MOSS

My mother told me that when she was a little girl, people used Spanish Moss to make mattresses.

When I was about 5 years old, I decided to make a pillow for my dolls using the soft moss I pulled from the low hanging limbs of the oak in our back yard. That night I was covered in red bumps that itched like nobody's business. My mother dabbed each dot with kerosene and told me all about Spanish Moss.

First, she told me those bites were chiggers, or red bugs, that loved living in the moss, and were now living right there underneath my skin. Of course, I certainly do NOT recommend kerosene as the remedy these days. That is one of the folk remedies old timers used since that and turpentine were about all they had. Nowadays people use 'modern' treatments like nail polish and hemorrhoid cream. It seems those might be folk remedies as well.

Nothing expresses southern ambiance more than Spanish Moss hanging from live oak trees.

Then she told me that when pioneers used moss, they boiled it to kill the insects before stuffing mattresses. Call that a lesson learned the hard way. As she smothered those pesky little critters, she told me a lovely story I will always remember:

"When Europeans first came to the New World, they found Native Americans living all along the coastline. Usually the Indians were helpful and made friends with the explorers. Near here, along the shores of Mobile Bay, one Spanish soldier fell in love with the daughter of the chief. The chief, however, did not want his daughter to marry the soldier, so he ordered the soldier tied to the limb of a live oak tree. He made it clear that if the Spaniard would denounce his love for the maiden and promise to never see her again, he would be released.

"Of course, he would never disavow his love, so day after day he remained tied to the tree. He was guarded to prevent anyone from feeding him or bringing him drink. The Spaniard swore that his love would continue to grow even after his death. As the maiden kept watch at the foot of the tree, her love grew as well. They looked into each other's eyes until his death.

"The chief ordered that his body remain in the tree, warning would-be suitors. Each day the maiden continued to kneel at the base of the tree. Soon she began to notice that his long black beard continued growing. The wind entangled the long strands in other limbs, the hair began turning gray, and still it continued to grow. The maiden knew then that his love was truly continuing to grow. And so did hers.

Typically, Spanish explorers wore the designated uniforms with metal helmets

"The chief then ordered the body be removed, but the Spaniard's gray beard could not be disentangled from the branches, so it was cut from his face and left in the tree. As the tribe moved from place to place along the coastline, the gray beard seemed to follow as it spread from tree to tree. The maiden never married and was often seen sitting in the low branches of a southern oak tree surrounded by the gray moss. It grows there to this very day."

The legend stuck in my mind and I always think of it when I am overwhelmed by the beauty of this plant. It is, indeed, a plant – a member of the pineapple family, of the Bromeliacae division. It is not a parasite, as many people think, but rather an Epiphyte, drawing nutrients and moisture from the air. The only damage it may cause is the breakage of weak limbs due to its weight.

A vintage postcard depicts a lovely oak-lined street and walking path. The card reads "Lovers Lane."

The Alabama Department of Tourism encourages the growth of Spanish Moss, declaring that when travelers from the north first see the long strands of silver they feel like they are truly in the South. Moss can be very successfully "planted", according to Donnie Barrett, a self-proclaimed moss farmer. He uses a long bamboo pole with a forked end to entangle the moss in the branches of live oaks. He warns that if it is just tossed into the tree, the birds will soon carry it away to line their nests. Donnie points out that the moss he planted is slow growing, but his efforts of the past 25 years are paying off. Some of the beards on his trees are quite long now.

Spanish Moss can live on some other varieties of trees, but the symbiotic relationship with Southern Live Oaks seems to be the most productive for the growth of moss, probably due to the strength of the oak limbs enabling them to bear the weight. You may see it on other surfaces like fences, but it will die if not on a tree.

As is usually the case in folklore, there are several versions of stories associated with Spanish Moss. An oft-quoted poem tells of a wicked Spaniard Gorez Goz, who chased a lovely Indian maiden. As she fled, she climbed an oak tree and at the end of a branch overhanging a river, she jumped. He followed her, but as he attempted to pursue her into the waters, his beard was caught in the branches and he was hung. His beard continues to grow to this very day.

Another story tells of a wedding of two Indians which was ended when an enemy attacked and killed them. As was the custom, the hair of the maiden was cut and hung in the tree, where it continues to grow.

Nonetheless, the name Spanish Moss, reportedly dubbed so by early French explorers, has become a part of life in the south, even though it is neither Spanish nor a true moss. But as my husband always says, "Who would want to ruin a good story with the facts?"

So, to me, when I relish the sight of a long beard of moss flowing in the breeze, I remember that true love does indeed continue to grow after life on this earth is over. I also remember to boil it if I want to make a mattress.

GHOST FLEET

The morning was perfect for what I had planned. There was a fog advisory; the temperature was cool enough to slow water moccasins but warm enough for me to sit awhile on the banks of the Tensaw River. Just before dawn I followed the beam of my flashlight down the abandoned steps at Hall's Landing. Then I heard it. The clanging of iron and the creaking of ancient ships bumping the wooden bulkheads. Large shapes began emerging from the mist. I was in the presence of the Ghost Fleet. I lost myself and was transported back in time.

I grew up hearing stories of ghost ships like that of Billy Bowlegs' sometimes seen in the bay, but when Daddy took me fishing early one morning, I saw a real ghost fleet that is now just a memory in Baldwin County.

My father always dreamed of having a fishing camp house on the Tensaw River at Hurricane Landing, his favorite launch. We often left home long before daybreak, pulling the skiff behind our 1950 Ford pickup, and just as the sun was rising, put in the boat. We jumped in and he cranked the ancient outboard motor. Just around the bend, we beheld a sight that will never be erased from my memory: out of the fog hanging over the silent delta waters, arose row after row of ships. As we drew closer, the armada of hundreds grew larger and larger, more than 300 rusted gray ships tied together and anchored in the river. Then he told me all about them.

"I remember when the war broke out, the Alabama Dry Dock and Shipbuilding Company began production of a new class of cargo ship we called "Liberty Ships." They used prefabricated parts and could put a ship together in just 70 days. An awful lot of men moved to Mobile to work there, like your Uncle Fleming. I was so proud they used paint we (Mobile Paint Manufacturing Company) produced.

"When the war was over, the government came up with a plan to recondition those ships so the Merchant Marines could be ready if war broke out again. They had a channel dug between Mobile and the Tensaw River, so the ships could be anchored right here at the Tensaw Shipyard. I think about 300 men had jobs to keep the ships in running order. I guess that averages about one man for each of these ships.

"Of course, the ships looked much better when they first came in than now. The ones you see here are rusted because they need a good coat of BLP paint.

After WWII, transport ships were "mothballed" on the Tensaw River. A shipyard was built there to maintain them in case they were needed once more. Photo courtesy of John Lewis

"As years passed, some ships were sold, but others were called back into service during the war in Korea. We still occasionally see them moving in and out through the ship channel.

"I will tell you one thing. This is the best place in the river for catching bream and shellcracker feeding on the barnacles on the bottom of the ships. And these wooden barriers between the ships really attract those fish. So, let's stop talking and bait these hooks."

Daddy did not live many years after that, but I kept tabs on the Federal Reserve Fleet as it was officially named. Every time I read any news about the mothballed ships, I would take a drive up the river and see them one more time. The US Maritime Administration ordered the phasing out of the mothball fleet in 1970 when there were 101 ships remaining. There were only 42 caretakers still employed when the shipyard was officially shut down about 1973. Many of the ships were sold as scrap metal, but some were sold to private companies which refitted them. The last 15 ships were towed out into the Gulf and sunk as fishing reefs. I remember seeing the last one go out in 1976. As we stood on the banks of the Tensaw River, I thought that would be the last time I would see one of the ghost ships. And it was, until this morning.

Lots of locals tell me that sometimes they, too, can hear the creaking and the clanging of the anchored boats. You can even see the ghostly visions from your own boat if you get out early enough on a foggy morning.

The ships docked on the Tensaw River became known as the Ghost Fleet. Most were eventually sold for scrap or used to create artificial reefs.

The pontoon boat tour from Blakeley Park that goes out every month or so sometimes passes by Gravine Island and the guide will point out the places all along the river where the spirits of those noble vessels will remain forever. Believe me, it is worth your time to see the places that hold our heritage.

This eerie staircase is one of the few remaining signs of the shipyard that maintained the ships of the Ghost Fleet.

MARYETTA

"Old ships may wreck or rot or burn but their legends live on to be told and retold by those who knew them in their glory. Many a schooner never dies but becomes a legacy left for the future." -Food, Fun and Fable by Meme and Charley Wakeford.

Can you imagine looking out over the Bon Secour River 100 years ago and seeing the sleek, magnificent schooners sailing the river? Many of those legendary boats on the Bon Secour had been blockade runners during the War Between the Sates, carrying the salt from the Bon Secour Saltworks, slipping past the Union blockade at the mouth of Mobile Bay to cargo the life-giving salt to other southern ports. Through the years, many were refitted and rebuilt time and time again to become oyster dredge boats and shrimpers, and eventually given gasoline engines, saying goodbye to the beauty of the unfurled sails in the bay. Some sank, some burned, and most are gone now, but their legends will never die. One of the most powerful stories of man and boat is the story of the Nelsons and the *MaryEtta*.

Mr. John Ray Nelson was just about the nicest guy you could ever have met. He welcomed me into his den and acted like he was tickled pink to talk to me about his beloved *MaryEtta* – and he charmed me into his spell! He was a born storyteller!

We have to go back three generations to start the story where Mr. John Ray began it. His grandfather came from Denmark, where his name was really Frank Nielsen, but was changed during immigration procedures in Mobile. He started Bon Secour fisheries with a family-run oyster house on Oyster Bay. It was this ancestor that acquired the *MaryEtta*, one of the most legendary boats in Baldwin County. In fact, she seems to have had a life of her own. Her keel was laid in New Orleans in 1860 as a single masted schooner; she was launched as the *Curlew*. Her cypress construction gives reason to believe that she was a member of the New Orleans Lugger Fleet, ships named for the shape of their sails and used primarily as oyster dredge boats

In the south, boats often become family members. The MaryEtta was a part of the Frank Nelson family. She was used for fishing and shrimping.

She was purchased by Pat and Tom Lilly who lived on Fowl River in south Mobile County. Mr. Lilly widened and lengthened her; she then had two masts, schooner rigged. Mr. Lilly renamed her after his daughter, MaryEtta, and then in 1896 sold her to Frank Nelson, who used the 50-foot boat for oystering. Once while delivering oysters to Mobile, and being towed into the harbor by launch, the *MaryEtta* was hit by the *James C. Kearney*, one of the many bay boats running between Mobile and the Eastern Shore. The *MaryEtta* sank; the Nelsons used another boat to tong the oysters while *MaryEtta* was in the docks in Mobile. She was repaired and soon returned to Bon Secour. In 1920 a 16-horsepower gasoline engine was added, and the Nelsons were among the first to actively catch shrimp for commercial use.

Frank retired in 1935 and his son John Andrew moved the business to the north shore of Bon Secour River, its current location, in 1939. John Andrew loved the *MaryEtta* as much as his father had. In fact, he named his daughter after her.

Old timers remember these days with fondness. Joy Callaway Buskens, author of *Well, I Never Met a Native*, narrates the story from her Aunt Minnie Lee's perspective. Minnie Lee was married to John Andrew and became one of the first women to go out on the shrimping boats. Minnie Lee said that oysters sold for $3 a bushel for select. Large oysters were called "Plants" and smaller ones called "Cullins." She named Arnold Frost as the champion shucker in Bon Secour.

John Ray joined in the business after WWII when he was discharged from the US Navy. John Ray married Jane Byrne, and the *MaryEtta* was still regarded as a family member. In fact, the *MaryEtta* was one of the boats blessed at the very first Blessing of the Fleet held at Swift's landing, with the porch of Patterson's store used as the platform for the service. More than 350 people gathered there on Sunday, August 7, 1949, to ask for blessings on the captains, crews, their boats, and their families. Maybe they even prayed for a much-needed successful season. John Ray was one of the organizers of that event. Episcopal Archdeacon J.D.C. Wilson led the event with the help of Rev. H.L. Redd of the Friendship Baptist Church. John Ray led the responsive readings of Psalms, Rev. Redd read the scripture lesson and Archdeacon Wilson delivered the message. Church choirs sang songs loved by "seafaring folk." I can guarantee that there were hundreds of prayers lifted up that day. The Blessing was an annual event for many years, and

During Hurricane Camille, MaryEtta was washed ashore at Bon Secour Fisheries. She was a favorite subject of photographers. Photo credit John Lewis.

I have memories of the water parade of boats always held after the blessing, such a beautiful site.

The *MaryEtta* served Bon Secour Fisheries well as a shrimper for many, many more years. The year Hurricane Camille hit the Gulf Coast, 1969, the *MaryEtta* was put out of service and towed up on to the beach, where she continued as a symbolic icon in her old age. She stood as a gallant lady photographed by hundreds who came to see the boats and purchase seafood. Shortly before the 1979 killer storm Frederic, John Ray moved her further from the water, where her remains lie today, as beautiful in death as she was in life.

If you are lucky enough to walk around her skeleton, you will feel a sense of reverence and awe. The MaryEtta speaks of those days of the past, telling us that death does not end life.

GHOSTS OF HURRICANES PAST

For those of us living on the Gulf Coast, hurricanes stay on our minds even when they are not breathing down our necks. Like Scrooge, we sometimes have visits from Ghosts of Hurricanes Past. Those who have lived through a hurricane know what I mean. The hurricane memories revisit time and time again and haunt us all our lives.

Storm lore flourishes as tales of survival and death during hurricanes are told on Gulf Coast porches. Everyone can tell a story about someone who survived by hanging onto a tree or a power pole. Many photos of listing buildings after the 1906 Hurricane show how people tried to save them, only to be again blown to pieces ten years later.

Robertsdale School
1906 Hurricane

Robertsdale, Alabama, is miles from the coastline, but buildings suffered tremendous damage in 1906. Here, efforts are made to save the Robertsdale School. Below, Fairhope Methodist suffered irreparable damage in 1916.

Some tell the tale of the Catman of Orange Beach, a baby who survived the 1916 hurricane and was then raised by a panther. The 1926 storm spurred many immigrants to pack up and return to the Midwest after the loss of their crops. Camille, 1969, hit the Gulf Coast trying to erase the historic homes. True tales of folks who were swept away while hosting hurricane parties in Biloxi have a way of sticking around. Old folks remember a hurricane dancing offshore for two weeks before heading right up Mobile Bay. So, don't ever get cocky about predictions of the path. Frederic was historic, changing the coast forever. People will show you the high watermark of Ivan's storm surge and the Grand Hotel tales about Katrina are part of her history.

A storm becomes a landmark in life. After a hurricane, all events are referenced to 'before' or 'after' the storm. For now, 1979 Frederic is the storm of reference for Baldwin County time, for things were never the same after he hit the Gulf Coast. The devastation was heartbreaking, but afterwards, the area took on new life and has developed into the top attraction it is today. Some younger folks now use Katrina as the timeline – and Texans will always remember Harvey as the most traumatic event in their lives. And now, Irma…

Damage caused by Hurricane Frederik was monumental and changed the face of the area in the south part of Baldwin County.

Most people laugh when I say that my bones know when a storm's a-comin', but I've had that phenomenon confirmed by others who feel the same thing and by my doctor who says that barometric pressure does indeed cause body responses. Folklore always includes tales of those who could predict storms before radio and television. One of my favorite stories is about Susan Swift.

Storms caught many by surprise in the olden days, but Susan had that sixth sense of impending danger. Maybe it was because she was in tune with nature, or maybe her motherly instincts gave her abnormal powers. Nonetheless, her intuition and determination saved the lives of her children.

Each year at the end of the summer before school began in October, the Swift children were allowed to go to the shores of the Gulf of Mexico for a camping excursion. Usually, Mother Susan went along, but in 1906, she needed to stay home with two small children. Therefore, Augusta Martin, the schoolteacher/governess, chaperoned the children and their friends, about 16 in all. Mr. Swift let his lumber boat captain take the party across Bon Secour Bay to Shell Banks. Then the group carried the camping gear across the peninsula to the sandy white beaches, where they set up their campsite. The boat captain then returned home to Bon Secour..

Late that same night, Susan suddenly woke up with a jolt. She insisted that her husband go and bring the campers back right away. He tried to assure her all was fine, but by daybreak he relented and sent his boat for the children and Augusta. However, the captain had no luck in convincing the camping party to return. Miss Augusta declared that the weather was beautiful, and they were having a great time. They all said they would stay and told him to go back and tell Mama that all was fine.

When the boat landed back at Swift Landing that evening, Susan was fit to be tied. All night she fretted and finally convinced her husband there was impending danger. At dawn, several other parents joined Charles and Susan boarding the boat. When they arrived at the beach, all still seemed well weather wise, but Mama's conniption fit threw them into a frenzy of breaking camp and loading the boat with their gear.

By the time they reached home about dusk, the weather had rapidly changed. The wind started to howl, the rain pelted down and the waves were at a record height. Everyone sprang into hurricane readiness mode tying down everything that might blow away. Sure enough, all night the hurricane dealt its fury on everything in its path through Gulf Coast counties. The Hurricane of 1906 was one for the history books.

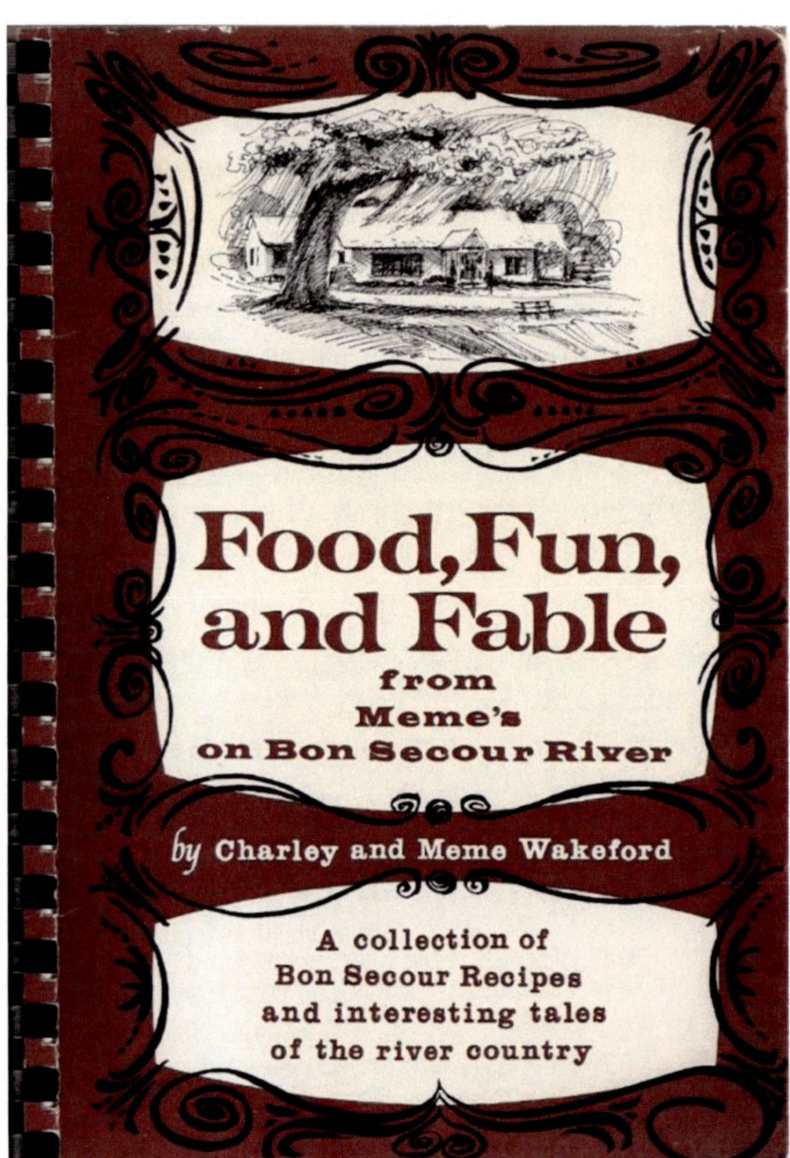

Meme's Cookbook. **Food, Fun, and Fable** *is filled with stories of the Bon Secour area. "Mama's Intuition" is one of those stories.*

The story of *Mama's Intuition* has been told over and over again, as are all good stories. I hope you take time to tell those stories that you have heard. Don't wait until there is power outage due to a hurricane. Do it tonight on your porch. If you don't have a porch come sit on ours and tell us your story – unless there is a storm brewing offshore.

DOUBLE DOG DAYS

My Daddy said I would live to see it, but I didn't believe him. Double Dog Days. He told me that in every generation there is one summer with two sets of Dog Days. This was the summer for mine. 2017 was the year. And now… 2024 saw another eclipse. Will we have 80 days of heat or rain?

Dog Days are traditionally a period of forty days in the summer when there is either rain every day or there is not a drop of rain. In the unbearable heat, dogs are most likely to be infected with rabies and tales of them foaming at the mouth are abundant. One is in the way that Harper Lee used the scenario in *To Kill A Mockingbird* when Atticus had to kill a rabid dog. Some people say the name came from the idea that it is too dog-gone hot. The term actually began when the early Egyptians connected the rise of Sirius, Orion's Dog as a precursor to the flooding of the Nile and the rise of heat and pestilence.

Sirius, known as the Dog Star, is at the bottom of photo.
The constellation Orion is to the right.

Greek poets also acknowledged that the rise of the star brings plagues. Homer referenced the impending doom for Hector that was to come during Dog Days. In medical writings, such as *Clavis Calendria*, the Dog Days are a time wherein wine sours, the sea boils, and men rage with anger and "burning fevers, hysterics, and phrensies." In 16th century Anglo-Saxon England, canonical rituals were observed from July 7 to August 5. I grew up hearing that they lasted forty days because the Great Flood lasted forty days and Jesus spent forty days in the wilderness with no water and food. I figure that makes belief in Dog Day lore somewhat religious.

The time period has a connection to miserable days of insects, humidity, and diseases. Here on the Gulf Coast it also means excessive numbers of jellyfish and yellowflies. My mother always told me that most infant deaths took place during Dog Days, especially during the child's second summer. Now I realize that was probably true due to the fact that the child most likely started eating table food, and bacteria growth in foods was much more prevalent before refrigeration. To speak nothing of the severe illnesses spread by mosquitoes.

We heard of many people dying with typhoid and yellow fever during Dog Days as well. My parents' greatest fear for us was polio. They kept us away from crowds and public swimming pools in the summertime. The homes on the Eastern Shore of Mobile Bay were built by families who had the means to move from the city during the deadly time, living a more secluded life while enjoying the bay breezes. Of course, none of us would eat an oyster in a month that does not have an "R" in its name.

The summer of 2017 was my once-in-a-lifetime experience with Double Dog Days with its two sets of forty days of unusually rainy weather. Typically, the six weeks of Dog Days start in June or July. The dates are flexible and change each year. 2017, however, brought the first set of forty days of rain beginning in June going almost to the end of July. Just when we thought there would be a break in the weather, record-breaking deluges again set in. Usually, Dog Days start to wane when the first hurricane hits the coast, but that is not the case that year. 2017 was a year to record in our journals.

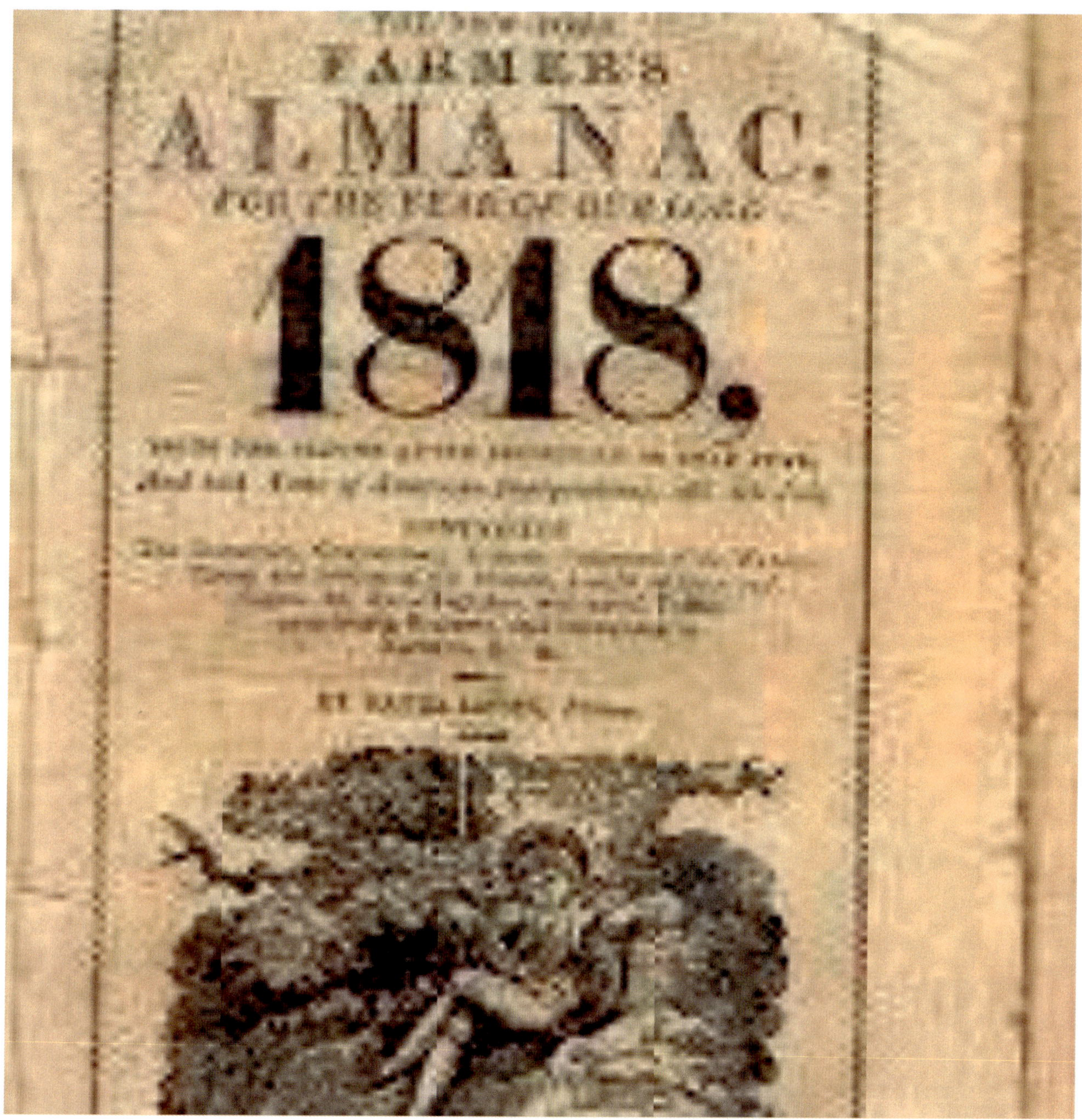

Farmer's Almanac predicts the best time to plant crops among other most useful information and tips.

If Daddy were alive, I have a feeling he would say that year's phenomenon was due to the eclipse of the sun that occurred that year. Maybe he would say it was because during the previous fall the trees got all confused and budded out early. In October 2016, our pecan trees with all the new leaves looked like it was April, and the winter was really a mild one; only one or two hard freezes. That means the mosquito cycle was not broken at all.

Some people declare that Double Dog Days are related to eclipses of the sun. I that is the case, then 2024 summer is due for Double Dog Days!

Old folks knew how to read the signs and their predictions are mostly accurate. I still depend on the *Farmer's Almanac* to plan activities. Farmers actually prefer a dry season during the summer growth period, as taught in this old adage:

Dog days bright and clear
Indicate a good year;
But when accompanied by rain,
We hope for better times in vain.

I will have to say that those wet days sure caused me to cut grass a lot more often than the dry spells. No matter wet or dry, I am thankful I live in the day of air conditioning, good medicines, and a riding lawn mower. I wish I could tell my Daddy about it. I hope he knows he was right. I Double Dog guarantee one thing – it is not hot where he is now!

CHAPTER 5
PLACES WITH A STORY

Many times, while visiting a certain place, emotions can erupt for no explained reason. Well, I think there is always a reason. I will tell you why I think that is true of some of my favorite places in the Deep South.

STRING OF PEARLS

The Foley Railroad Depot is one of the most charming historical buildings in the coastal area. Of the many stories taking place there, the story of Pearl is the most endearing.

Pearl lived in Daphne, and turned 16 on Dec. 7, 1941, the same day as the bombing of Pearl Harbor. The next year as she entered her junior year in high school at Fairhope, most of the young men in her school had already enlisted. On the home front, girls worked hard in the war effort rolling bandages and working at the USO Hall in Foley (today the Gift Horse Restaurant). On the weekends, Pearl often visited her friend Olivia, whose father ran the potato shed near the railroad tracks in Foley. The girls decorated the USO Hall and made lemonade and cookies for personnel stationed at nearby military bases.

Pearl often hitched a ride to Foley from her home in Daphne on the military supply bus, and she developed a friendship with the driver, who was stationed at Barin Field. Their romance grew, and many a Saturday night they were seen dancing on the wooden dance floor to records playing on the Victrola. Their favorite number was *String of Pearls* by Glen Miller, and Joey called her his Precious Pearl. One Saturday night, he asked Pearl to come outside, and there in the moonlight he asked her to marry him. He gave her a lovely strand of pearls as a token of their engagement.

The building that is now the Gift Horse Restaurant was once the USO.

Local citizens provided refreshments, entertainment, and dance music for the military personnel stationed at nearby Barin Field and Fort Morgan.

They married shortly after her graduation from high school, but all too soon Joey received orders for deployment to Europe. It was a quite an emotional day when the trainload of sailors pulled out of the Foley station. As Joey waved from the window, Pearl fingered her beloved pearls with one hand and blew him a kiss with the other. The tracks all the way to Bay Minette were lined with citizens waving flags and cheering for the men.

Pearl began eagerly awaiting his return, making a habit of walking to the depot every afternoon just to see if perhaps he was on the train. Sadly, the dreaded yellow telegram came soon after Joey arrived in Europe. From the moment she read the message, she was never the same. Every evening about dusk, she would don the blue dress that was Joey's favorite, put on her pearls and walk through town to the depot, where she would sit awhile on the benches there, fingering her pearl necklace. After the war ended, her mind grew even mistier, and so did her physical being. She seemed to glide about the streets and often she appeared in the hardware store, which was in the old USO Hall, and ask if anyone would like a lemonade. When the building became a skating rink, sometimes she would walk right out onto the skate floor and waltz with an invisible partner.

Soon after her death townspeople once again began to see Pearl. They often saw a misty blue dress seeming to float along the sidewalks. She was seen at the depot many afternoons, sitting on a bench awaiting the afternoon train from Bay Minette. Even after the train stopped running and the tracks taken up, she waited on her bench. She disappeared for a period of time when the depot was moved and lovingly saved by Mr. John Snook, but when it was restored to its original place, Pearl once again was seen awaiting the afternoon train.

Pearl is often seen sitting near the now defunct rail line waiting for Joey to return.
Photo credit: Penny Taylor

Pearl still heads to the train depot every evening about dusk. The most precious evenings, however, are the Saturday nights when Joey joins her. Sometimes diners at the Gift Horse Restaurant notice the dinner music change to the big band sound of Glen Miller's *String of Pearls*. Then they see a young couple dancing among the dining tables. He is dressed in a WWII Navy uniform; she wears a lovely blue dress and a strand of pearls.

BLAKELEY COURTHOUSE

Did you know there is a real ghost town in Baldwin County? Let me tell you a story about the once "booming" town of Blakeley.

Let's go for a walk down the dirt streets of old town Blakeley, bare feet in the cool dirt under magnificent live oak trees shading the town that was once a city to rival Mobile. The streets are lined with lovely houses, the *Sun* newspaper office, and many businesses. The roads are dusty with the heavy horse and buggy traffic because Blakeley is the county seat of Baldwin County – the beautiful brick courthouse dominates the town. Follow the road down to the wharf where there are riverboats at the deepwater harbor. Some of those boats had been built at Blakeley at one of the major shipbuilding companies.

This town was the brainchild of Josiah Blakeley and was a major city until about 1830 when it began its fall into ruin. One by one businesses closed; people moved away, mostly due to Yellow Fever epidemics and a decline of shipping business. Many buildings were moved brick by brick to Mobile or nearby communities. Even after the town was almost deserted, the courthouse remained active and the county business was supposed to be conducted there, but in reality, much of it took place in the city of Daphne. The Blakeley courthouse was still active during the well-known Battle of Blakeley at the end of the War Between the States although there were very few residents in the town. It was the county seat until 1868 when the county seat was officially moved to Daphne.

The courthouse stood in ruins for many, many years and the abandoned town was a destination for people searching for adventure. When I was a child, my friend, Alan, was one of those lucky enough to go there to explore. At this time the property was still in private ownership. Alan camped there with friends and told us wonderful stories about his discoveries and experiences. We loved to hear him tell about one night they camped out in the ruins of the old courthouse. They put their sleeping rolls over the area they figured had been the jail cell. The old cell was actually built part ways below the floor level of the lowest floor and had windows at the top just above ground level. The courtrooms were in a second story room. The jail cell had heavy iron doors and locks and the boys told tales about the prisoners held there.

By the time Alan camped there the cell doors had been long removed and the jail filled in with dirt. The boys were awakened in the middle of the night with a loud clanging crash and the ground rumbling underneath where they lay. He said the quaking was strong enough to shake some of the bricks loose to rain down all around them. They said it sounded like prison cell doors slamming shut followed by an earthquake.

Blakeley was the Baldwin County seat until well after the town's decline. The county seat was moved to Daphne in 1868 and then to Bay Minette in 1901. The ruins of the Blakeley Courthouse stood until the twentieth century

Since those long-ago days the park has been preserved and is a state park. The park has amazing nature trails and preserved breastworks, often the site of reenactments of the battle that took place there. Downtown has markers indicating the streets and the gazebo in the center of the square is a lovely venue for events.

The courthouse ruins have been excavated and are under a protective covering. Still there are reports of nighttime quakes. People who spend the night in the campground report being awakened by what they think is a mild earthquake or a plane breaking the sound barrier. A group of paranormal investigators spent the night downtown and most abandoned the search after no readings, but the one remaining, who spent the night in her car, said that she was awakened by crashing sounds that shook her car. JoAnn Flirt, the park director at the time, said that she thought those mysterious rumblings could indeed have been long buried live shells from the Battle of Blakeley that somehow explode. As for Alan and me, those are the doors of the jail cell slamming shut on a prisoner who would be hanged from a branch of the hanging tree, which is another story you will hear another day.

IRON CAGE

I certainly hope you never have to spend a night in a jail cell. However, if you do, I hope it is not in the one in the old Fairhope Jail.

The city of Fairhope was founded on the theory of the "Single Tax Colony" and has a colorful history going back to its founding in 1896. The Single Tax Colony Cemetery is noted as a favorite of paranormal specialists, and several houses in the city are haunted. It seems that the free spirit environment welcomes all who come, alive or not. One could spend all day or night in the Fairhope City Museum and never be alone. There are always activities in the old building, whether the museum is open or not. Former Director Donnie Barrett is a walking encyclopedia of all things past and present -- an expert on every subject imaginable, except that he does not know who keeps making noises and appearances in the former city hall.

The City of Fairhope museum occupies the building that was once the City Hall, Mayor's office, Fire Department, and jail

The building was built as a city hall in 1928 by Oswalt Forester using Clay City Tile. It housed the mayor, the police department, the fire department, the city council chambers and the city clerk. As additional city buildings were constructed over the years, all of the offices except those of the police department moved to new facilities. The police department was headquartered in the old building and the jail was in use until 2001. The old jail cell was used mainly as a holding cell during processing, and longer-term prisoners were housed in a more "modern" cellblock built to the rear of the station. Fairhope wisely saved the original building and converted it to a city museum, which has become the focal point of all things past in Fairhope thanks to the foresight of the directors, the mayors, and council members, and countless volunteers who care about preservation of the heritage of this unique city. The museum today replicates the original use of its spaces but has displays covering every aspect of the town's history. Everything is extremely well presented, and the museum has become a repository for all things of value, including those spirits that want to be heard and felt.

The former director, Don Barrett, has had personal experiences that he cannot explain. Once he was at the top of the stairs writing on a clipboard and heard someone's footsteps coming up the stairs toward him. When the footsteps reached the top, he turned to greet the guest, but no one was there. He has heard the jail door slam shut several times when he has been alone, but every time that he went down to check to be sure no one was in the building, he found both doors standing open. Three ladies who love to search for ghosts have amazing stories to share. Sherry got permission to go to the jail one night with her recording equipment. She asked if anyone was there with her, and she heard and felt a powerful *swish* go right past her ear. A wind came out of the cell and blew right into her face. When she listened to the EVP later, she distinctly heard, "cannabis high."

The old jail cell in the original jail in Fairhope was probably the same cell used in the old county jail in Bay Minette. Some historians believe it may have earlier been used in the Blakeley Courthouse.

Local historians are researching the origin of the cell that is now at the museum. It is believed to have been in the courthouse at Blakeley, consequently moved to Daphne and then Bay Minette. It was saved when the old Bay Minette Jail was demolished and most likely moved to Fairhope. The original cell was described as an iron cage, exactly describing the cell in the Fairhope Museum of History. If so, there have been more than 150 years of inhabitants locked behind those doors. No doubt the stories of those men and women need to be heard. At least one of them thinks so.

FIRST HANGOUT

It seems amazing that things that happened just a few short years ago (well, 60 or 70 years) are now the stuff we tell our grandchildren. When we talk about going to the Little Casino, we don't mean a gambling hall. Casino was the name given to recreation facilities, usually near water. Fairhope and Daphne each had one where there were dances, skating rinks, and canteens. The one at Gulf Shores is the stuff of which folklore is made. Oh, the stories we can tell of the good ol' days. Sounds like we are making it up, but this story is really true!

Nowadays, as the end of the school year approaches, plans are made for proms, graduation ceremonies and, of course, parties. Things were the same back in the day at Foley High School. The annual senior trip to Gulf Shores was planned in detail. On the given day near the end of the school year, students with their beach gear climbed into the back of a dump truck (Yes, I mean dump truck.) The short drive to the beach was filled with laughter and singing along to popular songs on a transistor radio. The truck parked right at the end of Highway 59 at the beach. There were only four or five establishments there in the 1950s: Neal's (Fannie Flagg's family store), Romeo's, A&W Root Beer, and the Casino, which was right where the Hangout is today.

Gulf Shores, Alabama, has some of the most pristine white sand beaches in the world. Once very scarcely populated, the Golemon family vacationed there and decided to open a Casino to serve tourists.

The Casino was the real happenin' place on the beach. Built by the Golemon family right after WWII using salvaged Quonset huts, the Casino was the result of a trip to the beach shortly after the Golemons had moved to Mobile from Birmingham. Floddie was thirsty, and there was no place close to the beach to buy a drink, to have a hamburger, or take a shower after a swim in the saltwater. Her husband James saw the opportunity to start a new venture – with a chance to live right in this heavenly spot.

They purchased property at the intersection of 182 and 59, put up the metal curved-roofed buildings, and opened The Casino in 1947. Right away, a hurricane claimed their buildings, but the Golemons just purchased more surplus Quonset huts, and this time used anchors in the concrete. From then on, hurricanes succeeded only in washing loads and loads of sand onto the dance floor. Oh yes, the dance floor: the reason the Casino became the mecca for teenagers of the 1950s. It was a place to jitterbug the days away, right on the shores of the Gulf of Mexico. The jukebox was seldom silent. Bill Haley and the Comets sang *Rockin' Around the Clock* almost 24 hours a day. There was magic in dancing barefoot on a sandy floor.

After the State of Alabama built a large pavilion named the Casino at the State Park down the road, the teenagers started calling the Goleman place the Little Casino. About that time, hip youngsters started using the slang, "Let's go hang out." The new informal name caught on.

Floddie and James Goleman raised their three children there. I had a visit with Jim, the eldest son, who was at that time an insurance agent in Daphne. He can tell you all about the winters there when there was no one to be seen for miles around. He rode the school bus to Foley, crossing over the new Intracoastal Canal via the old cantilever bridge. Even after the family moved to Spanish Fort in 1957,

summers were spent at the Casino, where Jim continued to shovel sand off the dance floor every night and spent days skin diving at the Whiskey Barge wreck.

When I talk with people who hung out at the Little Casino, they always smile. I am not sure they tell me all the things they did at the Hangout for fear their children will find out. I do know that many children were not allowed to go there because they actually sold beer.

If you kids want to see what it was really like in the days of *Beach Blanket Bingo,* go to the Foley Railroad Museum and take a look at the old Foley High School Annuals that are on file there. You may learn a lot about Grandma and Grandpa that will surprise you. But don't tell them I told you so.

Foley High School seniors had a traditional field trip to Gulf Shores beach at the end of their final year. They went in the back of a dump truck and spent the day at the Hangout.

BURNT BY LIGHTNING

Nik Coles purchased the historic Swift Coles Home in Bon Secour in 1976. He filled it with fine antiques, one of which holds a fascinating tale. Here is the story he told me a long time ago.

"Let me tell you the story of this dining room table. This is one of those places where the emotions of the past are so powerful they are still around. You can almost hear the clanking of the silverware and people laughing out loud. This table has been the center of many episodes throughout its life even before it came here to this house. It is a 14-foot cypress table. The cypress is one piece of wood in width, cut from a magnificent black cypress tree from the swamps in Louisiana.

"In fact, I bought it from an antebellum plantation in Louisiana where it was used as a worktable in the open-air work area under the upper main floor of the house. Do you see this dark cut in the wood? Only something very powerful and sharp could have made that black scar because cypress is one of the hardest woods there is. It is used for cutting boards and chopping blocks that never wear out.

"Many of the slaves in Louisiana were brought from the West Indies where the practice of voodoo and the mysterious arts is a part of the culture. The slaves brought some of those practices with them when they were brought to New Orleans and sold to work on nearby plantations. The slaves at this particular plantation were some of those. Their culture mixed the beliefs from their ancestors in Africa with those of the West Indies and then, as they learned of Christianity, they adopted those beliefs, but their heritage could not be forgotten, and the old ways carried on as well.

"As the slaves worked around this table, they sang the spirituals that have become an amazing collection of cultural art. Sometimes I imagine I can hear them singing, *I'll Fly Away* or *Swing Low, Sweet Chariot, Comin' for to carry me home* -- all the while working away here making biscuits, cutting up chickens to fry, or chopping okra for gumbo. These songs were plaintiff calls for freedom and hope for a better future in heaven if not here on earth in their lifetimes.

"Sometimes while the owner's family was gone on a trip up the Mississippi River and the overseer was in a drunken stupor, there would be a gathering here around this table. Hands were placed flat on top of the table and spirits were called upon in a séance.

The large river home of the Swift family was purchased by Nik Coles, who furnished it with fine antiques. The long cypress table holds a black mark that could only have been made by a red-hot force.

"The last gathering here was the night of April 9, 1865, the day that Gen. Lee surrendered at Appomattox Courthouse -- the final night of the War Between the States. Of course, the slaves here around this table had no way of knowing they would be given their freedom the very next day. Unfortunately for the slaves, the overseer got word of the session and suddenly appeared at the head of the table.

He took out his whip, cracked the whip on the table. He yelled for the slaves to return to their quarters. Just at that moment, a bolt of lightning flashed, streaking right under the house where they were gathered. The bolt ran the length of this table, shocked each of them and they fell to the ground. When they regained their composure, there on the table was this mark that you see here. The smoke coming from the scorched cypress filled the air. The overseer had been struck by the bolt and lay there dead.

"They knew that something powerful had happened, and when they heard the news the next day, they were convinced that the lightning had been a sign from the other side. The lightning had been sent as a message that their pleas had been heard and were answered, and the mark on the table was left as a reminder of that night.

The jagged black scorch on the table refuses to be removed. Even after being sanded, the mark reappears on the surface of the cypress table.

"After the War, some of the former slaves stayed in the area and the story of the table became one of the tales they told around their homes in the evenings. Old folks would bring their children here and tell them the story, lest the memory be forgotten. One of the grandchildren of a slave there told me this story. Sometimes even now when people sit here at this table, they feel an electric current come through their hands on the table. More often, a smell of smoke is detected here in this room. Yes, indeed, the past is still with us. "

STAGECOACH INN

Imagine traveling southward on a stagecoach, stopping at crude layover inns along the way.

The stagecoach line owner William Kitchen had built the house near Stockton as a place of accommodation along the line. Down the original road lined with magnificent live oaks, the property also had a post office, smokehouse, and the stagecoach barn. When I had the joy of visiting, the estate was owned by Carl Hixon, whose family treasured the place not only for its setting, but for its place in history as one of the few remaining stagecoach stops in Alabama. The house was charming and the creaking wood floors told of the years of wayfarers and families who had stayed there. However, the strongest sense of the past was found in the barn. There where old tack, ropes, tools, and wagon wheels hung from ancient posts and walls, it did not take much to imagine the stagecoach pulling into the barn, and the passengers dismounting to go to the house for a meal or for an overnight stay.

The Federal Road ran from Milledgeville, Georgia, to Mobile. Stagecoach stops such as the one in Stockton provided overnight accommodations for travelers and a change of horses was kept in the barn.

Most people know the legend that farm animals talk at midnight on Christmas Eve, but the Stagecoach Stable yields even more. Many times, on Christmas day, the cries of a baby are heard coming from the tack room. In fact, the descendants of Joe and Marta have told me that the family story is true and that they had witnessed the Christmas miracle there in that barn, reminding them that love lives forever. May the memory of babes born in barns behind inns be the center focus of every Christmas.

Marta was getting ready for a Christmas journey. This trip was not a holiday trip; it was a move to the new state of Alabama. Her husband, Joe, had gone by wagon six months earlier and built a log cabin on the land he homesteaded, and he then sent for Marta to join him. She packed her traveling trunk and boarded the stagecoach in Milledgeville, Georgia, to travel on the newly cleared Federal Road all the way to Stockton, Alabama, where she was to continue on the spur line south to her waiting husband.

The stagecoach stop in Stockton was at the Kitchen Inn. Mr. Kitchen provided housing for the guests and livery for the horses. There were extensive outbuildings.

The Federal Road was not well developed, and the journey was difficult with stops about 16-18 miles apart to change horses. Some of those stops provided overnight accommodations and meals. As the journey progressed, the road became even more treacherous; winter storms were coming in early. If all went as planned, she would meet her husband on December 24, and they would spend Christmas in their new home. She was excited as she thought of the letter her husband had written. He had a Christmas present for when she arrived, and she carried her present for him under her cloak near her heart.

When the coach made its regular stop in Stockton at the Kitchen Inn and horse exchange station on December 23, Marta enjoyed staying in the lovely house. It was a one story with the attic converted into extra bedrooms. The house was toasty warm as the roaring fire in the fireplace in the center of the house opened into all four downstairs rooms. She awoke the next morning looking forward to the final leg of her journey; she would see her beloved husband this very day.

She tried to enjoy a lovely breakfast on that Christmas Eve, but she began to feel strange and said she would go outside and be in the stagecoach when the driver was ready to leave. When she went into the barn where the stagecoach was already hitched up to the horses, she felt even worse and thought she would lie down a minute on the fresh hay in the tack room. She must have fainted because when she awoke, she could hear the sounds of the coach and horses rattling down the lane. By this time, she was in too much pain to move and she lay there until she heard Mrs. Kitchen come into the barn. When Mrs. Kitchen found Marta and realized what was happening, she decided to keep Marta there in the warmth of the hay, fetched blankets, boiling water, and swaddling clothes. Together the two women worked during the night until almost dawn.

Just as they heard the sounds of a horse galloping up the road and into the barn, the cries of the new baby rang from the rafters. Into the tack room rushed Joe, just in time to be a part of the miracle. When he had found that Marta was not on the coach at the designated spot, he realized she must have missed the coach; he had mounted his horse and raced north to the Kitchen Inn in Stockton.

Joe and Marta were the ones whose love was so great at that stagecoach stop, that sounds are heard there in that barn even yet. Especially on Christmas morning.

The original barn of the Kitchens Inn holds remarkable memories and the sound of a precious baby born there.

DAPHNE MASONIC HALL

Many people comment on the brilliant and mysterious light displays which were seen outside of the old Masonic Hall building in Daphne when it was standing. The flashing lights were not, however, an installation of Christmas decorations, but rather were made by residue of events that happened there long ago.

.

On the Old Spanish Trail in Daphne there stood an eerie stucco building. It was once a Masonic Lodge, later used as housing, the police station for the city, and stood abandoned for years before it was demolished in 2020. Throughout its colorful history people had strange encounters there and in the surrounding woods. The old Masonic Lodge was built near Yancey Branch on the Old Spanish Trail, the major thoroughfare of the day. A nearby well was shared by several families in the community. It is common knowledge that silver and gold were hidden in the well during the latter years of the War Between the States, when news of the Union march toward Spanish Fort and Blakeley reached the residents along the branch.

There are those who saw fireballs flying up and down the street which is now the remnants of the ancient byway. They described them as brimstone orbs which seem to be hurled with great strength. The fireballs were really the shots fired here in a skirmish during the War Between the States. A troop of Union soldiers transporting munitions was attacked by a small contingency of guerilla Confederate soldiers. There were several killed and more wounded before the Union was driven away. The injured Confederates were taken to a makeshift hospital at "Uncle Johnny's" house in Daphne on the bay, with plans to return to retrieve the dead from the skirmish site. One Confederate soldier had suffered a bullet to the head and was left for dead. However, upon reviving from his unconscious state, the soldier stumbled into the woods where he came upon the well. Here he met some women and children who immediately began to clean him and give him fresh water to drink. The soldier was not able to speak or hear, seemingly in a state of shock.

The women and children heard horses and wagons approaching and ran into the nearby woods motioning for the young Confederate to follow them. The young man seemed in a dazed condition as the Union troops came into the clearing; the Major called to the soldier to halt. But the young soldier simply turned and started walking away. After firing warning shots, the Major took aim and shot the soldier in the back. The Major approached the body and turned him over to see his face. He was terror-stricken, for the young soldier was his brother. Just at that moment the Confederate forces returned, and the Union contingency fled. The women and children came out of the woods, dragged the body away, and hid it. They returned at night to bury the body, but it was nowhere to be found. To this day, no one can explain the disappearance of the body, but the sightings in the area keep the story alive. Some say they can hear the rumblings of wagons and the hooves of horses. The apparition of the young soldier has been witnessed by enough people that it seems to be common knowledge that he haunts the woods and even inside the Masonic Lodge after it was built.

One of the now-gone historic buildings in Baldwin County is the Masonic Hall that was built near a community well on the Old Spanish Trail.

Joan White Crowder, author and historian, had personal experience with the sightings, as she wrote in her wonderful book, *Tell It To An Old Hollow Log.* During World War II she and her family lived in the two-story Gothic building which had been converted into two apartments. Joan's grandparents lived upstairs and Joan lived downstairs with her parents and her paternal grandmother. She vividly recalls the uneasy feelings her family experienced while living there. Several incidents made them aware that there were other presences in the building.

One of the first ways the spirit made itself known was through the kitchen faucet. It seems that Mama Net was always fussing about someone leaving the water running, although each time everyone would deny having even touched the spigot. The water came from the old well on the property. They assumed that maybe the spirit of the well was revealing a secret to them. Often people searched the well for treasure, but so far, none has been found. In truth, no one even seems to know the location of the well.

There were several other incidences with the spirit in the house, such as missing clothing and footsteps heard. Joan describes an encounter with the spirit that ended their fear of its pranks. During one manifestation of the ghost upstairs, her grandfather felt himself pushed against the headboard. When her grandmother began reciting the Lord's Prayer, she felt the whoosh of a cool breeze through the window take the place of the intense heat they felt in the room. Joan relates that the family still had some experiences in the house, but because her grandfather and the ghost had reached a "mutual understanding," they all began to laugh about the tricks played on them.

Later the building housed the Daphne Police Department. The officers and staff working in the building were reluctant to relate their experiences in the building, but tales continued to abound about the happenings taking place there. People outside still noticed strange occurrences as fireballs were seen flying up and down the street and in the nearby woods. Maybe they are shots fired from 150-year-old muskets, or perhaps they are really a Christmas light display.

PINE NEEDLES RETREAT

People say they have seen a light in the upper floor of the historic American Legion building on Mobile Bay. Let me tell you the story as it was told to me.

Across Mobile Bay in the port city of Mobile, women have always led active roles in society, as well as politics and business. Even before the Single Tax Colony had founded the lovely city of Fairhope in 1896, it was a destination for outings and retreats for residents of Mobile. Several hotels dotted the bayshore and religious retreats numbered at least four. It became a place of respite from the big city life in Mobile and represented relaxation and restoration for the soul.

A group of Mobile women had formed the Mobile Business Women's Club. The group decided that they would like to have a retreat and determined that Fairhope would be the ideal location. They were able to obtain a piece of land but did not have enough funds to build the retreat. After several years of fundraising, they decided to join the ranks of those women who had learned the power of peaceful protests. They made plans to raise canvas tents on the property and camp out there until funds would be garnered. They stayed away from homes and families until the husbands grew tired of their womanless states and contributed enough money to build the lovely resort. It was completed in 1912, a wooden three-story building with porches on all sides to catch the bay breezes. The third floor had dormer windows on all four sides to allow the flow of air through the building. Windows opened upstairs would draw the cool air from downstairs and expel it, keeping the retreat cool even on the hottest of days. They named the well-loved gathering place Pine Needles. The women considered it a female counterpart of the all-male Mobile Yacht Club on the western shores of Mobile Bay.

Pine Needles remained in ownership of the Mobile Women's Club for many years, and some women even lived there year-round. The ladies retained a housekeeper who cooked and cleaned to pay for her room and board. As the club's interest in the resort declined and financing the maintenance of the building became an issue, rooms were rented out to boarders. Eventually the club sold the building, and it became rental property.

Women from Mobile decided to build a retreat on the Eastern Shore of Mobile Bay. They raised funds and constructed the magnificent house which now houses the American Legion.

In the 1930s one family to rent it was the Arnold family with their eight children. One of those children, Elsie Burtegerite, has distinct memories of the second floor showers built in the overhang part of the building and the sound of the water falling all the way to the ground. The children learned to swim in the bay and spent hours on the porches of the old place. The fireplace was so large that it would hold immense logs. It is now boarded up, but some say the smell of the smoke from the fireplace is very real at times.

The place was used as office space in the 1950s. During this period the third floor was rented out to promoters who held boxing matches there. Seats were placed around a makeshift ring in the center of the room. Clamoring from the spectators could be heard for miles around until complaints caused the boxing business to fold.

In 1961 the building became the home of the American Legion Post 199. It was the first building in Fairhope to be named on the National Register of Historic Places. However, it was soon enclosed with clapboard siding covering the porches, making more indoor space. Inside rooms are still very much as they were in the earliest days of Pine Needles. Clawfoot bathtubs and unpainted walls take a visitor back 100 years to the days of the 1920s or earlier.

Paranormal investigator Barbara has visited the building to glean information about the spirits who inhabit the place from its one-hundred-year history. It is known that there are waitresses at the club who will not work alone in the building, and many people have heard steps sounds from the second floor where the bedrooms were. Barbara spoke aloud introducing herself and the others with her. She spoke in a calm voice encouraging dialogue. She asked if those present were upset that the place had now become a bar. The answer was distinctly, "No, I love it." When asked if she minded that women also drink at the bar, the answer was a definite, "Yes."

The Pine Needles retreat is now the home of American Legion Post 199. The bayfront is the spot many gather for music and bay breezes.

Servers say that when they come in to work as the place opens about three o'clock in the afternoon, they often find glasses turned over on their sides and once they came in to find the water running in the sink. Many say that doors are heard opening and closing on the second floor when no one is upstairs. The inhabitant has come to be known as the housemother, reminiscent of the days when the women came there for a little retreat. Perhaps this is because one resident said they repeatedly heard the sound of a broom swishing across the floor.

The most annoying of all the incidents is very loud thumping and pounding on the third floor – not so different from what would be heard at a boxing match. Most who have heard this, have been fearful and do not want to discuss it. Even though the upstairs does not have electricity, occasionally lights are seen from the upstairs dormers. Several motorists have reported seeing them from their cars as they pass by on Scenic 98. People are probably seeing the reflections of passing car lights – or are they?

BAREFOOT ANNIE HIDE AND SEEK

There is no family in Baldwin County nicer than the Morris family and there is nothing that says "country home" more than the sound of bare feet running across the wooden floor of a porch. That is exactly what makes the Morris Farm in Stockton special to all who believe. The Morris family certainly believes, for they have shared stories about the little girl whose bare feet are not only heard but seen!

Her name is Annie, and she does not like to wear her shoes. Her feet can be heard *pitter-patter*ing around the porch gracing two sides of the house. She plays hide-and-seek with her beloved dog, behind the swing on the corner of the porch. She is a five-year-old charmer with cotton-top blonde hair, tangled in the back as a little girl's hair is wont to do. It flips up at shoulder level. She wears a dress with aqua and white stripes adorned with puffed sleeves and a collar. Annie lives in the house just as surely as the Morris family does. In fact, she made herself known to Bill even before he bought the place.

Scarlet had told her father, Bill, that there was an estate sale in Stockton. He and his wife drove from Bay Minette to the Bryant homeplace. As soon as he parked the car on the dirt drive, he told his wife that he was going to buy that house. She thought he was crazy, but he did buy it that very day: the house and three historic outbuildings.

The estate was the homeplace of the Vaughn family, who ran a large plantation and boat landing. In 1851, the Vaughns had built a small house and a barn on their plantation, and later built the larger house. The Bryant's purchased the plantation from the Vaughns and lived there for about 100 years. The place has become known and the Vaughn-Bryant- Morris Home

The first encounter with the beautiful little girl happened on the very day Bill first saw the house. When his cellphone rang, he walked toward the rear of the house to talk. His granddaughters were with him that day. When he felt a child lean against the back of his leg, he assumed it was one of them. He reached to pat her head, and as he looked at her, he saw a blonde child who was not his granddaughter. She then ran out onto the porch. He took that as a confirmation that he should go through with the purchase of the house.

Work began on the place immediately with the assistance of two longtime helpers, Virgil and James. One day, James had his back to Mr. Morris, and Virgil was looking toward the corner of the porch at the porch swing. Mr. Morris saw that Virgil was upset and asked what was wrong. Virgil had seen a little girl run to the porch swing and then just disappear.

When Bill Morris went to an estate sale at the historic Vaughn Bryant planation, he decided then and there to purchase the home and grounds. He spent hours restoring the home and outbuildings. Some experts have designated the barn as one of the oldest in the county. Photo courtesy of Penny Taylor Balme

Immediately after that, Scarlet and Lynn, Bill's daughters who had been cleaning on the east side of the house, came out the front door to ask if the men had seen a little girl. The sisters had heard running footsteps on the porch and assumed it was Scarlet's two-year-old son, but when they looked, they saw the little girl run from the front porch swing past the window and then disappear. They could not see her feet, but they did see a dog run after her. When they went out to the side porch, they could still see the dog, which ran down the steps into the backyard, but the little girl was gone. The dog stayed around a long time after that, so the dog was "real." And Annie became real to them that day.

The Morris home in Stockton is almost exactly like it was one hundred years ago. The original porch swing is a favorite of Barefoot Annie. Photo credit Penny Taylor Balme

Soon after that, Scarlet's young son was spending the night with his grandparents at the farm, and Mr. Morris heard him playing in the front parlor happily talking with a playmate. When asked who he was talking to, he said, "I was playing with Annie." He then showed Mr. Morris the door that Annie had gone through, a closet access to the attic by means of crude ladder.

Once Scarlet was in the kitchen and heard a little voice call, "Mama," through the screen door. When she went to the door to check, there was no one there. They have also heard Annie calling for her mother from the front bedroom.

One Mother's Day, Mr. Morris came into the house through the kitchen door and something caught his eye up on the ceiling. There was a magnificent footprint of a barefoot child. The footprint was dark, like the child had played in the dirt or soot. The toes were perfect. It was there until Mr. Morris had the ceiling painted—

the workers did not realize that the footprint was a treasure and painted over it. Mr. Morris and his two workers have often noticed Annie playing in the yard or running on the porch, and when they make eye contact with her, she disappears.

Who is Annie? Do her bare feet tell us anything about her? The dipping vat may hold a clue. A cement pit had been built here on the farm so the cattle could be treated with pesticides. There in the cement of the floor of the slab are two perfect footprints of a five-year-old girl. The date is legible there: 1910.

The Vaughn estate had a concrete dipping vat in the back yard. The cement has the precious footprints of a little girl. Photo courtesy of Penny Taylor

Neighbors say it was rumored that a child visiting the Bryants fell off the porch, broke her neck and consequently died. Perhaps that child loved the farmhouse dearly and comes for visits. Annie hasn't been around much lately. Perhaps the children are too old to be her playmates, and when there are children once again running in the house and on the porch, she will come back for a play date. The Morris family emphasizes there is a wonderful, happy feeling in the house; Annie brings wonder and laughter with her visits.

The porch swing has been there for one hundred years, and the porch steps are exactly the same. Walking up the steps to the front porch takes everyone who comes there back a century to visit with Annie. Take off your shoes and sit a spell. Or play hide and seek with Annie.

LADY IN BLUE

Fact and Fable sometimes collide. That is when the best folklore comes to life. Such is the case of the Lady in Blue I saw one night under the full moon at Fort Morgan.

We were participating in a living history weekend at Fort Morgan, camping inside the fort, eating food cooked over the open fire, and conducting educational tours and reenactments for the public. Before turning in for the night, we shared stories of eerie events that many people have experienced, such as seeing a man hung from the rafters in the barracks, a man in uniform marching across the parade ground, and the sounds of gunshots and sobbing. Many people say that Fort Morgan is the most haunted fort in the south.

Not surprisingly, sleep did not come easily, and I got up to sit out under the stars and soak up the silent atmosphere. My eyes scanned the dark outline of the walls of the fort against a sky lit by the full blue moon. A blue moon occurs when there are two full moons in one calendar month, and I was fortunate enough to be there on that magical night.

There she was – the Lady in Blue walking the north wall ramparts. I had heard of her but did not fully believe until I saw her. Her face was a shadow, but the long flowing dress was luminescent and translucent, just like the blue moon. There was no doubt in my mind that this was the lady of lore, the tale told for almost 100 years.

I first heard about her a long time ago, when Mike Bailey, Director of Fort Morgan at the time, told me that several people claim to have seen the lady, although he had never had that privilege. As we chatted about the possible explanations for her supernatural presence, he related to me the story of a gentleman named Louis Pepin who came to visit the fort in his latter years. He wanted to see once again the place where he was born. He was born while his dad was stationed there when the fort was training young men for World War I. His father was then sent to Hawaii for duty and returned to Fort Morgan as commanding officer when Louis was about eight years old. Louis and his brother loved living in the officer's quarters, attending the school right there on the grounds of the fort, and most of all, playing in the sugar white sand of the beach on the Gulf of Mexico, searching for treasures that washed up every day. One discovery they made on the beach was heartbreaking, because it was the body of a lovely young lady, dressed in a long blue gown. Louis' father, for a reason unknown to his sons, had her body buried in the northwest corner of the fort, perhaps in the long-lost cemetery of the fort. Louis remembered that among those at the graveside was one officer's wife, who was inconsolable. After the burial, it was not long before people began to see a lady walking along the ramparts on the highest walls of the fort.

One of the best-preserved star forts in the United States is located at the western tip of the Fort Morgan Peninsula. A top tourist attraction, the museum is a comprehensive summary of the life of the fort. The walls hold many secrets and occasionally figures from the past are seen.

Who was she and how did she get there? The mystery of the lady lies in the hold of another legend of Fort Morgan. The ruins of the beautiful Rachel, a three masted schooner, are visible after the sands about five miles east of the fort are washed away from time to time by storms that hit the gulf beaches. The wreckage is sometimes called "The Mystery Ship," and many want to claim it dates back to the War Between the States, but Mike knows the truth behind the waterlogged remains of the ship. When it last arose from its sandy grave after Hurricane Ike in

2008, several media reports, including a national network, featured the mysterious ship.

The fact is that the wreckage is actually the remains of one of the largest ships ever built in the DeAngelo Shipyard at Moss Point, Mississippi. The Italian Shipyard on the east bank of the Escatawpa River was established by John De Angelo, who came from a family of shipbuilders in Italy. The Rachel was completed in the early 1920s, but met her fate in her first year, when she ran aground just off the shore of the Fort Morgan peninsula in October. Her cargo of lumber and most of her outfitting hardware were saved, but she was later mysteriously burned. The reports say that no lives were lost. But is that a fact? The crew of eight survived, but were they the only ones on the Rachel?

The schooner Rachel ran aground on her first voyage in October 1920. Reports say that the crew of eight survived, but legend says there was a secret passenger.

Now, this is the point in the story where fact and fable merge to make the moving tale of the Lady in Blue. Lorna lived in Moss Point, married to a cruel and heartless husband. She wrote to her twin sister, Lois, who was the wife of an officer at Fort Morgan and told her that she would have to escape her tormentor before he took her life. From her home, Lorna watched as a large new ship was being built at the shipyard across the river. An escape plan began to grow. She wrote to Lois that she would come to her sister aboard the new schooner Rachel, plotting a way to stowaway in the hold of the ship.

When the wreckage of the Rachel first appeared after a storm, enthusiasts hoped it was a vessel from the War Between the States, but scientist believe it is the Rachel.

When Lois heard of the wreckage of the Rachel, her heart feared for her sister, but was bound to silence for fear of her sister's husband. She sensed that Lorna had been hiding in the hold of the ship, and stayed there even after the cargo was removed, somehow undetected. Lois walked the beach daily searching for her, praying she had made her way to shore and safety. However, when the ship was in flames, she had that feeling that close sisters can have. She knew her sister had been aboard when the ship was torched. Her body washed to the beach many days later and no one else made a connection with the Rachel, until now as I read a journal hidden away for 100 years in my mother's trunk. It tells of fear of the sister's husband and the secret of her quiet burial under a blue moon in October.

I hope that one day I can see the wreckage and feel the hope that was hidden there in the hold. At least, I know that I have seen the visage of that hope. In a blue dress on the ramparts of Fort Morgan.

Thanks to Ken DeAngelo, descendant of the original shipbuilder and author of ***The Schooner Rachel****, and to the wonderful staff of Fort Morgan.*

TANK TALES

You may be old enough to remember the opening scene of television series "Petticoat Junction" where three girls are obviously taking a dip in the water tank, with their clothes hanging over the side. I have searched for anyone who has actually been inside a water tank for fun, and still can't find anyone who will admit to it, but I sure have heard some stories.

Water tanks hold a mysterious air, for all of us wish we could fly above them and see inside. Of course, nowadays, the covers are secure but that was not always the case. Water tanks were found on almost every farm of any consequence, and most did not have tops so they could catch rainwater to supplement the supply. They were at every stop along the rail line spur for the steam engines to take on water. Most towns built one early in the twentieth century as indoor plumbing was becoming more common. The tank was (and still is) usually located on one of the highest places in the area to enhance the gravity-based pressure of the water coming from the tank.

Earliest ones were made of wood and the water was pumped into the tank by means of a windmill. As gasoline engines were developed, turbine pumps were cranked up to send water up into the tanks. Sometimes rams were used to help with pumping the water. Later, electric engines made the process much more efficient.

It is hard to believe that everyone did not die from contamination in those days, for the water was used for drinking, too. Before days of water purity testing, they cleaned out the tank whenever the water got to tasting "funny."

The family home of Al Guarisco is the site of an unusual water tank. Al's father, Agostino, was a man of many talents. His work is admired today in many buildings in the area. He decided to enhance the 1930 water tower on his family place on Randall Road in Daphne. During WWII he put his sons to work helping him build a structure around the tank to serve as storage and a laundry room. The results are a charming tower reminiscent of the old world. Al told me that he remembered well working on the tower one day that they were listening to the radio.

The regular program was interrupted with urgent news. The D-Day Invasion had begun. Cheers erupted from the worksite and the women came running from the house to join the rejoicing.

Visitors passing the old Guarisco home are fascinated by the structure they think may have been a lighthouse, but it was indeed the family water tank.

Al said that he and his brother had the job of running the turbine engine pump at least once a week. It usually took about two hours of pumping to fill the tank. They knew it was full when water started running over the sides.

One of my favorite tank tales was told by Mr. R. Leslie Smith, Mr. History in Baldwin County. The north Baldwin County native authored several publications about the life he lived, which was approaching the century mark at the time of the telling. He clearly remembered the tank at the State Teacher College in Daphne, where he earned his teaching credentials. He says the water tank there was wooden and was known to attract squirrels. Of course, as the thirsty squirrels stretched to get a drink, they often fell in. When the water finally became too putrid to drink, the tank was drained and cleaned.

Daphne Teacher Institute was housed in the former county courthouse.

I have to mention this reminds me of urban legends of a human body found in one tank, with the same investigative strategy. When the water developed a very distinctive smell and taste, the tank was drained and the body of a young woman was found. Take notice, I don't think this was in Baldwin County. Although my parents always talked about the goat that fell in the reservoir in Mobile and was never recovered.

The 1940 water tank at Daphne High School, today Daphne Elementary School, was one of the finest, as was everything in that school when it was built. Mr. Smith was a teacher, principal, and superintendent of Baldwin County Public Schools. While in the position of Director of Buildings and Grounds, he supervised the demolition of the elementary school tank, and snapped three photographs. How I would have loved to have been there. A piece of it is on display in the school.

When Daphne High School was built, it was the state-of-the-art institution with its own water tank. When the tank was dismantled, crowds of people came to bid it farewell.

The concrete water tank in Bay Minette may be the only one of its kind in the world.

The water tank in Bay Minette is on the Register of Historic Places, for it is one of only two or three concrete water tanks ever constructed, and as far as can be determined, the only one still standing. The contract to build the tank was awarded to a Birmingham firm in 1914 for $3000. It was built next to the old county jail, which was demolished in 1999 and replaced with the current corrections facility.

The 130-foot-tall tank was used until a lightning strike during Hurricane Frederic disabled it. It has since been inspected regularly for safety and maintained by North Baldwin Utilities. However, the roof of the tank is no longer there. Rainwater flows through the tank onto ground level. Wouldn't you like to see inside that tank? I hope someone will send a drone to take a photo and send it to me. I want to see if there are any squirrels in it.

I wish I had a nickel for every time someone comments that they would love to have lived in the good ol' days. Next time you are tempted to say that, think about old water tanks and be thankful for modern water supply. I sure am.

The Malbis Plantation, a Greek community, was almost completely self-sufficient. The water tank was a landmark until demolition in 2024.

WELCOME TO THE HOTEL MAGNOLIA
SUCH A LOVELY PLACE

In February 1979, we were invited to a special evening at the Hotel Magnolia. Oh, the stories we heard ...we will never forget. Two great storytellers in one night!! What an experience.

We were welcomed at the magnificent front door of the Hotel Magnolia by John and Marjorie Snook who were hosting an evening with the renowned Alabama storyteller Kathryn Tucker Windham. We were escorted into the parlor where the other members of the Baldwin County Historical Society were eagerly anticipating hearing Mrs. Windham share from her book *Thirteen Alabama Ghosts and Jeffrey*. John introduced the speaker and, as usual, the audience was spellbound by the talent of the guest of honor. Mr. and Mrs. Snook then presented each guest a copy of the book, which was personalized with a nameplate and then signed by the author. It is still one of my most treasured volumes.

John Foley built the Hotel Magnolia to house the visitors and especially prospective settlers to the new town he had established.

As entertaining as the program was, there was more to come. Little did we realize that the stories told by John Snook would be just as much fun as those we had already heard. We were led on a tour of the historic hotel by Mr. and Mrs. Snook. They shared the story of the hotel built in 1908 by John Foley to house prospective real estate buyers during the earliest years of the new town. The Snooks were at that time, the final in a line of several owners and operators of the inn, and as he told us of those earlier years, he showed us places where some of those stories took place.

He called our attention to the large mirror on the wall and pointed out one on the opposite wall. When one stands between the two mirrors, a "Tunnel of Death' or "infinity" tunnel is perceived; the reflections seem to go forever, perhaps even into another dimension. Old beliefs hold that the lady of death resides in mirrors and is sometimes seen beckoning for the unlucky person to join her in the journey through the tunnel. ***"Such a lovely face..."***

The parlor had matching mirrors that reflected in each other, creating a ever ending corridor. Guests are wary of looking into the mirror for fear of seeing the Angel of Death.

There were several residents who lived there for years. One was a Mr. James Clark, whose family hailed from England. He was quite the dapper gentleman, some even saying he claimed noble English blood. He often wore his formal clothes, complete with cape, top hat, and cane. He loved the rounds of Christmas and Mardi Gras parties and balls, and attended some event most evenings, often returning home in the wee hours of the morning between 3 and 4 o'clock. Mr. Jimmy was most thoughtful of his fellow residents and as he came in the front door, he removed his shoes before climbing the staircase. Because he did this so many times, the soft creaks of the steps are still heard nearly every morning in the early hours between 3 and 4 o'clock.

Mr. John told us of doors that open by themselves, and of one room upstairs that will become locked from the inside even when vacant. He pointed out the nook under the staircase where the first phone was installed. Many a business deal was negotiated there, and he said you could still hear voices there on occasion. There was no doubt in our minds that Mr. John Snook was a believer.

John's wife Marjorie Younce Snook grew up in Foley and was a loving partner in all things that her amazing husband undertook. I was privileged to have a little visit with her and her love for the old building was evident. Her parents spent their wedding night there on April 3, 1913, and she has lived there at times. When

I asked Mrs. Snook if she thinks the hotel is haunted, she reported that the paranormal investigators had spent the night there in 1996 and did not record anything, but that does not deter her belief. She says that she has heard humming in the house when she was alone and that there is a door that often opens on its own. She said, "Yes, there are some guests who refuse to stay in certain rooms." Probably the most famous bedroom of all is the second floor Red Room or as John called it, The Brass and Red Room. I talked to someone who stayed there in November of 2016 and he told me that during the night he was awakened when he felt the bed give and creak as if someone were sitting on the side of the bed. He asked if they wanted anything, but he got no answer.

Another fascinating part of the hotel is actually underground. Some folks have been lucky enough to enter the tunnel that Mr. Snook had built running from the hotel to his Gulf Telephone Company building. Local news channel reporter Darwin Singleton of WKRG Channel 5 produced a story on the mysterious tunnel, but no mention of anything too unusual going on down there. The tunnel is sealed up now for safety's sake, but the video is almost as good as being there.

Even though it has changed ownership, The Hotel Magnolia remains one of the premier inns in the south. Its charm and character make the guests feel that they are personal friends with the owner. A word of warning, however. When you stay at the hotel and look into the Tunnel of Mirrors, if you see Lady Death beckoning to you, remember

"You can check-out any time you like

But you can never leave!"

The Hotel Magnolia is once again breathing life into the downtown area of Foley. Proprietress Dianna Rohe Pennington and her husband welcome overnight guests and diners in the attached restaurant. Such a lovely place.

VILLAGE POINT

Village Point Park Preserve is an example of a city taking pride in its heritage.

The City of Daphne has done an amazing job preserving those historic sites that first put Daphne on the map. Village Point Park Preserve has bayfront access with a pier and sandy beach, a pavilion, and walking trails that pass two significant spots. One is the D'Olive (dough-leave) cemetery and the other is Jackson's Oak. The city has also constructed a fantastic boardwalk, which crosses D'Olive Creek and connects with the Eastern Shore Trail. It has been lovingly nicknamed "Gator Alley" because of the numerous alligators visible from the walkway.

In Village Point Park Preserve are the graves of many members of the D'Olive family in early years. A photo taken early one evening revealed a man dressed in colonial clothing.

Village Point is located where the earliest town, the Village, was located on the eastern shore of Mobile Bay at an Indian fish camp named "Neutral Ground." Dominique D'Olive had financial interests in the Village and is considered one of the founding fathers of the settlement. The area changed hands as the European countries fought for control in the New World. In 1787, when the county was a part of Spanish West Florida, Louis D'Olive, a son of Dominique, was granted an 800 arpen (about 800 acres) Spanish Land Grant and came to the Village to build a home for his family. He developed a hotel, which he named La Belle Rose, and purchased thousands of additional acres, where he raised livestock. The family cemetery marks the final

resting places for members of the family who lived and died here. One of the daughters, Louisa, married Major Lewis Stark, who owned a brickworks factory that furnished some of the bricks to build Fort Morgan. Louisa and Major Stark are also buried in the family cemetery.

The photographer who captured a rare sighting found a picture of a comparable uniform, showing the likelihood of this being was from the 18th century.

Many reports of encounters at the cemetery are documented. One prominent businessman and his son were visiting there and snapped a photo with a phone. The image of a colonial man is clear in the photo, which is unfortunately of a very low resolution, but extremely convincing. Several groups of investigators have gone there at night and obtained readings after calling to the family in French.

The cemetery is not the only haunted spot in the park. The Jackson Oak is named for the famous Andrew Jackson, who addressed his men there as they prepared to march to the Battle of New Orleans in the War of 1812. A historic marker on Highway 98 reads as follows:

Standing on a low limb of a giant oak tree hear here, General Andrew Jackson made a pep talk to his troops, fresh from their victory at the Battle of Horseshoe Bend and poised before advancing on the British and Spaniards at the Pensacola, and the British at New Orleans.
Victories in all these battles speak well for the rest his men enjoyed here, as well as the talk.
Probably the only occasion in Jackson's long career that he was on a low limb.

Experiences near the tree have mainly been orbs, but some investigators report the wind whistling through the branches on even the stillest of nights. Andrew Jackson has been known to make other appearances as well. Many people have seen a soldier in a War of 1812 uniform riding on a white horse in the middle of both D'Olive Creek and Yancey Branch.

People say they have seen orbs in the branches of Jackson's Oak in Village Point Park Preserve in Daphne.

A walk in the park can take one through the stories of settlers and soldiers who are all still there. There are also reports of experiences with Native Americans along the shoreline. One lady was having a drink at a place near the bay. She looked into the mirror behind the bar and saw an Indian dressed only in a breechcloth standing behind her. He had a headband with a string of beads and feathers hanging down almost to his waist. The lady turned around to talk to this person who must be in costume for some party nearby. There was no one there. Looking again at the mirror, she saw him start to fade away. She quickly called the bartender to witness the apparition, but by the time he was there, and she pointed out the spot on the mirror, the Indian had completely disappeared. Well, maybe not completely. The mirror had a cloudy spot that could not be wiped away. No one could remember if the mirror had that spot before this incident, but it certainly did afterwards. The misty mirror stayed that way and many a night the story was told to customers by the bartender. It was still there when the building burned to the ground. All along the bay near Bayfront Park were camps where Indians came to gather and dry seafood for their winter stores. Mounds of oyster shells left by them give proof. Perhaps one of those Natives stayed when the rest of the clan went home.

CHAPTER 6
CHURCH GOIN' FOLKS

When Lorenzo Dow of evangelical fire and brimstone fame, came to Blakeley, he declared it would fail because there were no churches in town. Soon after, his prediction came true when yellow fever hit the town with a vengeance, leading to its demise. Most of the south, however, is known for its little brown churches in the wildwoods and the people who met there each and every Sunday.

HE'S PREACHED LONG ENOUGH

If you know the Earles, you have a connection with everybody in north Baldwin County – at least that's how it seems. No matter whose name I mention, either Agnes or her sister Martha say, "Oh, yes, we are kin to them." I guess that can happen if your family has been around for nine generations.

I met with Martha Earle Smith and Agnes Earle Smith at the historic Montpelier Church in the Baldwin County Bicentennial Park. They grew up in the house next to the church when it was in its original location in Blacksher. Their family donated this absolutely amazing nineteenth century building to Baldwin County and it was moved to the park in the twentieth century.

The Montpelier Church is a centerpiece historic building in Baldwin County Bicentennial Park. It was originally in Blacksher and was donated by the Earle estate.

This was a perfect place for them to tell me about their ancestors because they remembered attending church services in this very building. Each week Martha swept the church and arranged fresh flowers on the altar. She laughed telling about the time their father, about age 4, had been sitting in the hard wooden pew listening to the sermon that ran on and on until he just got too hungry. He announced, "He's preached long enough. I am going home to get a sandwich and I'll be right back." He slid off the pew and under legs so fast that no one could grab him. The others were probably wishing he would bring back a basket full of sandwiches.

In those days, the Methodist preacher had several churches on his "circuit" and traveled quite some distances between at least four churches in his charge. The Earle family always hosted him on his Sunday in Blacksher, and just about the whole congregation came to Sunday dinner at their home. Most in the church were family anyway. There was no heat in the church, so on really cold Sundays, the services were held in their living room. In the summer, the swing-out church windows were slanted open with a stick to hold them in place, and everyone had one of those paper fans with a picture of Jesus holding the lamb.

Their family was among the very first English settlers in Baldwin County. James Manuel Earle was a true pioneer, traveling the treacherous journey from South Carolina in the 1700s. He married Elizabeth Tarvin, who was part Creek Indian, and immediately built a cabin. Within a few years they realized that there may be trouble with the local Red Stick faction of the Creek Indians, so he joined his neighbors to travel to the home of Samuel Mims. After looking around the hurriedly constructed fort, he decided it was just not safe enough. He got his wife back in the wagon and continued on the new town of Blakeley. If not for that, the family would have probably been massacred.

The northern part of Baldwin County was first settled when the county was a part of the Mississippi Territory. Many settlers traveled the Federal Road from Georgia. The Earle family was among the first pioneers in the territory.

When they returned to Blacksher, they found their home had been burned, but they immediately built a new double pen cabin. When a traveling vendor came by in his wagon with a new-fangled invention, they put chairs in the front yard and had a photograph made. The cabin was known as the place where Andrew Jackson stayed for several months on his way to Florida to take the governorship. His wife, Rachael, was with him. She wrote home to Nashville most uncomplimentary about the area. At the time this cabin burned down several years ago, it was said to be the oldest house in Baldwin County.

Agnes and Martha both told stories about their grandmother, Agnes Earle. She ran the store in front of the house they grew up in next to the church and was also the postmistress for years and years. Little Agnes had to help in the store by selling the Jack's Cookies and the ice cream; she learned to make change by age four. She eagerly awaited the candy delivery man each week because he would slip her a whole bag of Hershey's Kisses. She would run behind the store and 'have her way' with the candy until her grandmother caught her.

These young ladies remembered getting their first telephone and their first television. They remembered when Highway 59 was a dirt road. In fact, while the road was being paved, they had a grand time playing in the new road and returned home covered in black tar. I would love to have been around to see their mother Martha scrub them with kerosene to try to get them clean. The clothes probably had to be burned.

The original Earle cabin was burned during the Creek Indian Wars while the family took refuge at the town of Blakeley, but it was immediately rebuilt by the Earles.

The Earles have certainly left their mark in Baldwin County history from the time that James Manuel Earle signed a document requesting that Baldwin County become part of Alabama. Each generation has made its contribution, and the rich family heritage is a treasure.

Agnes and Martha had a wealth of memories to share about their kinfolk and schooldays. This may be enough for a whole book! These sisters agree that they were blessed to grow up in Blacksher, "Even though Rachael Jackson may have described northern Baldwin County as a howling wilderness filled with dangerous critters, those of us who grew up there remember it as an absolutely beautiful area and it will always in our hearts, be home."

Historic Marker in Blacksher

Blacksher was a 19th century farming and timber community first known as Montpelier. Jeptha and Uriah Blacksher, large landowners from Monroe County, set up a sawmill in this area in the 1880s. They established a post office in 1889 renaming the community Blacksher. Later postmasters included William Bryant, Edward "Ned" Blake, John William and Agnes Atkinson Earle. Montpelier Methodist Church, built in 1986, served the Charles Earle, Frank Earle, Thomas John Earle, and James Thomas Bradley families until 2013 when relocated to Baldwin County's Bicentennial Park. James Manuel Earle I, a product of both the American Revolutionary War and the War of 1812, was among those who signed the document requesting Alabama's statehood in 1817.

First known as Montpelier, the historical locale and origins of Blacksher lie in the 1812 war with Britain. The Creek Indians were encouraged to rise in arms, massacring several hundred settlers who had taken refuge in Fort Mims. After the battle of Fort Mims in 1813, two more forts were built, Fort Montgomery and Fort Montpelier. Before his presidency, Andrew Jackson and his wife, Rachel, stayed at Montpelier hosted by the James Manuel Earle I family for five weeks. With his troops stationed in Blacksher at Fort Montpelier, Jackson resigned as governor of Florida on May 31, 1821. One of the few survivors of the Fort Mims massacre, Edward Steadham was a descendent of James Manuel and Elizabeth Tarvin Earle and is buried on the family property. John William Earle petitioned the Baldwin County Commissioners to survey and build a road connecting north Baldwin County to Atmore.

PREACHER BOY OF BLAKELEY

THE War, 1865, Blakeley Battlefield.

A horrible accident took place and the precious boy still haunts the fields trying to reach those lost souls.

Jeremy lived with his large family very near the dying town of Blakeley. His father had been a slave but was given his freedom at the death of a large plantation owner in Selma. He moved to Baldwin County where there was plenty of work to be had. He worked at Sibley Lumber Mill and his mother raised nearly all of their food right there on their homestead. Early in the 1860s, the family knew there was a war going on, but it did not seem to affect them, and their lives went on as usual. They had all they could do to keep food on the table for their 6 children.

Jeremy's favorite place was the church. He listened to every fiery word spoken when the traveling preacher came a-riding to the community of Bromley. He could sing every hymn ever sung in that little unpainted rickety country church. The songs were those which were born in the cotton fields. They promised deliverance and a heaven where streets are paved with gold. He could feel that starry crown as he lost himself in the spirituals.

All God's Children Got Shoes

Go Down Moses

He began to practice delivering sermons like he heard the fire and brimstone evangelist preach. He preached to his brothers and sisters and to the dogs. He even set up a little church in the woods, using logs for pews and a tree stump for his pulpit. When his message reached a fevered climax, even the birds and squirrels stopped to listen.

It wasn't long before the entire community came to hear his message in the woods and then he was asked to preach from the real pulpit in the little rickety church. Such singing and stomping and praying as you've never heard came from that little nook near Blakeley. Folks said he had The Gift.

The ruins of an old country church are reminiscent of the churches that grew up in every community. The houses of worship often were used by several denominations and also as a community gathering place. This one had been converted to a barn in later uears.

Then the war came close to home, and with it came the soldiers who built earthworks and redoubts and set up tents all within yellin' distance of Jeremy's home. Instead of fear, Jeremy saw a new opportunity to spread the gospel. He soon made friends with the country boys now wearing the gray and butternut uniforms, boys who loved hearing him preach the sermons they missed so much from home. They loved the spirituals he sang and the prayers he lifted for their safety. Jeremy became the unofficial chaplain of the boys in gray. He walked the lengths of the earthworks, stopping at each camp along the three-mile defense line, welcomed at each one.

Somewhere along the line, a soldier gave him an old kepi, a faded and ragged cap, almost devoid of color and shape, but he loved wearing it. Another gave him a haversack taken from a fallen comrade. Jeremy put his Bible in the sack and carried it over his shoulder as he trekked back and forth over the earthworks for months on end.

Then came the Union forces. The ground rumbled before the enemy could be seen. Caissons and cannons and cavalry. Then the dust rose in clouds as the troops advanced toward Blakeley. Northern armies surrounded the land approach to the fort at Blakeley. The boys in gray saw the artillery coming in. They saw the massive numbers of infantry troops. They saw the banners flying for miles. So could Jeremy. He felt the battle looming over their heads and his sermons reached each heart needing peace. His words lifted the souls of the boys in Gray.

Jeremy walked home each night. At dusk on April 2, 1865, he headed home as usual, but now his path home had become no man's land between the lines of battle. A lone shot rang out and his friends looked in horror as Jeremy fell to the ground. There was not a moment's hesitation as a Missouri boy jumped over the southern breastworks into the line of Yankee fire. He was running toward Jeremy when Union General Steele yelled, "Hold your fire. It's only a boy."

Soldiers on the Blakeley Battlefield took the preacher boy's messages to heart. They loved this little boy who fervently preached the word of God and led in singing hymns.

Both sides watched in silence as one Confederate soldier bent to lift the limp body of the boy preacher and gather his haversack and kepi. He sensed a shadow over them, and he looked up to see a lone Yankee boy bending to help lift Jeremy. They began to walk the length of the earthworks toward Jeremy's home. They left him in his mother's care and returned to face the enemy fire and each other on opposite sides of no man's land.

The battle continued for long days and nights. The Union troops far outnumbered the rebel defense, yet the boys in gray held their posts. In fact, one of those posts was right on the front porch of Jeremy's family cabin. Two Johnny Rebs were stationed there day in and day out to protect the family from Union attack.

Just as the command was given to surrender the fort on April 9, the cabin front porch guards heard the first sounds of the keening wails of Jeremy's mother, and knew that he, too, had surrendered. The first shot of the Battle of Blakeley had taken the life of the boy who had come to save all who would hear the Word. He had clung to life for the sakes of the souls he loved, but when the time had come, he left this place on earth.

Or, did he?

Somehow, Jeremy knew he still had souls to save, so his spirit remained there to search for his friends. He was seen by the Union forces. He was seen by his family. He was seen by those who came years later to view the battlefield. During a Peace Convention attended by both Union and Confederate veterans in Mobile, former officers in blue and gray made a trip to Blakely and looked across the battlefield now being reclaimed by young trees. They saw a boy, a knapsack slung over his shoulder and his clear voice lifted in song.

For years before the site became a preserved park, relic hunters roamed the battlefield, and one named Alex had an encounter with a young African American boy who said he lived nearby. He asked Alex if he had been saved, and then he disappeared in a sudden fog.

Recently, David, a park ranger, had a personal visit with Jeremy, who was sitting on one of the picnic tables, reading a Bible. My favorite encounters with Jeremy take place during the reenactments of the battle held each spring. Modern day soldiers take on the personae of those who were there more than 150 years ago. They become those soldiers in Blue and Gray. And they hear the soulful singing of spirituals coming through the woods -- coming from the visage of a rickety wooden church. One character there at the battle is not a re-enactor. He is real. He is Jeremy. Still searching for his friends and praying to save a lost soul. Sometimes both armies see his ghostly presence walk between the lines of fire. This time he does not fall when shots ring out; he keeps walking and singing.

And the people said, "Amen.

Jeremy's family home still stands. His family descendants still live in it. I paid a visit there and was one of those few people who has seen the treasures the family keeps in a trunk – a Bible, a haversack, and a kepi.

PREACHER IN THE WINE CELLAR

If you take a trip to Maschwanden, Switzerland, you will notice that a river runs between it and the village of Muehlan. Something happened more than a hundred years ago that divided families from these two hamlets. Descendants in Elberta can tell you the story.

It all started in 1912 when Walter Salzmann left Maschwanden, Switzerland, to come to America. It was common for young men to leave home and start their own lives after they became of age. So that was what each of the eleven Salzmann boys did.

Walter came through Canada to get to the United States, but within a few years he went back to the old country to get his betrothed. When he got home to Switzerland, however, his fiancé had already married someone else. Walter then asked her sister Anna Kaeppeli to go to America with him – and she did just that. That was a hundred years ago but the stories live on. The two families were still at odds with each other when Walter's granddaughter Frances Salzmann Bush went back to the homeland to visit in the 1970s. She was not able to talk to her grandmother's family in Muehlan, but years later when her brother Paul Salzmann made the trip, he had a nice visit with both families. I guess all must have begun to heal over by then.

Frances and Paul enjoyed telling the stories of their ancestors who came straight from Switzerland. When Walter and Anna came to America on the SS Bergensfjord in April 1917, they were processed through Ellis Island, and soon were approached by a salesman who recognized their Swiss German language. Ended up, he sold Walter 160 acres near a German settlement named Elberta in Alabama. Walter and Anna were married April 30, 1917, in New York, and headed south.

Upon arriving by buggy in Elberta from the Foley train depot, Walter and Anna began building their new life. There were actually three Salzmann brothers who came to Elberta: Walter, Werner, and Emil. It was not long before Emil decided to head back north to Philadelphia. Werner, however, stayed in Elberta and opened a blacksmith business. Anna and Walter started building a home on their land

Developers actively advertised in newspapers in the Midwest and in New York at Ellis Island. The Salzmann family story is one of many of the Eastern Europeans who traveled to the southern United States to buy land and build homes and farms.

three miles north of town. They walked there and back every day from Elberta. During this period, they were in dire straits at least a couple of times. Walter left Anna in Elberta and went to Philadelphia to work as a baker until he saved enough to get them through a few months.

Their son, Joe, who was born in 1926, spoke only German when he started to school at St. Benedict Catholic School in Elberta. He rode a pony named Danny to school every day. "That pony lived a long, happy life," said Frances. "We remember riding on him when we were children. He was a member of our family, and Dad had a hard time when he died."

Frances had copies of the naturalization papers for Walter and Anna, their son, Joe, and Emil. They traveled to Cleveland, Ohio, for the swearing in ceremony and adapted to the life of patriotic Americans in every way. Even though most

Pictured on his pony, Danny, is Joe Salzmann at age 4.

residents of Elberta spoke German in the home, they always spoke English outside the houses. "All business was started on the street and then taken inside to work out the details to be sure they had a clear understanding of the money involved," Paul laughed.

During the years of prohibition, Elberta residents were allowed to brew wine and beer for their own use, and taverns were allowed to sell it. Paul's grandfather Joe was still making wine in the cellar when Paul was little. One day when the Baptist preacher came to visit, Walter took him to show him the cellar and asked him to taste a new batch of wine. Then, taste it again and again. During the same time, the propane gas deliveryman came, and Walter took him a jug out near the henhouse. I can just see Walter going back and forth between the two until he decided it was time to let them get together. Maybe it would not have been so bad if the gasman had not been a deacon in the same church. Somehow when they were leaving, the fence was knocked down. The next day the deacon dragged the preacher to help him repair it. There is no hangover as bad as one from homemade wine, so I imagine fixing that fence was indeed due penance.

The family struggled with truck farming until industrious Walter contacted the Naval Air Station in Pensacola and was awarded the chicken and egg contract. It took two days to haul the goods in a wagon crossing Perdido Bay on the ferry. This is the break that helped them get ahead.

They often wondered about the other Salzmann boys who left Switzerland to make their homes around the world. Some went to California, and in a strange incident, Paul met a son of one of them. While on a fishing trip in Alaska, the tour guide told Paul that his brother was in a recent fishing trip group. Paul was dumbfounded. The tour guide said, "Well, maybe you don't know him, but there was guy here last month that looked just like you, talked just like you and his name is Salzmann." So, sure enough, they made contact with each other, discovered they are indeed cousins and filled in some missing links in the family records. This was without *Ancestry.com* or DNA tests!

Anna helped transport the egg delivery to Pensacola Naval Air Base

The Salzmann family in Elberta has farmed the same land since 1917, and now the fourth generation has taken over the reins of the old legacy. They are not struggling with truck farming or hauling eggs to Pensacola, but instead are raising some of the best turf in the world, preserving that heritage of the land for generations to follow.

SLAVE GALLERY

The Methodist Church Museum in Daphne holds hundreds of amazing artifacts. It also holds the story of a former slave named Daphne, who is said to have saved the town from yellow fever.

The old building now part of Bayside Academy was once a lovely hotel named Belle Rose, built by Captain William Howard. His wife, Elizabeth, quite educated and well read, often charmed her guests with Greek myths. She was enamored with the laurel trees that abounded in the area and often told of the ancient story of Daphne, the goddess who was changed into the laurel tree to protect her from an unwanted pursuer. Mrs. Howard told people they should always be on the lookout for the lovely maiden running through the magical woods, as it may well be the lady of lore.

The Belle Rose Hotel was owned by the Howard family.

As Mrs. Howard approached the spring one day, she heard a sweet voice singing and saw a lovely young lady with a laurel wreath woven around her hair. Mrs. Howard was delighted to meet the girl and told her the story of Daphne. The young woman was legally a slave who lived not far away. Mrs. Howard invited the young woman to work at the hotel, so the arrangements were made for her freedom and the young maiden moved into the Howard Hotel. Mrs. Howard would call her nothing but Daphne, so that became her legal name.

Daphne soon became a part of the life at the hotel. Her gracious manner and pleasant nature added to the reputation of the resort, and she was soon considered a part of the Howard family. When a terrible yellow fever epidemic hit the community, she helped nurse many residents through the deadly disease, using remedies she had learned from her mother.

In the 1850s, the Howards gave the land adjacent to the hotel for a new church to house the Methodist congregation. The wonderful building built in 1858 stands today, intact with its balcony for the African American population who attended. Many of these were slaves, thus the term slave gallery is used to define the space upstairs. The upstairs parishioners joined the others in prayer and singing of hymns. Daphne especially loved the hymn singing and always added her special harmony and rhythm, echoing her African heritage. Her voice rang out above most in the congregation and she inspired all who heard her.

The Methodist Church was barely complete before it was occupied by Union forces encamped on the way to attack Spanish Fort and Blakeley.

The idyllic little town and church were invaded in 1864 by Union troops who were advancing toward Spanish Fort to capture the forts on the Eastern Shore of the delta so that they could approach Mobile. They camped at the church and on the grounds, and Daphne was among those cooking for the men. After the war, Daphne continued to live at the hotel, and she still attended the Methodist Church, sitting in the balcony, singing her heart out. When she died, her funeral was held at the Methodist Church and she was buried nearby.

When the first post office was established in Daphne, a name was needed. Mrs. Howard asked her husband, who became the first postmaster, to name the town in honor of her dear friend and also of the maiden of Greek myth, so the name Daphne was given to the lovely Eastern Shore town.

Parishioners of the church missed her voice coming from the balcony. At least some missed it. Others heard it during services. Sometimes when the altar guild was inside the sanctuary cleaning and preparing for the Sunday worship, they were serenaded by a lovely spiritual humming coming from the rafters. Daphne Methodist was an active church until the congregation built a new sanctuary and the old one was in danger of being lost. It was used for community meetings until a devastating hurricane nearly destroyed the historic building. The City of Daphne stepped in and purchased the building to house its artifact collection. The City of Daphne Museum opened in 2001 and preserves the heritage of the "Jubilee City." When timing is right, humming can be heard from the balcony. Those who hear it say it might be the wind, but to me it sounds more like a rich female voice, somewhat distorted. The tunes are not always discernable, but one witness knew the hymn was *"Go, down, Moses."*

One of my friends went into the slave gallery to sort some boxes and felt sure she was not alone. Every time she heard a sound, she turned to look, but there was never anyone there. Chills went up her spine and hair on her neck and arms stood on end. She began to sing an old spiritual, one of her favorites. She was joined in the hymn by an amazing harmony and rhythm. She knew that Daphne was there with her and she continued to sing until she had finished her work and went downstairs. That evening, she locked the door and went away with a beautiful secret in her heart.

A lovely voice is often heard coming from the slave gallery, the upstairs balcony of the Old Daphne Methodist Church, even when no one can be seen there.

THIEF IN THE ATTIC

Montgomery Hill Baptist Church in Tensaw is the oldest active church in Baldwin County. Oh, the stories those walls can tell. Come sit in one of her ancient pews and listen to a story.

The preacher's booming voice echoed throughout the wooden building; the pews filled with devout churchgoers. When the pump organ began the introduction to *Amazing Grace*, the congregation stood, and the rafters rang with the music. In fact, the echoes of the singing seemed to take on a different voice than any of the congregants had noticed before. It was almost as if the deep bass voice came from heaven above. Church goers looked all around to see if they could discern who was singing in such a magnificent way.

The Montgomery Hill Baptist Church in the community of Tensaw in north Baldwin County is the oldest continued church in the county.

After the service, at the Dinner on the Grounds, the neighbors caught up on the news in the Tensaw Community. Mr. Bradley began to tell of a strange incident out in his henhouse. He had heard a raucous, grabbed his gun to shoot the raiding fox, but when he got outside, the chicken coop door was actually open, and he could hear the hen squawking in the woods nearby. Mr. Earle said that was nothing compared to his experience. He found his smokehouse door had been unbolted and a ham had disappeared. Others chimed in with similar stories that could not have been the result of foraging animals.

Sheriff Richerson was called in to help solve the mystery. His hounds were known as the best trackers in the county and he put them to the test. They did find

Sheriff Richerson poses with his dogs famous for tracking criminals.

some scents and the trails led right to the church. Some of the men set up a night watch of the building and, sure enough, they saw a man leaving the church. They followed him, saw him steal a link of sausages, carry them back to the cemetery and have a picnic on one of the gravestones. Afterward, he began to rake the grounds and clean the tombstones.

He then went into the church. When they slipped in behind him, they saw him climb into the attic. They followed him and apprehended him right then and there. Come to find out, he was a convict who had escaped the jail in Bay Minette several months ago and had been living in the attic of the church. The sheriff locked him back up in the jail in Bay Minette and soon he was preaching to the other inmates. That's right, he had heard the preachers and the singing, felt the Spirit, and had reformed his ways while in that attic.

When the church members found out about that, they dropped the charges, posted his bail, and brought him back to the church grounds, where they built him a little hut near the cemetery. He lived there the rest of his life, cleaning the cemetery and preaching to the souls in residence at the graveyard. No one can remember his real name. They just called him the Thief. When he died, he was buried there in that cemetery, but as he had requested, there was no tombstone erected.

He is there in that Montgomery Hill Baptist Church cemetery which is often cleaned without anyone claiming to have done it. On Homecoming Day each fall, members will talk about the olden days while they are decorating the graves. Sometimes they find a few ham and chicken bones at the edge of the graveyard. And sometimes locals still find a link of sausage missing from the smokehouse.

CHAPTER 7 WARTIME FOR HOMEFOLKS

Much is written about those who bravely fought for our freedoms. Homefront folks played roles important in the wars as well. Their stories are worth the tellin'.

BLOODY BARIN

I took my young children to see Uncle Everett in the nursing home, I think about 1975. He was a "Wounded Warrior of the Greatest Generation." We arrived about an hour before the Fourth of July Program was to begin.

Sitting in his wheelchair, he opened his pocketknife, and said, "Yeah, the Navy taught me to be tough; watch this." He jabbed it through his pants into his leg just above the knee, where it stood upright. The children's eyes opened wide and they were speechless. Smiling, he lifted his trouser leg and showed them his wooden prosthetic leg. He was one of those people who had that special way of looking at life. I wanted to try to capture that attitude, so I pulled out my brand-new portable cassette recorder and asked him to tell us about his Navy years.

When Pearl Harbor was bombed nearly everyone he knew went to fight the war to end all wars. Uncle Everett was a senior in high school, but he and most of his friends decided a high school diploma could wait until after the war. "I chose the Navy because their uniforms were the best looking," he chuckled. "We knew if we volunteered, we could choose the branch of service we wanted. But, by golly, we really did want to help win that war."

In 1942, our family heard he was chosen for mechanical aviation school at Naval Air Station in Pensacola. Wonder of wonders, he was stationed close to home at Barin Field in Foley, built on 950 acres including the old Foley Airport site. He was there when the first group of flight students entered the facility at its commission on Dec. 5, 1942.

"At first there were 111 SNJ planes there, but by April 1944, the number was more than 400. There were four hangars, the main office building, and stores. Oh, yes, there were two runways, busy day and night.

"I think one time there were as many as 800 pilots being trained, and the ground crew numbered in the thousands. For every pilot there was about 10 of us support personnel. We were housed in typical two-story open barracks with double bunkerbeds and lockers. It was hard, but we were willing to do what it took to win that war. We kept thinking about our buddies overseas.

"Training was tough for those pilots, I tell you. There were at east 40 men killed and soon people called it Bloody Barin.

The United States Navy base in Pensacola, Florida, was supplemented by Barin Field in Foley, where pilots were trained.

"Man, the mess hall was something else. Can you imagine peeling potatoes for that many men? We also had a baseball team, just like we had at home in Rosinton. In fact, we even played against Rosinton one time at the big field there. We won.

USO Hall in Foley offered entertainment every weekend.

"I guess the most fun we had was at the USO hall on Laurel Street downtown Foley. Girls from all over the county came to dance with us. They served cake and lemonade and sometimes the locals, my sisters included, put on a show for us. That first Christmas we were at Barin, Commander Brigg landed his SNJ with Santa Claus in the back seat. Now, that was a hoot."

My daughter asked him how he lost his leg. He stared into the air awhile, his eyes watered, and when he spoke his voice cracked.

"I wanted to make a career of the Navy, but that just wasn't to be. It was a freak accident; the plane we were working on was not securely anchored and it fell on me while I was underneath. It coulda' killed me. All during recovery, I kept thinking of my buddies that weren't coming home and kept asking why I was spared. I have always felt lucky.

"The Navy has taken care of me pretty good. I learned to walk on this wooden leg and worked as a mechanic my whole life. That is until the last year or so. I can't stand by myself anymore."

Barin Field Tower and Main Hangar

At one time, there were more than 800 pilots being trained and there were at least 10 support personnel for each pilot being trained.

One of the children asked if Barin Field was still there.

"I used to ride down to the field after the war. It was out of use, but the Navy still stored planes there and used it as a landing field. Big old fence all around it. In 1948 they started back training there and in 1952 the Korean War came along and suddenly Bloody Barin was in full swing again.

"I could see those guys landing and taking off. Sometimes the instructor's plane pulled a target sleeve. That was when there was gunnery training going on. Out over the gulf, six SNJs practiced hitting that target. I never heard if any of those 0.30 caliber guns hit an aircraft by mistake!! I sure hope not. I hope Bloody Barin didn't live up to its nickname.

"Yeah, those were the good old days. Actually, every day is a good day. I've had a wonderful life."

It was time to go down to the activity room where the program was to take place. Jessica and Joe pushed his wheelchair right up to the front row. When the "Star Spangled Banner" was played, we realized that Uncle Everett was attempting to stand. I reached to help him, and he pushed my hand away. He struggled a little holding onto the arms of the chair but rise he did. His right arm raised in salute, tears rolling down his face. There were tears on my face, too.

I am not ashamed that there are still tears each and every time I stand for our National Anthem, I think of the sacrifices he and so many others made for me just so I could stand. And stand up, I will, every time.

GERMAN SUB

Come sit on the screened porch of the old Fairhope cottage where octogenarian Lila Marie Pennington Ryals tells stories of her childhood in Fairhope. She lives in Canada in the summer and comes home to Fairhope every winter to her wonderful original cottage, once lived in by the Wilmers, who ran Fairhope Hardware. She is the reason the headlines once read: **German Sub Sighted in Mobile Bay! Spy Captured**

"Mama died when I was just nine years old. My little brother was seven. We were living in a house on Grand Avenue overlooking the gulley and Mobile Bay. There was a clear view then out into the water. Out from the beach aways, maybe about a block, were two crossed poles, everyone called them "Two Stakes", a landmark for sailors. About 50 feet away my father had about 10 poles stuck up in the water to hang his cotton nets on to dry. He tied his little skiff there, too.

"After mother died, and Pearl Harbor was bombed, my Daddy, Captain Penny (Pennington), and his large fishing boat were drafted into Civil Service stationed at Brookley Field in Mobile. He could come home to Fairhope only one day per month, riding the Greyhound Bus. He patrolled the waters of the bay and worked at the fire station on the base. My two older brothers enlisted in the military and one sister went north to work in a uniform factory. My other sister was taken in by a family in Fairhope. We saw her often, but just my brother Buddy and I lived in the old Miller home my dad rented. Yes, just those two children lived all by ourselves during the war years, actually for seven years. Oh, the life we led – it needs to be written in a book – more interesting than any fiction.

"But for today, let me tell you about the German submarine we saw in the bay. Buddy and I struggled just to eat. We sold scrap rubber and metal we found in the woods to earn a little money for a few things, dragging the scrap to the filling station on Section Street owned by Mr. Rugghe, who was mayor of Fairhope at that time. He was a good wartime mayor. Mostly, we ate raw vegetables we grew in our Victory Garden and the fruit we foraged in the woods around. We did have an old kerosene stove, but if we had fuel, we did not have matches. And if we had matches, we did not have fuel! There were a couple of pomegranate trees in the yard, a Japanese persimmon tree, and a wild persimmon tree. We ate it all. The police chief, Jack Titus, took to checking on us about once a week. He was a good man.

The Pennington children in Fairhope were victims of the war in a most unusual manner. After their mother died, their father was drafted for the Civil Corps stationed at Brookley Field in Mobile. The children were left to fend for themselves for several years. The oldest daughter was taken in by a Fairhope family, but Marie and her brother lived alone in the house her father rented for them. They foraged food and often slept on the beach or a boat. The police helped keep watch over them.

"Our bedroom was in the middle of the house, and we were often afraid that if anyone came in either the front or back door, we would be trapped, so we slept outside most nights. We slept on the screened porch some nights, but mostly we slept on the beach. We felt we could always run or swim away from danger. We swam like fish. We sometimes slept on my father's skiff tied up at the poles he used to hang his nets; we kept blankets under the bow of the boat. I loved the way the waves rocked us to sleep in the boat.

"One time, when we were walking home, we saw a man wearing a white shirt in the attic window of our house. That really frightened us. We later found a mattress up there and leftover wrappings of food he had eaten. In those days, tramps were common. Most were good men, but we were afraid, nonetheless. We rarely went into the house at night.

The house once the home of the Pennington children was refurbished to its original glory. The owners graciously welcomed us and enjoyed hearing the story of the children fending for themselves during WWII.

"Now, to the submarine. One moonless night when we were on the beach, my brother saw a large form coming out of the water right at the Two Stakes. We thought maybe it was a whale we had heard about. Soon we saw a man emerge from the hatch and start flashing a light of some kind. Then we noticed a light flashing from the point just north of our spot, called Sea Cliff. We stayed quiet and still and, of course, were scared to death. We saw the same thing for several nights. We knew about the Germans from the newsreels we saw at the theater on those few occasions when the owner would let us in free. We had heard there were U-boats in the Gulf which had sunk several ships and figured this was a scout sub sent into the shallow bay to gather information. We were right, but Daddy did not believe us at first. When he came home for his short visit, we convinced him to see for himself. And he did. He then called in some help, Jack Titus and some Coast Guard men. They hid behind my father's fishing nets and probably waited several nights before the sub emerged.

"They apprehended the German on the submarine and also the man on the cliff. It turned out he was a man we knew who owned a stable to rent horses for the rich people to ride. My father told us that both were imprisoned.

"I know that most of this was top secret. We were told that if we said a word we would be in danger. We kept the secret until many years later. My sister Wilma, who lived with the Foster family, also came one night and saw it. In fact, there were two other adults who had also seen it, and they confirmed it, too.

"About 10 years ago, a reporter did a story on our adventure, and he said all of our stories matched perfectly. My brother Joe died three years ago, and my sister Wilma died four years ago, so I am the only one left alive with those memories.

"I hope someone will remember after I am gone."

Kleinst- Uboot
"Molch"

The German Molch mini sub was less than 2 meters in height and could possibly have been the one sighted in Mobile Bay by Marie Pennington.

LADY SLOCOMB

As old folks tend to do, I often think back over my life and the amazing people who have been a part of it. As visitors pose for photographs with me here at Memorial Hall in New Orleans, I hope they know my story. – Lady Slocomb

The Battle of Spanish Fort was part of the last battle of the Civil War. The siege lasted for days and the gunfire was heard for miles. The Lady Slocomb cannon was abandoned by the Confederates as they evacuated the battlefield and was retrieved fifty years later. She tells her story from her resting place in New Orleans.

I was born at a Confederate Naval Gun Foundry in 1863 during that War Between the States. I was cast of Alabama iron and weighed five tons. Yes, I was quite a big baby! I was a Columbiad cannon with an 8-inch smooth bore; ten feet long and two feet in diameter. On March 24, 1865, I was taken to Spanish Fort to help protect Mobile. The men at Battery Blair were members of the 5th Company Louisiana Washington Artillery from New Orleans. The guys soon nicknamed me "Lady Slocomb" in honor of the wife of their beloved commander Capt. Cuthbert Slocomb. There were three other cannons and four mortars in Redoubt 3 with me.

I was mounted in a salient redoubt having three embrasures and could be pivoted either directly in front or to the left or right. I could see the men pile sandbags in front of me so that I was not easily seen by the enemy.

All too soon, March 28, the attack began. The Union forces were under the command of General Canby; there were thousands and thousands of them. I remember feeling a surge of power when my first shot exploded a caisson and killed seven men of Loomis' Michigan Battery. That began twelve long days and nights that seemed forever.

One incident keeps vigil in my memory. One day Sgt. Fitz Ripley of the 21st Alabama, which was assisting in Battery Blair, awoke with a depressed state of mind. He informed his men that he was firmly convinced that his name would be on the list of the killed that day. Everyone tried to cheer him up all day, but he remained resolute. As the night fell, the men were gathered around the coals, for a fire was too dangerous. One man undertook to rally him about his presentiment, which he took good naturedly and stood up to his full height, stretching his arms above his head, "You are witnessing a miracle." We all heard the thud of the bullet hit his fully expanded chest and saw him fall by my side. Like the soldiers around me, some things are embedded in your memories in such detail as to never be altered. This is one of those times. Our hospital was full, and "every night the boat which went to Mobile carried bad news to someone in the waiting crowd on the wharf that horror which all were dreading." *

During the battle I was fired 144 times, consuming 1440 pounds of powder. On the tenth day I fired my final shot. Immediately thereafter I was hit by two shells, almost simultaneously. For a few moments none of us could discern anything through the "blinding maze of dust and smoke" * until I was then seen upon the ground as only a broken gun – a gun no longer, but an altar, because my "heated metal was red with blood still warm with love of home and duty."* Three of my men lay lifeless beside me, one of them with his arm thrown over me, and thus I was silenced. One of my trunnions was blown away, but my men who were still living, a determined bunch, propped my right side up on an iron bar and loaded me with canister. Before I was fired again, the garrison was ordered to evacuate. My men rolled me down the earthwork mound into the slushy bog at its foot so that I would not be captured by the enemy. After the men left to trudge to the wharf at Spanish Fort, I lay silent, buried in the graveyard of spent ammunition.

Members of the Gray and Blue Union searched for and found the discarded Lady Slocomb. They had her moved to Mobile, but she just lay there almost forgotten

There I lay 26 years, reclaimed into the earth by nature herself. Then, one day I heard the veterans of the Gray and the Blue Union gather at the redoubt. They officially formed an organization whose purpose was stated to aid and foster fraternal feelings between those opposed to each other during the Civil War and commemorate the valor of American soldiers and the last battle of the war, Spanish Fort and Blakeley. They took on the project of erecting a Peace Monument in Mobile and decided to use me as its crown.

They hired Capt. Loxley, who had a logging rail line, to move me. First, some of the experienced veterans removed the live charge that was still in my barrel. Loxley used two teams of Michigan horses to pull me to the rail line, but he had to rest them every rod. I was loaded onto a barge and tugged to the foot of Government Street in Mobile.

My goodness, what a gala event greeted me! Crowds of people cheered, a salute was fired by Battery A, Alabama State Artillery – a salute of thirteen guns, one for each day of the thirteen-day battle. I learned then that the battle had continued for another day after Spanish Fort fell. The Battle of Blakeley took place on April 9, 1865. This was actually the evening of the same day that Lee had surrendered at Appomattox Courthouse. Speeches given at my welcome rally in Mobile referred to my battle as the last battle of the war.

The next Monday morning I was pulled to a grassy spot on Government Street between Water and Royal for a temporary resting place until the completion of the Peace Monument. A photographer accompanied the Blue and Gray Veterans Union to the battlefield and followed me to Mobile. He took photographs of me that were sold to the public for 25 and 50 cents. The profits were to go toward the monument.

I felt so honored to have been chosen to be the symbol of a peaceful existence in a monument. However, that dream was not to be. The wound in my right arm pains me now, so I will have to tell you the story of my move to New Orleans another day.

Paul Brueske snapped a photo of the historic marker in Spanish Fort Estates that designates the location of Redoubt Number 3, the location of the Lady Slocomb. Shown are volunteer historians providing a tour of the battlefield sites. Photo courtesy of Paul Brueske.

The quotes used in this commentary were taken from articles copied by Caldwell Delaney in his book **Confederate Mobile. Paul Brueske has researched The Lady Slocomb extensively and published an account of the Siege of Spanish Fort in **Digging All Night and Fighting All Day.***

FORT MIMS

For more than thirty years, re-enactors have portrayed the events of 1813 on the very grounds that the Fort Mims Massacre took place. Those who camp there for the night have eerie tales to tell over the campfire breakfasts.

The grounds at the site of one of the greatest massacres in United States history still carry a sense of forbidding menace. The echoes of screams of settlers and war whoops of Creek Indians reverberate throughout the wilderness there in the northernmost part of Baldwin County. More people claim to have eerie experiences here than in any other place in Baldwin County, except perhaps at Fort Morgan. Death and destruction have left timeless messages at this place, messages of impending death.

The massacre marked the beginning of the Creek Indian Wars, a facet of the War of 1812. The Creek Nation was incited by the British to attack American settlers encroaching upon their lands. Even after a visit by the Chief Tecumseh, the Creek Nation was divided. It is important to note that many people in this area were of mixed blood, and the 'Americans' and the 'Indians' were often related. A vote was held among the Creeks who voted for or against war with white or red sticks or war clubs. Those wanting to fight the Americans won the vote and were therefore called "Red Sticks." Among their leaders was the famous Red Eagle, or William Weatherford, who was not a chief, but greatly respected.

After a group of Creek Indians was attacked by Americans at Burnt Corn Creek, the Indians were further motivated to attack. As news of the unrest among the Creeks spread, Americans in Tensaw were alarmed and many moved their families to the homestead of neighbor Samuel Mims on the banks of Boatyard Lake, an old channel of the Alabama River. A contingency of 265 soldiers was sent to Fort Mims to help protect the settlers there, and a stockade was built around about an acre of the Mims farm, including the Mims house. Living in the 17 buildings and many military tents were about 265 soldiers and at least 553 settlers.

Commanding the fort was Major Daniel Beasley, whose actions showed that he was not up to the job of protecting the fort. Beasley had become complacent; some historians even call him arrogant, in regard to the threat of an Indian attack. He blatantly ignored reports of the threat. Failure to heed the warnings resulted in lack of preparation for the Indian attack on August 30, 1813, which historians call one of the bloodiest horrors to take place on American soil. It is generally agreed that between 250 and 400 settlers, many of Indian heritage, and militiamen were scalped and murdered. Although scalping was not a common Creek practice, the rumor that the British were offering to pay $5.00 a scalp motivated the gruesome mutilations. The Creek Indians also captured 100-150 slaves who were living in the compound. The Creeks suffered major losses, perhaps up to 300.

Today the fort is designated as a historic site and The Fort Mims Restoration Association has rebuilt a blockhouse and a part of the stockade and placed four large markers. The group sponsors a reenactment of the battle in August of each year where the smell of smoke is not only from the black powder of the reenactors' muskets but is also residual odor of burning buildings and bodies. As one walks there, feet tread on ground that once soaked up the blood of victims who have stories to tell and unfinished business. Overnight campers report sounds and smells – and many specters. Paranormal investigators have spent numerous evenings here recording and communicating with some of those victims and perhaps even the attackers. Voices are clearly heard, apparitions are seen, and many, many orbs move about the battlefield.

One of the blockhouses was reconstructed by the Fort Mims Association.

One of the members of the Restoration Association reports the following:

A couple of years ago we allowed a group of paranormal investigators to stay overnight. My granddaughter and I visited them just as a storm was rolling in. We were huddled arm in arm, a little cold and a little uneasy. They were wide-eyed when they told us they saw a figure of a man at the East gate…thought it was someone playing a joke on them, but there was no one around. They also tried recording and called out Major Beasley's name…and got plenty of reply. The recordings were eerie, but occasionally words that I could understand…I decided not to stick around. Being in the midst and seeing orbs all around was really strange.

The words distinctly heard by all seem to be warnings of the impending attack. For, in fact, in 1813, warnings were repeatedly relayed and consistently ignored. Perhaps these frustrated returning spirits are once again warning of danger, hoping that this time, the alarms will not fall upon deaf ears.

Some feel it is Major Beasley, returning to try to rectify his neglect in preparing for an attack. General Ferdinand Claiborne of the Mississippi Territorial Militia paid a visit there on August 7, 1813, soon after Beasley arrived. After inspecting the fort, Claiborne sent a letter to Beasley recommending that at least two and preferably three additional blockhouses be built "to respect our Enemy and to prepare in the best possible way to meet him, is the certain means to ensure success." Beasley, however, apparently not feeling any imminent danger, did not strengthen the fort except to construct a second defensive wall inside the stockade facing the east gate.

Two slaves reported they had seen braves in war paint in the woods nearby on Sunday, August 29. They saw hundreds of Indians and hurried back to the fort to inform Major Beasley. To his credit, he did send a scouting party of ten men outside the enclosure. Two of these scouts rode within 300 yards of the camouflaged Creeks, who could hear the men talking. When the scouts brought back reports of no danger, Beasley ordered the slaves whipped. The owner of one of the slaves believed his trusted friend and would not allow the beating to take place, but the other received painful lashes with a leather whip.

The appearances of orbs are common at the site, many of which are about eye level along the perimeters of the fort. In constructing the original pine log stockade, advice concerning the gunwales was ignored. Orbs are seen appearing near the slits cut in the stockade in effort to advise the militia to raise them or completely seal them up. Unbelievably, the holes were at shoulder level. Good fort engineering designed the gun slits at a higher level with a ledge for the riflemen to stand on. The eye level slits enabled the Creeks to peer into the fort on the night of August 29, the Sunday evening before the planned attack. They saw men drinking whiskey that had arrived that day and rowdily playing cards. They saw settlers laughing and dancing, with no weapons readily accessible. The Indians planned to man the slits at the beginning of the attack.

An apparition at the gate is one of the most powerful indicators of the return of spirits to the battlefield. Many re-enactors think that the vision which appears often is one of their own making a nighttime ride through the campground, but as he disappears into the woods, a strange dead silence covers that place. A silence waiting for the screams that will follow. This is probably a messenger who was not there for the battle, but whose one last warning was scoffed by the militia. Before noon, James Cornell, a scout, galloped into the fort shouting to Major Beasley that the war party was advancing toward Fort Mims. Beasley, who was probably drunk, mocked Cornell, saying that he must have seen red cattle. Cornell yelled back at the major that those red cattle would "give him one hell of a kick before nightfall." Cornell made the statement that if the men were to prepare to fight, he would stay and join them to his death, but if the contingency was to remain unprepared, he would be no part of the battle. Major Beasley ordered Cornell arrested, but he turned and fled, escaping the soldiers and leaving the fort to its fate.

The infamous gate holds the story of the easy accessibility to the fort by the Creek Indians. It had not been shut for so long that the sand had blown against it and prevented its closure at the time of the attack.

So, the fort was unprepared for the attack at noon on August 30, 1813, and the rest of the story is grim indeed. News of the attack spread rapidly, and the cry "Remember Fort Mims" fueled a war. On the 9th of September a contingency of men under the command of Major Kennedy arrived at the gruesome scene to bury the dead. The description of the compound is beyond comprehension. They found what was left of hundreds of human bodies of all races. They had been burned, mutilated, and left to the elements of nature for several days. The soldiers dug a trench, put the decimated remains in it and covered it with dirt. Those unrequited spirits must be there to try to save others from their fate.

What would have been the outcome if those in the fort had heeded the warnings given them? The voices and visits from that terrible time seem to be warning visitors even now to escape before you become a victim of horrors not seen before.

CHAPTER 8
ART OF LOCAL FOLKS

Earliest indications of human existence are in the form of art. As a language that needs no interpretation, the universality of artistic expression is in our deepest selves. There is, however, something special about the deep south art, especially when it is right here at home.

JUST A PILE OF OLD ROCKS

Many people wonder about the wonderful monument of red rocks on County Road 32 in the Summerdale area. We set out to discover what they are all about.

Man has been piling rocks about as long as there were men on earth, and each man-made formation has a story. Earliest formations were probably to mark an area for future use, like signposts. Many early cultures erected steles to commemorate an event, and many to mark a person's life. Eventually, like Ogham standing stones in Ireland, they were carved with runes and later were even shaped into obelisks. Some early cultures used rocks placed in perfect formations like Stonehenge for religious purposes or as dolmen to mark graves, but the earliest ones found were simply stacked in ways that created a permanent structure. Here in Baldwin County, we call them rock piles!

A couple of years ago, high in the Rocky Mountains, I pulled over to the side of the road, jumped out and went to a pile of rocks by the side of the road. There I picked up a large one and leveled it good in the dirt. Then my husband added one on top of that base. In turn, each of my three grandsons added a rock to the pile. Then I explained the custom.

I am trying to remember just when I started doing this – it seems like I have always done it. On every trip I make, at the furthest or highest point from my home, I build an Ebenezer. We show our thankfulness for a safe journey thus far and ask for traveling mercies for our journey home.

Then we sing,

"Here I raise mine Ebenezer, Hither by Thy help I'm come.

And I pray by Thy good mercy safely to arrive at home."

Thinking of the Ebenezers I have made, I treasure the memories of each place. We built one at Machu Picchu, at Mount Sanai, at Vesuvius, and one at Alabama's own Mount Cheaha. We built one at the westernmost point of Hawaii on the isle of Kauai at the end of the Hanakape'ai hiking trail on the NaPali Coast (Glad I did that when I was younger.)

Piles of rocks are seen all over the world. They can be called Ebenezers, Wishing Stones, Inukshuts, and probably many other names. People take part in the ancient ritual of stacking rocks at significant times or places.

The Biblical reference is in I Samuel, where a stone monument was raised in Israel to commemorate victory over the Philistines, but virtually every culture has similar monuments. Some even take on personalities and other meanings.

Canadian and Alaskans use Inukshuts for welcoming and to garner good fortune. Earliest ones were single upright stones used as markers, as a means of communicating some message to those who passed that way. The name can be translated as "that which acts in the capacity of a human," and the later ones do seem to take on the image of humans. On our last trip to Alaska, our grandson Luke, built one on the Yukon River, our furthest point north.

In Vancouver, the official symbol of the Olympics was the Inuksuk, a traditional rock structure of the Inuit and other Native American tribes from Alaska to Greenland. This is a piece of jewelry made in the shape of the Inukshuk.

Here at home, everyone loves seeing the rock sculpture on County Road 32 in Summerdale. The farmer used local red ironstone to create a sculpture as wonderful as any we have seen in our travels. The owner of the land, Wayne Teem, lives across the road. He says that he leases the land to a cattle farmer. The rancher asked permission to dig a pond on the acreage and while doing so, the magnificent iron rocks were uncovered. He had them piled up in a formation visible from from County Road 32. Mr. Teem said that the cattle rancher talked about naming his spread Red Rock Ranch, the Triple R. The ranch is now expanded all the way through to County Road 28, where a similar rock structure can be seen.

I guess it is the permanence of rocks that makes them beg to be used to leave a sign of man's existence. The Jewish custom of leaving a small rock on a headstone is a beautiful way to show respect for the lasting memory of the deceased. The dramatic conclusion of *Schindler's List* demonstrates the honor paid to a person when the stone is placed at the gravesite. Scholars of the Jewish faith write that the custom signifies a more permanent tribute than flowers at a gravesite. It may be a tradition springing from the early days when graves were marked with piles of stones. Regardless of its origin, the custom is powerful today.

Every time I visit my great-grandfather's grave in Rock Cemetery in Robertsdale, there is at least one small stone on the headstone of Carl Alex Brill. I don't know who else puts them there, but I always add one of my own. We are connected by the bones of the earth.

I just read a teacher's blog which extols the value of building rock sculptures. It is not as easy as it looks. It takes understanding of physics and balance, usually by trial and error – which builds patience and persistence. Maybe we each need to pile some rocks.

Red rocks are piled to create monoliths on County Roads 32 and 28. Word has it that the creator calls his ranch Red Rocks Ranch.

SHOOFLY, DON'T BOTHER ME

'Like father, like son,' so they say. In this case, the saying rings true. Robert Lucassen, son of Johnnie Lucassen, who had the soda bottle sculpture at his place of business in Fairhope, has built a landmark structure on Highway 98 in Montrose. It is now a part of Baldwin County Legacy. But it is time for us to use the real name of this architectural wonder. It is called a ShooFly!

People always notice it – and make reference to the white structure built around a huge live oak tree at Lucassen Body Shop. No one seems to know just what to call it. Most use the word gazebo, but the old timey name is a ShooFly. The name comes from the idea that if you are sitting high above the ground, in the shade of a tree, the ocean or river breezes will help shoo the flies away. A ShooFly is definitely a part of southern lore. Can you imagine the stories that were told while sitting in a ShooFly?

Often called a gazebo, the wooden structure built above the ground around a tree is correctly named a Shoofly. Usually they were built near water where the cool breezes offset the southern heat and the height helped deter flies and mosquitoes. Pictured here is one built by Robert Lucassen.

Robert had his first one built in 1989. He had always loved seeing the one that graced an antebellum homeplace facing Mississippi Sound in Biloxi. It was in front of the antebellum home Montrose and disappeared during Hurricane Camille. He also had photographed the one that George Brown had built at his home at the end of County Road 10. The Brown's ShooFly was damaged during Frederic but was repaired and a wedding held there just two scant weeks after the devastating storm. It was featured in many publications about Baldwin County and was used by state tourism department for advertising the southern part of the state. When Hurricane Ivan hit in 2004, it was washed away, and has not returned thus far. Robert thought we needed a new one to enjoy!

At the end of County Road 10, a shoefly once stood overlooking the Bon Secour River.

In the early years of his business, people often asked directions to the shop, but still had a hard time noticing it from the car, so Robert thought, "A perfect place for the gazebo!!" The one he had built in 1989 immediately became a landmark; eyes were drawn to it as cars made the curve on Highway 98. It stood time well until just last year when it started to show its age. The first one was built dependent upon the oak tree for support, so as the tree grew, the structure suffered.

One day he was talking to Don Hill, Construction Engineer, who took on the challenge to rebuild the ShooFly and had it up and beautiful in a few short days. Robert had the specifications he wanted, and the result was true to his specs. The first one was held together with a cable around the perimeter, and when Don cut the cable, it "opened up like a Bloomin' Onion!" The new one is larger, about 26 feet in diameter and is free standing. You may notice that some of the older shooflies have staircases to allow access to the floor of the structure. A staircase access could be considered a danger, so it was not allowed for this one.

Robert had lighting installed so the structure is even more dramatic at night. The huge oak tree is estimated by arborists to be about 200 years old. One neighbor has lived for about 80 years in his historic Clay City Brick home next to Lucassen Body Shop. He says he remembers playing on the lower branches of the tree when he was a little boy and it seemed just as big then as it is now.

It is wonderful when a private citizen takes ownership of his community heritage and makes the effort to enhance the perception that people have of it. That is just what Robert and Weezer Lucassen have done. They have created a landmark that seems like it has been there forever – a leftover from a long-gone old home. Even if it is gone one day, people will talk about the ShooFly that was on Highway 98 in the Good Old Days. Aren't we lucky to have it? Thank you!!

YOUR FACE IS UGLEEEE

Baldwin County is rich in folk arts and also the folks who carry on traditional arts and crafts of our people. I know you've seen Face Jugs all around, but do you know their story?

The Devil Jug sat on the bottom stairstep in my home when I was little. It was so frightening it kept me from crawling up those stairs. I guess that was Mother's version of a child gate, and it worked. After I was older, the jug was returned to its regular place on top of the Hoosier Cabinet in the kitchen. Sometimes I saw Daddy get the jug and disappear to the barn with some of his cronies. I heard laughter and cuttin' up as those men passed that jug around taking turns downing a swig from it. Mother told me that I should never touch that jug, that it was made that way to let me know it was dangerous. Even though I knew the jug was forbidden to me as a child, I fell in love with the ugly old man's face and to this day am fascinated by Face Jugs.

The author placed a Rezner Face Jug at the foot of her staircase in hopes it would deter evil from climbing the

Collectors and enthusiasts mostly agree that Face Jugs were first made in America by African slaves in the Carolinas. They were perhaps from the Kongo culture, where the religious jugs held the spirits of the gods. They were believed to protect a home from evil, much like gargoyles. They also may have indicated that the contents were poisonous – the uglier the jug, the more potent the contents, just like my mother said. One custom says they were placed on graves to scare the devil away so the spirit could go on to heaven. Old folks said that if the jug was broken during the first year after the burial, that meant the deceased had wrestled with the devil and won.

By the 1880s other southern potters had adopted the craft form, spreading across the Appalachians to North Georgia and Alabama, where it took roots and thrived. The creations were sometimes called Ugly or Grotesque Jugs. Alabama is known for its fine pots and the artists who throw them like Jerry Brown and Steve Miller whose families have created jugs for generations. Their jugs are found in the Black Belt Treasures shop in Camden, but I declare why would anyone need to go all the way to Camden, when the most amazing potters are right here in our own backyard?

I mean backyard literally, for John Rezner has his kilns and store right next to his house in Fairhope. Surrounded by a buffer of shade trees, the well-known potter displays his variety of pots on tables outside and also in a charming shed. If you don't see him around, do as the sign says, "Honk 4 Service." Rezner uses old-timey methods in creating these works of art.

He gets his clay from a local pit, delivered about 18 yards at a time and dumped right near his shop. He pulls back the tarp and says, "I was lucky with this load, only a few sticks and rocks. I put about 200 pounds through a mill at a time, throw pots a day or two, then go back to the clay pile and start all over again."

Rezner has three kilns but uses the wood fired one for his Face Jugs, which have the traditional ash glaze. He explains the glaze, "With influence from outside Alabama the local potters had access to alkaline glazes and salt glaze processes, that along with wood firing gave rise to a new look for local pottery."

John Rezner was the first artist to create a six-sided Face Jug, saying he was inspired by the "Two Faced Horse Dealer" mask from Day of the Dead

Face Jugs were most likely introduced into the United States by slaves brought from Africa. Originally, they probably were known to hold gods or the spirits of ancestors. The art is continued by southern potters like John Rezner, who maintain the original methods of throwing and firing them.

celebrations. Each of the six faces shares an eye or nose with another. The first one he made can be seen at the Mobile Museum of Art and two of his works are built into the sign in front of Bay Medical Family Practice.

Tom Jones Pottery is usually a busy place. Here he is throwing one of his one-of-a-kind pumpkins that are always in high demand in the fall.

Rezner is quick to give credit to Tom Jones who trained him. Jones, a delightful host, is usually found at the wheel in his shop near the old Clay City brickworks. He was throwing pumpkins when we visited, and we could hardly take our eyes off the magic of his hands in the clay.

Tom first learned to work with clay under the tutelage of Edith Harwell at the Organic School in Fairhope. She came from Seagrove, NC, and it makes sense that she was influenced by the work there and brought it to south Alabama.

Tom told us he had recently made a Face Jug in the image of his son, Dallas, who has it on display in his barber shop – the likeness is uncanny. However, this one is NOT an Ugly Jug!

Every Face Jug is unique with a personality all its own, but I think the best one of all is the jug which is on my bottom stairstep, just like when I was little.

You may be wondering what happened to that Face Jug of my childhood. When my Daddy died, I was eighteen and I well remember his burial. That night, I went back to the graveyard toting along his old Devil Jug. I placed it on the fresh mound of dirt, just as he had asked me to do. After a week or so, the flowers had been removed, but the jug remained. Then a week later when I returned to the grave, there were only the shattered shards of the Devil Jug. Some say that vandals or a lawn mower were to blame, but I know better. Daddy wrestled with the devil and won.

When I die, put my Face Jug on my grave. I plan to wrestle with the Devil and I know I will win.

SODA ANYONE?

As a little girl I can remember coming to Fairhope to follow the footprints painted on the sidewalk all through town to see the window displays of collections and artwork. These early days of the Arts and Crafts Festival were an annual outing for our family. Every time we came to Fairhope, however, the highlight of the trip was to drive by the folk sculpture of a soda bottle. I wanted to make one at our house!

Can you remember where the cement sculpture of a soda bottle stood in Fairhope? It was on the corner of Morphy and Mershon next to the Corner Store. The sculpture was made of cement with real glass drink bottles of all colors and brands imbedded in it. I remember it well and wanted to find out what happened to it; so, my quest began. As anyone around here knows, if you want to know something about the Eastern Shore (or all of Baldwin County for that matter) you pay a visit to Donnie Barrett, then Director of the Fairhope Museum of History. Of course, he had some answers for me. Even better, he told me it is still in existence!

Old-timers in Fairhope love to recall the concrete and bottle statue which stood at the Corner Store on Morphy Avenue. It was one of the iconic symbols of Americana in the south. Photo courtesy of Baldwin County Historical Development Commission.

The store was owned and operated by Johnny Lucassen. Robert Lucassen, Johnny's son, told me the story of how it came to be. Mrs. Frances Lucassen decided to have a surprise made for her husband, so she engaged local mason, Joe Klein, to create a fine piece of folk art. They designed and constructed a nine-foot-high cement soda pop bottle and installed it right there on the store grounds in the mid 1960s. Mr. Johnny was indeed surprised and was thrilled with the distinctive icon for his store. During the 1950s and 60s, as automobile travel was becoming more affordable, America was caught up in building roadside attractions to call attention to businesses. You may remember Wig Wam Motels, and of course, the giant root beer mug on A&W Root beer drive-ins. Those works of art still around are dubbed Americana and are once again the roadside attractions they were 50 years ago.

Fairhope has always been a magnet for interesting characters and art, so the drink bottle sculpture was embraced as a part of the town. Lots of traffic came by the store. It was right across the street from the town baseball park, which is now the city tennis complex. After the tragic death of Mr. Johnny during a robbery attempt in the late 1970s the family closed the store and the bottle was vandalized during years the store was vacant. In 1985-86, John Sledge conducted a survey of historical structures for the Baldwin County Historical Development Commission. He photographed the bottle sculpture at its original location while the cap was still intact.

Mrs. Frances Lucassen eventually sold the store and it was remodeled into a private home. But Mrs. Lucassen was determined to save Johnny's beloved drink bottle, and the structure was moved further out Morphy Avenue onto family property, where it stood for about 15 years. It attracted old-timers searching for it, and surprised sightseers when they spied it on the corner of Bishop Road and Morphy Avenue. Bobby and Debra Green, owners of Green Nurseries and Fairhope natives, saw that the work was once again in danger of being lost, and asked if they could move the sculpture and preserve it. They secured the artwork, and had it moved to their private home, where it stands today. Thank goodness!!!

The sculpture has about 45 rows of bottles inserted neck first into the concrete. A bottle cap was created atop the sculpture but has since been lost. During the years of vandalism, the bottles which were underneath the ground were preserved. There are Coca-Cola, Nehi, Barq's Rootbeer, Grapico, and RC Cola, just to mention a few. The Greens are conscious of the heritage of our area and are interested in preserving as much of it as possible. They have considered restoring the piece but say that people seem to like it as it is. It tells a great story. As we looked over the artwork, the Greens and I laughed about the how the cost of the sculpture had to include the amount the bottle deposits would have been worth. Yes, you may need to explain bottle deposits to the youngsters you tell about this and show these photographs

The remains of the soda bottle were rescued and are on private property today. It is still indicative of the master craftsmanship of its creator.

Now, Donnie, Debra, Bobby, and Robert -- and other interested folks -- we need to make a reproduction and put it at the Fairhope Museum! Of course, that depends on whether we can find enough glass bottles. Soda anyone?

FOLK ART TRAIL

I miss the old days when nearly every yard had some piece of art created by the owner of the house. Nowadays you can buy fancy, production line yard art, but somehow it is just not the same as the kind that is home made from scrap. So let's take a ride..

On County Roads – a virtual Folk Art gallery – right here in our own backyards. Well, maybe not your backyard if you live in a town or in a subdivision that has covenants. I get it – covenants can certainly protect your property value, but then again, I guess it is all in how you define property value. I am one of those people who just can't see the point of paying a group just so they can tell me what I can or can't put in the yard. So, if that means I am a country girl, or even a redneck, I will take it as a compliment. That is one reason we live on a County Road! It was still country when we built, but the tentacles of nearby towns have reached out to ensnarl roads all around us. It seems that with the encroachment of city life, folk art begins to disappear. What a price to pay for progress.

Southerners are known for their love of beauty and have unique perspectives for creating art to enhance their gardens and homes. A drive on county roads in the rural south can bring delightful surprises at every turn in the road. The artist changes the decorations on the mailbox tire with each season.

It has been way too long since I have seen tractor tires cut and painted white, creating amazing flowerbeds for red amaryllises. What happened to those days when people painted their trees white halfway up? What a sight to behold. Better yet, I long to spot a yucca plant decked out with flowers cut from Styrofoam egg cartons. If they are put on with the artist's eye, they are absolutely beautiful. Every time you see a work of folk art in a yard, someone has been touched by a calling deep inside to use what is around to make this world an even more beautiful place.

Nowadays I might have to drive a little further out in the county to see the yards that say something personal, but it is sure worth the drive. I don't have to go far on County Road 34, to enjoy the wonderful mailbox wreath my neighbor created from a tire. I can hardly wait to see the new ribbon or flowers with each change of season or holiday. Right up County Road 13 is another of my favorites. The Williams had a tree trunk in their yard that just called out to them to create the perfect stand for a birdhouse. With paint, tinsel, and decorations, the artistry is revealed. Go see it!

County Road 13 in the middle of what is known as Jacksonville, the Williams family creates amazing works of folkart. Here is a birdhouse on a tree stump, painted and decorated with skill.

In Foley there is a storybook yard, filled with characters and scenes loved by all. The Tin Man, Dorothy, and the scarecrow were all handmade by Roger Falk. Of course, this is on a county road -- 65. He says makes the artwork, then sneaks out at night to add it to the scenes so the next day everyone will think it appeared magically. Actually, it is magic.

Follow the Yellow Brick Road, otherwise known as County Road 65 in Foley, to find the Land of Oz complete with characters that appear magically overnight.

A house on County Road 10 was for the longest time graced with three totem poles. The last time I went to see them, one was gone. It is worth a drive down to the south end of the county just to see them if you can.

Bottle trees, which once were almost forgotten, are now beautiful products sold by metalworkers. Mine is a natural cedar branch brought to me by two of my favorite people, Debbie and Tony Ayers, self-proclaimed "river rats' who rescued it from Fish River. They may have even helped me empty some of those blue bottles you can see there. By the way, blue is the color that will deter "haints" from your home.

Some bottle trees are created by craftsmen and sold at shops throughout the south. This one, however, is made with a waterlogged cypress limb rescued from Fish River.

Those who are handy with a saw may cut out plywood figures – and paint them. I call those sophisticated yard art. You can see Amish buggies, cowboys, Bigfoot, and other loveable characters, mostly painted black. Except for the amazing pink flamingos seen south of Fairhope on County Road 3.

The most elaborately decorated home I can remember is Mr. Shanks' home in Stockton. John Lewis produced an enhanced photograph that will take your breath away. Mr. Shanks used a little of everything he found. That, my friend, is recycling to enhance our time here on earth. His house is gone now, so I am so thankful I took a drive to see it years ago.

While out riding last week, I asked a man sitting in his front yard if he knew of anywhere that had tires made into white painted flowerbed borders. He laughed and said they would be "called out" these days. My goodness, what a sad commentary on what we call sophistication. Every piece of folk art represents a person who is expressing a sense of wonder in this world. Let's never lose sight of what is really important: respect for each other. Take a ride. If you see someone in a yard with folk art, stop and tell them you appreciate the effort they made to share their art with the world.

CHAPTER 9

CEMETERIES

Our people, our past, our heritage.

Cemeteries are full of stories.

Let me tell you some of my favorite ones.

GRAVEYARD DOGS

Why do cemeteries seem to be a vital part of our lives? Because they are.

Grandpa Bill Coon was my mother's father, a dirt-poor tenant farmer in Ohio. Many of his neighboring Amish families had moved south for warmer climate and cheap farmland. In 1919 he took his meager savings, packed up his wife, Leafy, and two daughters and boarded a train heading to Baldwin County, Alabama. As fate would have it, just about that time the Amish, discouraged by terrible hurricanes along the coast, were returning to Ohio, family by family, and selling their farms in Baldwin County.

When the Coon family reached Bay Minette, they stayed at the Hamilton Hotel, where Leafy and the girls were thrilled with the bustling town. Grandma bought her first ready-made garment, a Georgette blouse, at Kahaly's store. The girls had their first ever ice cream cones, and Grandpa bought his first ever piece of land, just east of town in Phillipsville.

The Coon family rented a house from the Beachy family who had returned north to their Amish community in Ohio.

Bill spent the last of his savings on two mules, a wagon, and a plow and moved his family into the old Beachy place next to his farm. It was the home of a family who had lost their fruit crops, and much more tragically, their daughter Mary had died before she was two years old. They buried her in the little graveyard up the rise a piece and joined other Amish farmers returning north.

The Coons rented their house. Grandpa started work farming and building a cabin and the girls started at Pleasant View school just down Still Road. Grandma started making the house into a home.

One day soon after moving there, as Leafy washed clothes in the washpot over the fire, she could see the little graveyard just up the rise. A movement caught her eye and she said the white vision looked like an angel. She left her wet clothes in the basket and trudged up the rise a piece. There among simple crosses and headstones was a German Shepherd dog as white as the snow. She had never seen anything like that dog.

As Leafy returned to the house, the dog followed and soon the two were inseparable. Neighbors said the dog had been devoted to little Mary, but when the Beachys moved back to Ohio, the dog was left behind. The dog soon gave his love to the Coon family, especially Leafy. She called her Angel. Angel never left my grandma's side, except to meet the girls every day as they walked home from school. Of course, Angel went with them when they moved into their little cabin, which they called "Coon Holler."

When the girls entered high school, they rode one of the mules into the town of Bay Minette to attend the new brick Baldwin County High School. Bill struggled to eke a living out of the poor farmland, but still they were a dirt poor farm family.

One day during their senior year in school, the girls noticed their Mama looked peaked, and as they helped her to bed, they realized she was going to have a baby. They were all worried about her and dreaded the worst. Angel stayed by her side every day, except to meet the girls after school.

One day after school Angel was not there to meet the girls. They knew something was wrong. The baby girl had come much too early, and both she and Leafy had died that day.

The two girls washed and dressed the bodies while Grandpa built the coffin. All this time, the dog stayed under the bed where the bodies lay. The girls and their father sat up around the bed all night to keep the "Wake" and Angel stayed right there with them. The next morning, both mother and child were wrapped in a quilt, then tucked in the crude coffin.

The cemetery on the outskirts of Bay Minette holds the remains of some of the early Amish settlers and of others in the community. It also holds visions.

As the coffin was carried up the little rise a piece to the graveyard, the dog went right along beside it. After the last shovel full of dirt was placed on top of the mound, Angel lay down on the mound. And she stayed there.

The girls took her food and water, but she refused to eat. They figured it was because their mother had always fed her before. The dog grew weaker and weaker, and one day she went on to join the mistress. The girls dug her grave next to their Mama.

Several months went by when the girls started noticing that the grass over their Mama's grave looked like an animal had slept there, maybe a deer or a free range cow. Then one day coming home from school they looked over at the little graveyard. There was Angel. Not believing their eyes, they jumped off the mule, calling to the dog. You can guess what happened. The closer they got, the weaker became the image of the white German Shepherd, until it vanished completely. The girls looked at each other in disbelief. They had both witnessed the same thing. After that, they saw Angel many times in the graveyard, and let her be.

The girls graduated from high school and went to business school in Mobile. Grandpa left the old place too. Angel stayed in the cemetery.

Those girls were my mother, Harriet and her sister, Margaret. They both married and lived in Mobile. Grandpa eventually came to live in Mobile as well.

Jump ahead about 50 years to when I was in high school. My father knew he was sick and was trying to do what he could to provide help mother after he was gone. He worried for her safety and her loneliness. One day, he brought home a beautiful white German Shepherd. He was given the dog by a coworker, Bob Adcock, who lived in Spanish Fort and raised the rare breed. My mother was amazed, for she had never told anyone the story of Angel.

A rare white German Shepherd was seen after her death at the cemetery where Leafy Coon was buried. The dog was buried there as well but is still seen lying on Leafy's grave.

Mother named her dog Diana, and she gave my mother companionship for years after Daddy died. When Diana died, Mother asked me to help her take her body to grown-up patch of land on the road east of Bay Minette, sort of near the dipping vat. She went right to that hidden cemetery and told me about her Mama and Angel. There we buried Diana, wrapped in a quilt my grandmother had made.

Now there are now two white German Shepherds holding vigil in the lost cemetery in the woods on the Pensacola Road not too far from the dipping vat. People told me so. I guess there are still angels there.

OLD MAN MCDONALD'S GRAVE

Everyone who attended the old Rosinton School has wonderful memories of the wooden building that was built in 1919 on County Road 64, just east of the present day Rosinton School. When the old folks gather to talk about those days, the story of Old Man McDonald's grave always comes up.

Folks say that a man by the name of McDonald built a little cabin on a spot of land near the Rosinton School. He had a reputation for not wanting to work, but rather "borrowed" things from neighboring farms. Of course, McDonald's idea of borrowing was considered stealing by his victims. After one of his raids, the men around the area took the law into their own hands, as many local farmers were wont to do in those days. Several men went to his cabin one night, McDonald jumped out of his window and ran toward the woods. Shots were fired resulting in McDonald's death. The men simply buried him on the property near McDonald's swamp and went on about their business as usual. There is no record of any reports of his death or arrests of the farmers, but locals knew all about him and the legends grew and grew.

When Rosinton School was built it was a modern three-room schoolhouse, the first in Baldwin County under the State Aid Plan. It consolidated with the Antioch School and Miss Lillian Hodges was the first principal. By 1923 the school had been expanded to four classrooms for students through grade eight. Hollinger and Styx River Schools were then joined with existing student body and the school had at least 140 students. Generations of families shared the heritage of the amazing community school, and all have the same story to tell about the first graders' "initiation" that took place year after year after year.

Jeannette Ryan remembers the anecdote well. Her son Barry Ryan told me that the tradition continued when he was in the first grade a generation later. Jeannette's brother Ernest Dyess wrote up the story years ago. As a first grader, Ernest was baited to be brave enough to go out back of the schoolyard to the site of Old Man McDonald's grave, knock on the grave and say, "Old Man McDonald, whatcha doin' down there?" He was told that when did, Old Man McDonald would say, "***Noooothhhhiiiinnnnn.***"

Lovely wooden Rosinton School was built in the typical fashion of the early twentieth century: a central entry with two classrooms flanking the entry hall. Rosinton was a large community on the Wire Road connecting Blakeley to Pensacola. There was also a narrow gage railway running to Gateswood and Bay Minette for lumber transport. The old Rosinton School was demolished, and a new one built in the community.

So, Ernest bravely faced the task with all the other first graders. Each fearfully took a turn patting the mound of dirt and calling out to McDonald. They soon went running back to the teacher, Mrs. Higgins, and cried, "Mrs. Higgins, he didn't say "***NOTHING***."

Well, the wise teacher replied, "Well, didn't I tell you he would say, **'Nothing'**?" Ernest wrote that was when he learned that words can have multiple meanings.

When a new school was built just west of the old building, the old school was slated for demolition. Alumnae footsteps were heard in the halls as former students and teachers met to say goodbye to the building, but not to the memories. Every one of those people had their own story to tell – and most of them were about Old Man McDonald's grave.

Today the ruins of the 1941 brick gymnasium are all that remain on the old school site, and I can find no one who can point out the location of the unmarked grave, but the new Rosinton School thrives and continues to live up to the reputation built by years of educators and students. If you happen to venture out by McDonald's Swamp and find the grave, rap on it and ask, "Hey, Old Man McDonald, Whatcha doin' down there?" I guarantee he will say……

RUBY RED ROSARY

The Weeks Cabin was preserved and moved from Weeks Bay to Bon Secour by the Brown family, where it is now a private residence. Some local historians claim that it may be the oldest house structure in Baldwin County. Many stories were told on the porch of that ancient dogtrot cabin.

Glynis and her cousins ran across the grassy sand every day to visit old Grandma Weeks. They sat on the front porch of the old cabin facing Weeks Bay, watching the dolphins play and drinking the wonderful tea made from sassafras roots, sweetened with sugar cane syrup. "Tell us a story," the children begged every afternoon. This day Grandma Weeks told about her own grandmother.

The oldest cabin in the area is said to be the Weeks Cabin, moved from Weeks Bay to Bon Secour by George Brown.

"This is the very cabin my grandfather built using the trees all along the banks of this bay named for his family. They were devout Catholics, attending mass regularly nearby where there were many other Creole families with direct ancestors from France. He and my grandmother raised their children here, teaching them mostly at home and sometimes sending them to the parish school taught by the priest at the church. My father was the youngest of the children and he was about twelve when his mother died, but he remembered it his entire life and told us about that sad time.

"His mother and father slept in an old bed that had a bookshelf built in the headboard. It was in this bed that his mother lay dying with her children and priest around her bedside. My father said she was beautiful lying there, a lovely smile on her face and holding her rosary in her hands as the priest administered the Last Rites. She had prayed that rosary every day and the children thought that she had brought the rosary when she came from France. The beads were of rubies and the cross and chain of gold; she had told her husband that she wanted it to be with her in her coffin when she was buried.

"Her passing over was peaceful, and the room seemed holy with the presence of unseen beings. The tears and mourning were subdued and dignified, all assured that the amazing woman would live forever in heaven. The preparation of the body for burial was done by the daughters in the family and she was dressed in her wedding gown as a shroud. Her coffin was placed on a funeral bier in the parlor of the cabin and family members took turns sitting with her for an all night wake, the last night they would see her on this earth. Grandfather remembered her request to be buried with her rosary, so he went to the bedroom to get it, but it was not where he had put it on the bookcase headboard. The entire family searched the house from inside out and it was simply not there.

"With a heavy heart Grandfather went to bed next to the empty pillow where his wife had slept for their entire married lives. His silent tears were not only of loneliness, but of despair that he could not grant his wife's wish to be buried with the ruby red rosary. The rooster crow at daybreak sounded as mournful as Grandfather felt as he opened his sad eyes dreading the coming day. He turned his head toward his wife's pillow and his heart filled with peace. There in an indentation on the pillow was the ruby red rosary. The message from his wife was clear.

"He slipped into the living room and placed the rosary in her folded hands. The family gathered to pray the rosary one last time with my grandmother, and all felt her presence in the Holy Communion of the Saints. The sons were the pall bearers who carried the casket to the church where friends joined in the Mass before she was taken to the cemetery for burial. Afterwards, the ladies of the parish provided a meal for the family under the canopy of trees near the cemetery.

" Every day following the burial Grandfather walked to the cemetery just before daybreak to commune with his wife. One morning after he knelt before the grave and said a prayer, he lifted his head right at daybreak he noticed that there was a small red spot embedded in the marble slab that was over her grave. He scrubbed the spot to no avail. It would not be removed. He returned every day and scrubbed the slab until there was in indentation in the marble, but still the red spot was visible. As days passed, more and more spots appeared on the marble slab, always visible at daybreak right after his prayers. He was buried beside her when he died, his grave marked with a plain marble slab as well."

Look carefully at the slab of Grandmother Weeks to see the ruby red spots that can never be removed.

Glynis and her cousins listening to the story on Grandmother Weeks' porch asked if the red spots still appear. The old woman told them that she had seen them herself – but only at daybreak after she had knelt in prayer. The children awoke the next morning before daybreak and ran to the cemetery in the dark. Sure enough, they found the two slabs on in the Weeks plot, one with a slight indentation. They knelt in prayer and at daybreak, there in the indentation were the red spots, the ruby red spots of a rosary. The graves are still there – with no names engraved in the slabs, but all who come to that cemetery notice the slab with ruby red spots. That is, if they come at daybreak and kneel in prayer at the graves.

BLACK MAGIC, WAR HORSE

Late evening golfers on the Lakewood Golf Course at the Grand Hotel tell of unusual sounds near the adjoining Point Clear Cemetery. Neighbors and joggers even say that they have witnessed an apparition that tells the story of one of the soldiers buried there at Confederate Rest - of the bond that exists between man and horse.

Among the resorts lining the eastern shore of Mobile Bay, the Grand Hotel, has been in operation for almost 200 years. The first hotel was built in the 1830s but was destroyed by fire. It was replaced in 1847 by a grand two-story hotel and was put to use by the Confederate government to provide hospital care for the men wounded during the siege of Vicksburg, Mississippi. It was during this sad period that more than 300 soldiers died and were buried in the nearby cemetery named Confederate Rest.

The story of Edmund Smith and his beloved horse is so powerful that the vestiges of the story are visible today. Edmund enlisted in the Confederate Army and brought his horse, Black Magic. He had raised Black Magic from a colt, and he was one with his horse. Black Magic saved Edmund's life on more than one occasion before they were sent to Vicksburg, the last Confederate stronghold on the Mississippi River. Here they joined other soldiers and citizens alike enduring one of the most horrific experiences ever known. When hunger became the motivation for human behaviors, Edmund would rather have died himself than see his beloved horse sacrificed to feed soldiers. You see, Black Magic had a soul that Edmund understood. One night, while most were in a fitful sleep between bombardments from Union cannons, Edmund had a long talk with Black Magic and convinced the horse to run for his life. With a slap on the flank, he bid goodbye to half of his soul as he watched the horse slip through the enemy lines near the river.

Black Magic somehow evaded capture and stayed hidden the woods near Vicksburg. He saw the end of the siege when the Confederacy surrendered on July 4, 1863. He then witnessed his beloved master among those most seriously wounded who were loaded onto a barge, paroled, and sent to hospitals. Black

Magic followed the barge down the Mississippi River to the Gulf of Mexico and across the gulf coast eastward. In some mystical fashion, he was able to arrive at the Grand Hotel in Point Clear as his master was being carried on a stretcher into the makeshift hospital. The hospital was under the guard of the 21st Alabama Infantry which was stationed at the Tam Denton Plantation near Grand Hotel.

Black Magic was almost like a phantom horse even when he was alive. He could slip quietly in and out of places as if he were not even real. He found his master and put his head through the open window of the ward where Edmund lay dying. Edmund reached his wounded hand to touch the horse and died peacefully knowing that Black Magic had escaped the brutalities of the war and was alive. Tragically, most of the wounded who were sent to Point Clear died there and were buried in a cemetery near the hotel, many in a trench grave, all unmarked at the time.

Black Magic stayed nearby. The members of the 21st Alabama Infantry became attached to the loyal horse and cared for him as much as the horse would allow. They put meager rations out where he could find them, and often saw him near the cemetery.

Men may not have known where Edmund was buried, but Black Magic did. The elusive horse was seen coming to the cemetery every evening right after dark. He would paw the ground and whinny a forlorn call to his master. He never allowed anyone near him but would run into the deep woods to remain a refugee. He was seen for a couple of years after the war ended, until one morning, the horse was found dead in the cemetery, most think from exhaustion, old age, and most of all, grief. One former member of the 21st Infantry lived nearby and when the horse was found dead, he was determined the two souls would be together. He buried the horse in the cemetery.

Soon after that, the locals began to once again hear the whinnies of a mourning horse, and occasionally someone would see him run through the cemetery. Often the ground near the graves was churned and had been pawed by hooves. Reports of the mysterious horse have been told for more than 150 years, and members of the 21st Alabama Infantry Reenactment group, have had encounters with Black Magic. They and the members of the Admiral Buchanan Military Order of Stars and Bars organization have spent countless hours in the cemetery. Thanks to these groups, many headstones now mark the graves of those known to be buried there, even though the original lists were lost in a fire at the hotel. Several of the members have heard the neighing of a horse nearby while they were working. One even heard horse hooves gallop through the cemetery. The cannon, the entrance gate, and the gravesites are respectfully tended, and marked with flowers on Memorial Day. When ceremonies are held there, participants often think one of the re-enactors brought along his magnificent black stallion, for Black Magic is usually seen near the edge of the woods. The powerful connection between man and horse lives on.

During the War Between the States, the Grand Hotel was used as a hospital for Confederate soldiers and sailors. Many who died there were buried in trench graves without identification. The records were burned in a hotel fire several years later.

ABOUT THE AUTHOR

Harriet Brill Outlaw is the author or coauthor of six books and numerous articles relating to local history and folklore. She is a retired educator who lives with her husband in Fairhope, grandparents of fourteen grandchildren and two great-grandchildren so far. Her favorite hobbies are storytelling, traveling, and just about everything else you can think of like....

Exploring cemeteries
Talking with old folks who remember times long past
Reading mysteries
Decorating for Christmas
Hearing good jokes
Playing with grandchildren
Learning almost-lost arts and crafts
Maintaining ten acres (With a Scag mower)
Listening to historical lectures
Touring historic buildings
Visiting museums
Dancing while no one is watching
Writing stories without worrying about facts
Collecting post cards
RVing miles and miles
Having massages
Cooking for family gatherings (but not day-to-day meals)
Running into former students
Rocking on the front porch during a rainstorm
Sitting around a long table with family after a huge meal

She emphasizes that even if she is not sure she believes in ghosts, she thinks everyone enjoys stories of the mysterious. So, remember there is always a good tale out there worth"Tellin'."

www.taletellinbook.com

Made in the USA
Columbia, SC
08 October 2024

5982dd4e-5579-439c-ba63-c4825c3dbd65R02